CURSED PRINCE

NIGHT ELVES TRILOGY - BOOK 1

C.N. CRAWFORD

Copyright © 2020 by C.N. Crawford

All rights reserved.

No part of this book may be reproduced in any form or by any electronic or mechanical means, including information storage and retrieval systems, without written permission from the author, except for the use of brief quotations in a book review.

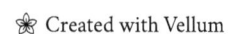

❋ Created with Vellum

CHAPTER 1

MARROC

*E*ndless solitude. That was my existence. Day after day. Year after year. Decade after decade.

Sometimes the guards looked in on me, but mostly, they kept their distance. They feared me. Even if they couldn't see into the shadows of my cell, or under the smoke whirling around my face, they knew *what* I was. They could feel the evil spilling off me.

Pale skin, eyes that shone like flecks of ice, my body smoking and smoldering—with just one glance at me, they knew to keep their distance. That I'd been cursed, my soul ripped from me.

My heart hadn't beat in a thousand years. My vocal cords had burned away; I hadn't uttered a word in all that time. Since I didn't eat, the guards didn't bring food. I no longer needed to breathe, though I continued to do so out of habit. So I was left in complete isolation. The only sound was the irregular *drip, drip … drip* of water from the rocks above me.

My companions were the granite under my feet, the iron bars, and the rat who slept by my side. I'd named him

Gormie, after the elf king who'd locked me away nearly a thousand years ago.

I'd had all that time to mull over my fate.

But time had become murky and confusing. Sometimes, it seemed like yesterday that I'd been thrown in here. That first day, I'd hurled myself at the bars, bashed my skull against the stones. Cursed as I was, I'd hardly felt a thing. Only the dull thrill of killing the guards—of grabbing them by the shoulders, pulling them toward the bars, my teeth piercing their flesh. I killed one after another, draining their souls through their blood.

They never learned.

So, I waited. My body might be damned, but my soul was intact, far away from me. Bound in gold and magic, it remained hidden outside the walls—waiting patiently for its match.

The one destined to free me.

CHAPTER 2

ALI

My muscles were completely stiff, both from nerves and the cold. It was nearly one a.m., and my teeth were chattering so hard that I thought I might chip one of them. Pretty sure I'd been lying on the same patch of roof for nearly six hours, battered by wintry winds. At least I had a faux-fur-lined coat to keep me warm, and boots to match. And being in the forbidden realm aboveground always sent a rush of adrenaline through my veins.

In any case, cold or not—I had a bank to rob tonight. As one of the chief assassins and thieves of the Shadow Caverns, my jobs weren't always cushy, but they were necessary. Robbing from the High Elves—killing when necessary—these were the only tools I had to help free my people.

"Ali, how's it going?" Barthol's voice sounded in my headset.

"Cold up here. Just trying to stay warm." I pictured my brother Barthol leaning against the wall of the alley on the opposite side of Silfarson's Bank. Out of the wind and a lot warmer than my rooftop perch. Of course, he'd also be wearing his cave-bear jacket, his hands stuffed deep in its pockets.

"You ready for tonight?" he asked.

Not really. "Absolutely."

Lowering my face, I peered down the sight of my crossbow and over the tip of the anti-magic-hex bolt. I had the crossbow trained on the window across the street, just above the gold sign that read *Silfarson's Bank*. While the bottom half of the old office tower was gilt and ornate, its upper floors had fallen into disrepair centuries ago, iron girders jutting out at odd angles like broken fingers. Icicles encrusted from them, glinting in the faint moonlight.

The crossbow's sight was like ice against the edge of my eye socket. What I really wanted, desperately, was to be at home with a hot cup of tea and my collection of ancient romance novels.

A bit of dread was spreading over me like blooms of frost, and I took a shivering breath. I started to hum, trying to calm my nerves.

"Ali, what's that tune?" asked Barthol. I suspected he sensed my nervousness. "I like it."

I smiled. He and I had the same taste in music. "Something I found on an old flash drive I bought on Newbury Street. Don't know the title, but the file was called *RickRoll.mp3*."

"Oh, I've heard of Rick Roll. He was super popular before Ragnarok. It's wild that you have music from a thousand years ago, isn't it?"

I was obsessed with the world before Ragnarok, when Boston's streets had thronged with people and flowers had bloomed in the summers. Before Thor, Loki, Odin, and the rest of the gods died. When the High Elves had lived in Elfheim, and Midguard was the world of men. But fate was unforgiving, and as foretold, civilization had crumbled into the apocalyptic, icy shit-show we had now. A world in which Night Elves like me lived underground. A world I was trying to destroy, one illegal job at a time.

"Does he have more than one song?" Barthol asked.

"Just that one." I hummed the melody over the headset. "Brilliant, though, isn't it? I don't know who Rick Roll was, but he just seems very… loyal. He was committed to someone. A warrior, maybe, thinking of returning to his lost love." I could feel my eyes getting misty as I tried to peer through the crossbow sight. "When we get back to the flat I can give you a copy—"

"Wait, hold on, sis," Barthol interrupted. "The last security guard just left. I think we're on. Is your side clear?"

My heartbeat kicked up a notch. "Let me check."

I tensed, then shifted forward, peering down at the street below. Empty. No cars, no bicyclists, no one out walking their dog. Just whirling snow and silence. My breath fogged as I exhaled.

This wasn't the first night my brother and I had spent studying the routines of the bank's security. I knew that the last elven guard went home at midnight, the bank stood empty until six a.m. During the day a manager worked exactly opposite my vantage point, in a room with dark wood and marble floors. I knew the manager sometimes slipped a gold piece or two into his jacket pocket when he thought no one was looking. I knew *all* the bank's secrets.

And, most importantly, I knew that I'd die if I failed.

The Shadow Lords had made that clear when they'd sent us here to steal a safe deposit box. The box held an object that might lead us to Galin—a High Elf sorcerer. Long ago, he'd worked for the king. He was the one who'd imprisoned our people in caverns deep underground. If we could find Galin, we had a chance at freeing ourselves.

If the High Elves caught me, I'd be executed.

But it was all worth the risk. If I could steal the safe deposit box tonight, we had a chance to free our people.

"My side is clear," I said, sounding calmer than I felt.

"Okay, go anytime."

My finger hovered over the trigger. "I'm going to take the shot."

"Okay," whispered Barthol. "Good luck, Ali."

I checked that my vergr crystal was ready to go before I resighted down the scope. This time, I allowed the pad of my index finger to rest lightly on the trigger. Then I slowly squeezed, and with a soft twang, the bolt shot over the street —directly into the center of the window.

Bullseye.

I leapt up, slung the crossbow over my shoulder, then snatched up my vergr crystal. As the glass shattered on the street below, I hurled the crystal. It spun, glittering in the moonlight, until it disappeared through the shattered opening across the street.

I slung my crossbow over my back, securing the leather strap. Time to get into the bank.

"Fara," I whispered under my breath.

Purple light flashed around me, and cold magic skimmed my body as the spell whisked me away. When the purple light dimmed, I found myself on the manager's mahogany desk. A rush of frigid wind whipped in through the broken window. I scanned the room until I spotted my crystal at my feet. Snatching it up, I slipped it in my pocket, then crouched perfectly still and listened to the silence.

I wasn't worried about the manager—he'd left hours ago —but I was worried about the runes. I'd seen them earlier— the protection runes covering the windowpane. Runes linked directly to the High Elf police force. At best, I had about two minutes to break into the vault before the law arrived. I jumped down from the desk and rushed into a hall of ivory marble and walnut walls.

That was when I smelled my first big problem.

There was still a guard in the building, one that I hadn't accounted for.

"They've got a draugr," I whispered into my headset.

When Barthol didn't respond, I stuffed my headset in my pocket. Probably the thick walls of the bank were interfering with the reception. Of course, my brother couldn't help me fight the undead from where he was.

My pulse started to race. I could already hear the heavy thud of footsteps lumbering toward me.

I sprinted down the hallway, arms pumping. In hindsight, I shouldn't have been surprised to meet a draugr here. They made excellent guards, as they were obsessed with protecting treasure. Undead and untiring, they shredded thieves like me into little pieces.

At the far end of the hallway, I spied what I'd come for—the vault. But it wasn't what I'd expected, and my mouth went dry. Not only did a heavy steel door lock it shut, but protection runes glowed over the metal. Not insurmountable, but with a draugr hot on my tail, I had no time to crack it.

I'd need to improvise.

Adrenaline coursing, I pulled my crossbow from my back, then kneeled to reload it.

The draugr shuffled into view. It was an animated corpse, its emaciated body sinewy and leathery. It licked its lips. Then, with a bellow, it charged. As it bounded down the hallway, I felt the floor tremble beneath me.

I raised the crossbow to my shoulder and fired. Satisfaction lifted my heart as I watched the bolt slam into the center of the draugr's chest, only ten feet away from me. It grunted, looking down at the tiny bit of wood, then took another step toward me.

That was the problem with draugr. They were undead. You couldn't kill a magically animated corpse just by shooting it in the heart, because they didn't need their freaking hearts.

Good thing I'd fired an incendiary bolt.

The draugr was nearly on me when flames began to lick its skin. Something deep within its dead brain must have registered that fire was bad, because it finally stumbled back, clutching at its chest.

Ducking past it, I sprinted back toward the banker's office. I knew that the gas filling the draugr's body was extremely flammable. Just as I rushed into the windy office, the draugr detonated. I covered my head as the building shuddered with the blast.

In the next breath, I was up again.

I grimaced as I stepped out. The once gleaming marble hallway was now coated with leathery bits of draugr flesh. But I grinned when I saw that my plan had worked. I'd lured the beast close enough to the vault door that the explosion had blown it clean off its hinges.

Sometimes I really was brilliant.

I hurried inside the vault and began scanning the safe deposit boxes. I'd been assigned to steal box number 314, and I couldn't wait to get my hands on it.

But my smile disappeared when I discovered that the explosion had done more than just open the vault. The rack holding the deposit boxes had fallen, and their contents had spilled across the floor.

I glanced at my watch. Thirty seconds left.

"Balls," I muttered, and began to search through the mess. Amid burning scrolls, I snatched up bits of broken unicorn horn, old spell books, even a velvet pouch of giant's teeth. Priceless relics.

Problem was, the Shadow Lords hadn't told me what was *in* box 314, so I had no idea what I was looking for. That sort of info was above my pay grade.

So, I stuffed anything that seemed remotely interesting into my pockets, hoping I was snatching the right thing.

"Crap," I said again as my watch buzzed. *Time's up.*

Then a gleam of metal caught my eye from under a faded scroll. I kicked the curling parchment aside and found a simple gold ring underneath.

Might as well take it.

I plucked it from the ground. But as soon as my fingers wrapped around the gold, a blinding flash of white light shattered my mind into a million pieces.

CHAPTER 3

MARROC

I woke with a jolt, feeling like someone had reached into my chest and squeezed my dead heart. I leaned back against the cold, slimy cell walls. As I caught my breath, I realized what had happened.

Someone had found my soul.

After all this time, would it finally come back to me?

I didn't move from the stone ledge at the back of my cell. Instead, I closed my eyes again. With the limited magic I had, I reached out to the astral plane.

I had no soul to send across it, but with my mind's eye, I could still look into the ethereal realm. Across the cosmic expanse, my soul shone like a star. I focused, trying to see who had found it. As I did, I felt the curse kindling. My body tensed as my blood began to warm.

I gritted my teeth. I could almost perceive her now. A woman.

Shock ignited me as she finally came into focus—the one who would free me. Horror wrapped around me like the coils of a serpent.

No.

One part of me was thrilled. At last, my magic had finally done what I'd commanded. It had bound itself to my twin soul, the perfect complement to my own. The one fated to lift the curse and join me for eternity.

And another half of me wanted to scream at the dead gods. My twin soul was a *Dokkalfr*. A Night Elf. Once she learned who I was, her only goal would be to send my soul to Helheim.

I lay back on the stone bench that served as my bed as I waited for her to find me.

Whatever happened next, I'd have to make sure she didn't figure out how to end my life for good.

CHAPTER 4

ALI

My head throbbed as I opened my eyes. I lay in the middle of the vault, my cheek pressed against a chunk of unicorn horn. I sat up slowly, and nearly screamed when I looked at my watch. A full five minutes had passed since I'd broken into the bank. I was all out of time.

I stood on shaking legs, but my head felt strange. Unbalanced. Like that time Barthol had brought home an old bottle of vodka and dared me to drink half of it.

Even with my head spinning, I managed to stumble into the draugr-coated hallway. Gross, but nothing I couldn't handle.

But my stomach flipped when a figure moved at the end of the hallway, just before the door to the manager's office. Not a draugr this time—someone with golden hair draped over white robes, eyes the color of honey, and a thin hawthorn wand in his hand. There was no mistaking what he was. A High Elf.

He stood about fifteen feet away, and he'd spotted me.

I whispered, "Skalei."

In an instant, a blade appeared in my hand—Skalei, the

dagger given to me by the Shadow Lords when I'd first received my commission as assassin. I remembered how Barthol had comforted me, holding my hand as the Lords carved runes into my flesh to bind the blade to me. All I had to do was say its name, and it would appear in my grasp.

"Don't move!" The elf's melodious voice floated across the hallway, angelic and forbidding.

The air near my cheek hissed as a spell whipped past my head, narrowly missing me. The High Elf wasn't messing around, but I wasn't about to obey his command. I took a step forward, dagger in my hand.

His golden eyes pierced me from the other end of the hall as I stalked closer, every one of my muscles tense and ready.

"Stay where you are!" he called.

I wasn't following his instructions. For one thing, it'd take him a few seconds to recharge his wand. And for another, if he caught me, I'd be as good as dead.

So, I threw the blade. It sank into his chest, and he fell to the ground, clutching his heart.

I muttered, "Skalei," again, and the dagger returned to my hand, now slick with his blood. It was a good thing I had it back, too, because I could already hear more High Elves heading my way.

I stepped over the High Elf's body and rushed closer to the manager's office with the broken window. At the edge of my vision, I saw another High Elf round the corner behind me, blond hair streaming off his shoulders.

He raised a wand. Magic buzzed in the air, and a burning pain shot up my leg. I had no idea what kind of spell that was, but I was sure I'd find out soon enough.

My leg felt like it'd been dipped in boiling water, but I made it back into the banker's room, slamming and locking the door behind me. I cursed when I realized I'd left my crossbow and the knapsack I'd been filling with relics in the vault.

My heart was a wild beast. So far, the robbery had turned into a complete disaster.

With a boom, the door shook. The High Elf outside was battering it so hard that I thought it might break.

I shoved my hand into my pocket, grinning when I felt a sharp chunk of stone. At least I still had the vergr crystal.

I hurried to the shattered window, reared back, and threw the crystal across the street. It soared over the road and landed on the snowy roof where I'd been hiding before.

A High Elf's fist slammed through the wooden door. It was time for me to get the Helheim out.

I shouted, "Fara!" And magic whipped over my body.

I reappeared on the roof, crouching to peer at the flashing lights beneath me. Silfarson's Bank, it seemed, did not mess around when it came to apprehending thieves. High Elves swept through the air, mounted on moths as big as horses. At any moment, I'd be spotted.

I needed help, and I needed it fast. I pulled on my headset. "Barthol, are you there?"

"Ali!" he whispered sharply. "What's going on?"

"Can you help me get out of here?"

"Are you okay? What happened—" A strange, strangled sound cut him off.

"What? Barthol?"

"Run! *Run!*" he shouted frantically, before cutting off again. My headset filled with the hiss of static.

I whirled and sprinted over the rooftop even as I tried to work out what was going on.

Then I heard a noise that explained everything.

"Ghhhroooooarrgh!"

My blood turned to ice, and I froze where I was. There was no mistaking the hunting cry of a troll. Born in the hearts of mountains and made of living rock, trolls were the size of maple trees and virtually indestructible.

The troll pounded the snowy street just below me. The building on which I stood shuddered as the creature barreled through the exterior wall. The whole structure began to shake, and I wondered if it would collapse.

Shit. Only sunlight could stop a troll, turning them to solid rock. But by my calculation, dawn was at least four hours off, and this thing was tearing through the building fast. Screams pierced the air, residents shrieking as the troll tore through the lower floor.

How did it know where to find me? It was at this point that it occurred to me what had hit my leg earlier—a tracking spell. The troll would know *exactly* where to find me, wherever I went.

Quickly, I scanned my surroundings. A building of similar height stood across the street to my left, and it looked like the best escape route. I started to run, but the roof juddered beneath me, and I sprawled flat.

Like a cannonball punching through the side of a ship, the troll burst through the shingles behind me. It was a deep, speckled gray, and it glared at me with tiny eyes that glowed like lava.

"Bllllroooooooahhh!" As it howled, molten saliva spewed from its mouth.

Covering my face with my arms, I knew then that I was one hundred percent, completely and utterly fucked.

Still, I flew to my feet, sprinting toward the rooftop to my left. As I neared the edge of the roof I was on, I threw my crystal across the gap between the buildings, then teleported myself in a flash of magic. I snatched the crystal off the icy surface.

The troll leapt after me, howling. With a splintering crash, it landed about ten feet away. The creature must have weighed at least a ton, because its bottom half instantly disappeared under the shingles. Trolls were big and strong, but not good for chasing people over roofs.

Unfortunately, the moth-mounted elves had no such limitations, and I soon heard the hiss of hexes whizzing past my head. I ran as fast as I could, darting under water tanks and behind chimneys as I tried to stay out of range.

But the next roof was… not there. I skidded to a halt before a three-story drop to a white expanse of snow, speckled with a few barren trees—the frozen remains of Boston Common. I'd be totally exposed if I went down there.

My knuckles were white over the crystal. Stuffing it into my pocket, I began to turn back, but the troll was closing in on me. The bricks were crumbling beneath its weight, but not before a stony hand shot out and snatched me around my waist.

As its other hand reached for me, the roof finally gave way.

There wasn't time to contemplate the disappointment, the failure to save my people. Already, we were crashing through wood and plaster, screams erupting around us. Something cracked the side of my head, and pain shot through my skull.

Four stories and three seconds later, we landed with a deafening crash. Pain rocketed through my body and I tasted blood in my mouth.

Fuck. This job had meant everything. This job would have meant freedom for my people, finally.

I tried to stand, but the troll was already pulling me through the building's wreckage. As an elf, I was sturdier than a human, but I was still in rough shape, and I hung limply in the troll's grasp. It began to drag me into the center of Beacon Street even as dizziness bloomed in my mind.

My body slid and scraped over the freezing pavement. I scrambled to remember what I needed to do next.

"Goott herrrr," the troll growled. Its molten spittle hissed on the icy street.

You got me. But you're not taking me alive.

"Skalei!" The dagger appeared instantly in my hand, its blade black and lethal. I might have failed my people, but I wasn't going down without a fight. I swung hard at the troll's forearm, but my dagger barely chipped his skin.

The troll grunted, then lifted me in the air by my arm and slammed me onto the frozen asphalt. Agony ripped through my bones.

With its stony fist pressing down on me, there was nothing more I could do. Within moments, the High Elves were locking iron handcuffs around my wrists.

CHAPTER 5

❦

ALI

A guard tugged on the chain connected to my manacled wrists. The whole situation had me walking at an awkward sideways angle. At this point, I could only hope they did not know I was a chief assassin. With any luck, they simply thought I was simply a thief.

My body had taken a battering in the past hour, and I winced with every step. Since they'd blindfolded me, however, I had no idea what my surroundings looked like. Footsteps echoed, and the air smelled of moss, dank rocks, and death.

In here, it was far too hot to wear my coat, even if the fur was fake. Sweat trickled down my neck.

Best guess was that I'd been taken to the Citadel. In the years following Ragnarok, when my people had been imprisoned deep within the earth, the High Elves had constructed a colossal fortress in the center of Boston. A thousand feet high, its stark walls were interrupted only by the heads of marble gargoyles. Pale gold spires ringed the tip of the tower, like a crown atop Beacon Hill.

It had always seemed so clean and beautiful—a fortress that shielded the ornate and mysterious world of the High Elves. I'd never been inside it, but I imagined lots of glittering parties and gilded ceremonies.

The elves called it *New Elfheim*. But to everyone else, it was just the Citadel, the seat of their power. All I knew was that it was part temple, part prison, part castle. It housed priests, prisoners, and royalty all within the same looming fortress.

Whatever the case, it was a constant reminder that High Elves now ruled the city, and that my kind wasn't part of it.

Clearly, I wasn't being taken to the royal section of the building. Even with a blindfold covering my eyes, I'd been able to work out that much. High Elves didn't live in places that smelled worse than a sailor's armpit. No, it was straight to the prison blocks for me.

Crushing disappointment pressed on my chest. I'd been so close to saving my people. The task had been to go to the bank, to steal the safe deposit box. And something in that box would lead us to Galin. He was the sorcerer who had locked the Night Elves underground, and I longed to kill him. His death would break the spell and lead to our liberation.

But it seemed I'd fucked it all up. Which item was even the right one? Would've helped if they'd explained that.

I felt like the tip of a blade was piercing my heart. When I was little, Mom always told me that was my destiny, that I'd bring the Night Elves into the light again. Before she'd died in the subterranean caves, she'd said I was the North Star, and I would guide the Night Elves to freedom. And I'd always believed her.

My thoughts shot back to Barthol. Fear streaked through my nerves when I pictured him pressed facedown in the snow, handcuffed by High Elves. I could only hope he'd escaped, that he'd made it back to our safe house.

I couldn't let myself think of any other possibility or I'd fall apart completely. So, I shut a mental steel door over my worst fears and tried to focus on the sounds around me.

The creak of ancient hinges pulled me out of my worries as the guard pushed open a door. As he tugged me deeper into the Citadel's depths, my right side brushed against a damp wall.

"What's happening?" I asked.

"You'll see soon enough," the guard replied, in that annoying singsong voice that seemed to be universal to High Elves.

Truthfully, tonight was the first night I'd ever encountered High Elves face to face. They were the mortal enemies of my kind, *Dokkalfar*, Night Elves. And now, the blond bastards ruled Midgard, what had been world of men. They killed my kind on sight, or for sport.

When they weren't slaughtering Night Elves, the High Elves were imprisoning us in caverns under the ground. Every Night Elf like me had dreamed of freeing our kind. And I'd nearly had the chance…

There it was again, that frosty bloom of regret spreading over my heart.

But revenge against the High Elves would never be easy. Here in Midgard, we were outnumbered. Barthol and I had spent the last year planning the robbery. We'd kept a low profile, sleeping in abandoned townhouses, scrounging food on the streets. We'd steered completely clear of the High Elves the whole time, never getting too close. Never risking death until we had to.

The guard slowed, and I heard him suck in a sharp breath. Something had him on edge. He stopped, fumbling with his keys. Judging by all the jangling, it sounded like his hands were shaking. What did *he* have to be scared of?

A low growl reverberated in the cellblock, and the sound slid right through my bones.

It was like nothing I'd ever heard. The hunting cry of the troll had been terrifying, but at least it'd sounded dumb. This growl was barely audible, yet somehow managed to convey a brutal savagery. It was a strangely haunting sound, shivering over my skin and turning my veins to ice.

The guard ripped the cell door open and pushed me to the ground. My knees bit into the cold, jagged rock, and I tried to stand, but the guard pressed a foot to my back as he undid my handcuffs.

Again, that low, quiet, forlorn growl slipped over the stone like wind howling through trees.

The guard gasped. He was terrified.

"What is it?" I asked.

He didn't answer as he ripped the blindfold from my face. I rolled over to look at him, catching golden eyes wild with terror. Then he stumbled back out of the cell, slammed the door shut, and ran down the corridor and out of sight without looking back.

I was left alone in complete darkness. Not that I particularly cared. Night Elf eyes were magically adapted to a life underground.

I squinted, studying my surroundings. Unsurprisingly, a row of thick iron bars separated me from the corridor's glistening stone floor. Jutting from the wall behind me was a granite slab, covered in straw. My bed, apparently. No sign of food or water.

My instincts told me to stay back, that something deeply unnatural and evil lurked nearby.

And yet—curiosity had me shifting closer to the bars, peering between them and into the corridor. I scanned the narrow hall, counting ten cells in the block, five on each side.

Iron rods barred each of them from floor to the ceiling. From this vantage point, I could only see into the cell across from me, but it was like the darkness was *thicker* there.

I squinted, trying to understand what I was looking at. In the back of the cell, where a stone bed should have jutted from the wall, pooled inky shadows that my eyes couldn't penetrate. As I stared, the shadows began to move, coalescing into something denser.

The low growl returned, skimming along the rocks and trembling over my skin. Across from me, the darkness seemed to lengthen into the shape of a man. An enormous man, looming over the back of his cell—six foot five at least, big as a god. What *was* he?

The hair on the back of my arms rose. Still crouching on the cell floor, I inched back. No wonder the guard had been freaked out.

Without warning, the man shifted so fast that my heart skipped a beat, a flash of movement in his cell. When the smoke around him thinned, my breath caught in my throat. His tattered shirt revealed a thickly muscled chest tattooed with runes gleaming with magic.

But from between the tattoos crawled a stygian darkness, like black ink that was also somehow alive. Shadows writhed around his face, so dark and thick I couldn't see his features until, for an instant, they flitted away.

In that moment, I saw what lay beneath—a heartbreakingly beautiful face, with cheekbones sharp as blades and eyes the color of a glacial stream. Most of all, his wicked smile made my blood turn to ice.

He was simultaneously the most beautiful and the most terrifying man I had ever seen, like someone sent by the gods to destroy everyone. But I had no idea what or who he was. He had neither the silver hair of the Dokkalfar nor the blond of the High Elves. Clearly, he wasn't human—his size and all the inky magic made that clear. So what the Helheim was he?

Whatever he was, I'd caught his attention, and it sent jolts of fear through my nerve endings.

With his gaze locked on me, he raised his right index finger and began to cast a strange sort of magic.

CHAPTER 6

MARROC

With my index finger, I traced *sowilo*, the S-shaped rune for sun. It was hardly a spell, but even so, the curse roared in my veins. I gritted my teeth and forced my hand to keep moving. When I finished, the air glowed with light, and I could see at last.

From the cell across the hall, a female Night Elf stared at me, silver eyes wide as saucers.

There you are, little one.

She was the one who'd woken me from my sleep. Silver hair cascaded down her back, and her wide cheekbones shimmered faintly under the golden light, her eyebrows and eyelashes black as jet. Although she wore a furry jacket, I found my gaze sliding down to her body. She wore tight leather pants that showed off her shapely legs.

Once, long ago, lust for her body would have raged in me as I looked at her. Now, it was a different kind of desire. I wanted to drink her soul, to press my mouth against her neck and drain her completely. Hunger for her ripped through me. Every guard I'd drained in here had been dull, their souls as mediocre as their lives. For a thousand years, I'd been unfulfilled.

This one, this beauty across from me—her soul would taste divine.

Every one of my muscles went tense, and I gripped the bars. I couldn't do it, though—couldn't let myself get close enough to give in. Draining her soul would be a disaster for me—it would cost me my own life.

Because from here, I could feel what had happened. She wasn't the owner of one soul, but two. When she'd stolen my golden ring, my soul had taken shelter within the thief, and she was now its vessel. That was what had woken me in my cell. And I had to do everything within my power to keep her safe—to keep my own soul alive.

She was the one living creature I could never kill.

But was that *only* because she had my soul? She was my mate, too. After all, that was what my spell had commanded: that my mate find the ring, even if she had no idea the part she played in my magic.

I could feel the mating bond, vaguely. A sense of protectiveness glowed, dull in my chest like a dying ember. Without the curse, it would have raged like a flame. Still, it was amazing that I could feel anything at all. I couldn't love anymore, but I still *felt* something for her, dimly.

And yet fate had truly offered me a poisoned dish. The gods had doubly cursed me with this Night Elf. Once she knew who I really was, she'd hate me for eternity. She wouldn't rest until I was dead. And possessing my soul as she did, fate had given her the means to kill me easily.

The elf had inched back when I'd revealed myself, but now she moved forward again, her slim fingers wrapping around the iron bars. She should have been terrified of me, but she looked curious.

Gold sparkled on one of her fingers. Even though I knew

she carried my soul, my heart thrummed when I saw the familiar circlet. It was the ring I'd forged a thousand years ago, the vessel that had housed my soul for millennia.

"Who are you?" she whispered.

The moment I tried to speak, blood roared in my ears, and my skin burned as though a thousand suns shone upon it. The curse heated my blood, and the words died in my throat.

I let out a long, slow sigh, then stepped back into the depths of cell. Maybe not right now, but I'd get to her, one way or another.

CHAPTER 7

ALI

At least an hour of silence had passed since I'd been thrown into this cell, during which my strange prison friend had disappeared into the shadows. As he'd slunk back into the darkness, the aches in my body had returned.

Now, I couldn't see him at all; inky darkness collected around him. Strangely, even my Dokkalfar eyesight couldn't pierce those shadows, and he wasn't making a single sound. I could smell him a little, though. And it wasn't a bad smell, either—like wood smoke and burned sage. I breathed it in. There was almost something alluring about it, despite how terrifying he'd appeared.

I sat on the stone bench, trying to work out a plan. Apparently, the guard hadn't seen me as much of a threat, because he'd hardly searched me. For safekeeping, I'd stashed the vergr crystal in my shoe—a possible route out of here, I had thought, if I could manage it.

And yet it couldn't get me out of here. I'd already tried.

About twenty minutes earlier, I'd slipped the crystal between the cell bars. I'd actually escaped my cell and walked to either end of the cellblock, only to find the doors to the block were solid and locked. There was no way to get my crystal through, so I was stuck here for now.

Unfortunately, waiting for someone to open the door so I could toss the stone through meant sweating in my winter coat. The acrylic fur was making my neck itch, the fake goatskin trapping in the heat. But there wouldn't be time to throw it on if the door creaked open.

I searched the darkness for my prison buddy again—the terrifying man with the cold eyes who seemed like he might eat my soul. *Nothing.*

"Skalei," I whispered, and the knife appeared. I wasn't sure what I'd do with it; I just felt better with it in my hand. The blade was magically sharp, and it could slice through the flesh of my enemies in an instant. Not, unfortunately, troll arms or iron bars.

I began to hum the Rick Roll song as I flipped the blade in my hand. Five full rotations of razor-sharp steel. Once with my eyes opened, once with them closed. An old assassin's habit to pass the time.

I *hoped* a guard would be showing up at some point with food. That was when I'd make my move. Although there was every possibility they planned to let me starve down here. Might explain the stench of death.

Just as I raised Skalei for another toss, light and voices flooded the cellblock.

"In with Marroc?" came a feminine voice, followed by tinkling laugher. "That *is* brilliant. She's probably pissed herself with fear."

I was getting the impression that they had no idea who I was.

Another voice, this one masculine but still with the mellifluous tone of the High Elves: "I still can't believe Father sent us down here. This place is *vile*."

"Sune, you know how he is. He only trusts his own family. I, for one, am *honored* to do as he asks." The woman's tone dripped with sarcasm.

I peered between the bars, and my stomach sank. A trio of High Elves had entered the cell block. If I threw my crystal, they'd almost certainly catch me.

So, instead of escaping, I watched as the High Elves walked down the corridor between the cells. Leading the way was a stocky guard with blond eyebrows. He tried to look confident, but his knuckles were white on the hilt of his sword.

Behind him walked a pair of taller elves—a man and a woman. They were dressed in the ivory robes preferred by nobility, and both wore a thin hawthorn-wood wand on their hip. The woman was beautiful, with the honey-colored hair and eyes typical of their kind. The man, however, looked too pale, like he'd faded in the sun.

I slid Skalei next to the crystal in my shoe to hide it as they drew closer to me. I tried to look peaceful when the trio stopped in front of my cell, folding my hands in my lap.

"You're the one who tried to break into Silfarson's?" asked the woman. Her voice was musical but unmistakably hostile, like a flute played in a minor key.

She irritated me already.

I sighed. "I *successfully* broke into Silfarson's."

"You know, she's technically right, Revna." The man laughed. I recognized the voice as Sune's. "She *was* caught escaping from the bank."

"Semantics," she snapped. I regretted my impetuousness, considering her expression said she'd love an excuse to rip my throat out.

Sune's eyes narrowed. "Tell us why you tried to rob the bank."

I shrugged, feigning nonchalance. I couldn't let on the truth. "Because I want to be rich."

Revna arched an eyebrow. "Even Night Elves aren't stupid enough to break into our banks without a good reason. We know your name. Ali, daughter of Volundar."

My throat went dry. Did they know what I did? That I wasn't simply a common thief?

"Volundar," said Sune. "As far as I can tell, he's just another dead Night Elf. Your mother's name isn't even recorded; that's how insignificant she was. Though I imagine she's dead too, rotted away in the caves. Is that right?"

Rage tightened its grip on my heart, but I fought to master control. I kept my mouth shut to stop myself from hurling curses at them. I didn't want them uttering a word about my parents.

"I would feel pity for your wretched kind, if it weren't for the fact that the Night Elves caused Ragnarok," added Revna. "You killed the gods, worshipping Loki like you did. Naughty, naughty. You're lucky we let you live at all, after what your kind did to the world."

I wanted to tell them that was a lie—at least, I'd always *felt* it was a lie. But I had to keep up the charade that they weren't getting to me. "Who cares about the past?" I spat. "I care only for gold."

The only comfort in this entire situation was that no one had mentioned Barthol yet, and he clearly wasn't here. I was growing ever more hopeful he'd made it back to the safehouse.

Just behind them, in the shadows, the blue-eyed prisoner began to stir. His shadowy magic condensed around him.

When I looked back at the two blondes, I saw that Sune was staring at the ring on my finger. "Where did you get *that?*"

I glanced at it. Somehow, in the shitstorm that had

erupted since the robbery, I'd totally forgotten the ring I'd found on the floor.

I held my hand up with a smile. "Like I said. I like gold."

"That ring belongs to us." Sune slid his hand between the bars. "Give it to me."

I kept my expression neutral. "I'll give it to you if you release me."

Revna folded her arms. "Don't be absurd. How about we agree not to torture you until you can no longer remember your name?"

"I'd love to peel back her face," Sune added enthusiastically.

A compelling counteroffer. I wasn't sure I had much negotiating power in this situation.

With a scowl, I gripped the gold encircling my finger—but when I pulled, it wouldn't budge. I pulled harder, with a rising sense of panic. Out of the corner of my eye, I saw tendrils of the prisoner's magic twisting across the stones between the cells.

"It's stuck." Some strange magic was binding it to my skin.

"She can't remove it," said Revna. "Guard, fetch my skinning blade."

I was not going to endure a face peeling just because I couldn't remove a freaking ring. I still had a chance to break out of here if I could manage to catch the door opening at the right time.

I pulled Skalei from my boot and pressed the blade against my finger, just below the ring. Immediately, blood welled against the blade. I was gritting my teeth, ready to cut into my skin if I had to, when an unearthly growl rose from the prisoner's cell.

A *boom* erupted from across the cell block as the prisoner slammed his hands against the bars once more, and the sound of the impact reverberated through the prison. The pair of High Elves jumped like they'd been shot with a hex, and the guard screamed like a baby.

"Take her," said Sune to the guard. With shaking hands, the guard hurried to open my cell. I slid my blade into my boot again, though no one seemed worried about it.

As soon as the cell door was open, Revna raised a wand. I had no room to dodge, and her spell slammed into my chest. My body stiffened as ice flooded my veins. With my muscles no longer responding, I teetered for a moment before toppling backward like a felled tree.

* * *

WHEN I CAME TO, I was being dragged by ropes bound tightly around my wrists. The words *face peeling* slammed through my mind. Though my body was still frozen by Revna's spell, the effects were starting to wear off a little. I could just about wiggle my toes and fingers.

Quickly, I took in my surroundings. I was outside. It was near midnight. The moon was out, luminous and full. A thin breeze blew icy cold, and my breath caught at the chill, the winter air stinging my cheeks.

A few golden spires loomed above me, but the massive walls of the Citadel were nowhere to be seen. Instead, short parapets rose on either side. The stone was the gleaming white of the Citadel's walls. We seemed to be on a curving walkway surrounding the fortress, towering somewhere above Beacon Hill.

Thing was, since I'd never been inside the Citadel before, I didn't have a sense of the layout at all. I had no idea what to expect next. Were they going to throw me off the edge of the tower? I remembered vaguely that used to be the punishment for treason in ancient times.

My head throbbed as I tried to formulate a plan, but I'd

been through such a beating tonight that I was nearly out of coherent thoughts. I still had the vergr stone, at least, but I couldn't get to my shoe with my wrists bound.

Skalei always came to me when I called for her, and the blade could slice through rope. But I'd need the guard to stop yanking me before I could pause to make that work. I'd get one chance to call Skalei and make my escape, so I'd have to consider it carefully.

Once again, I tasted blood on my lips, and my thoughts drifted a little. Somehow, it was hard to think clearly when your body was magically frozen, like Novocaine for the mind.

Vaguely, I remembered I was supposed to play Rick Roll for Barthol tonight, and I wondered if he'd manage to find it on his own. Would he be okay without me? He must be out of his mind with worry, and I felt desperate to get a message to him. He wasn't in the dungeon, and I hadn't seen him out here on the roof. With any luck, he was back in the Shadow Caverns. On a normal night, I'd be making mushroom soup for him, while he made up wild stories about a talking goat character he'd invented, or we would draw on the walls. When we were super bored, we would try to choreograph dances. In the Shadow Caverns, we had to do our best to make our own entertainment. Tonight, he'd be telling stories of Jeremy the Alcoholic Goat to the silent walls.

Assuming he got home safely.

But what would he do if he figured out where I was? I didn't want him taking off on a wild revenge mission, or attempting a prison break. He needed my guidance to undertake anything insane.

"Oh! The thing is awake."

Revna's singsong voice pulled me out of my stupor, and I realized I had to switch into survival mode again. As the numbing spell grew weaker, I could feel myself bouncing painfully over the stones.

Revna walked beside me, smiling placidly down. There was no one else with us besides the High Elf guard who dragged my bound wrists. At last, my legs were thawing a bit, and I could better feel the stones beneath me.

"I can walk!" I shouted. "You can stop dragging me."

The guard ignored me, not even a glance back in my direction.

I scrambled to stand on my tingling legs with a jolt of panic. For a few moments, I was locked in a tug of war with the guard. But after an awkward tussle, I managed to get to my feet, glowering eye to eye with the guard. An arctic wind whipped over the parapets, stinging my cheeks and rushing through my silver hair.

It was only at that moment that I felt the sharp pain in my hand, that I looked down at my finger. I felt myself going dizzy—

Revna pivoted. "I'm sorry," she cooed. "We had to take the whole finger off. It was frankly *disgusting*."

With horror whirling in my mind, I stared at the bloody nub where my ring finger had once been. When I glanced back over the long, curving walkway, I saw a long stream of crimson. In fact, the nub was still pumping blood onto the stones at my feet. My knees went weak.

I wanted to call Skalei, cut my bonds, and carve a permanent reminder of what Revna had taken from me across her pretty face. But now that I'd lifted my gaze from my mutilated hand, I took in the view around me.

On one side, the city of Boston spread out. And on the other—the walkway encircled an enormous amphitheater of white stone, with seats cascading down. The floor of the amphitheater was as dark as the night sky.

Tugging on the rope, the guard dragged me through a gate, into the top row of the amphitheater.

So, *this* was what loomed over Beacon Hill, on top of the Citadel. It was like a pale colosseum, ringed by spires like the rocks of a Neolithic stone circle.

I sucked in a sharp breath as I realized that, all around the amphitheater, High Elves filled the seats. It felt as if a thousand golden eyes were on me, all of them lit up with anticipation.

This did not bode well. I didn't imagine I was in for a comfortable evening, here among a legion of my enemies.

I tried to reach for my shoe—it was definitely time for my vergr stone—but the guard yanked the rope so hard that I stumbled on the top step. I struggled to keep up as he dragged me down the steps, one row after another. All around me, the High Elves stared as I trailed blood behind me.

When we arrived at the lowest row of the arena, Revna turned to me, her eyes flashing with malice. The wind toyed with her pale hair. "Is it true that your kind can see in the dark? I suppose it's a needed adaptation when you live in caves. I suppose you've grown used to all the disease down there as well, and the corpses piling up around you."

A flash of white-hot anger flamed in my chest, but I ignored her, staring at the floor of the amphitheater. Jet black, it looked like a piece of the night sky had dropped to the earth and filled the arena.

"Oh, do you understand now? *That's* where your life ends." Revna batted her eyelashes, and I imagined stabbing her in the eye.

But before I did anything rash, I needed to understand the layout of the place. As I scanned the entire amphitheater, I spotted a dais just below us. There, a tall elf stood, dressed in thick golden robes. By his gleaming, spindly crown, I recognized him as King Gorm, the ruler of the High Elves. Head of the very family responsible for everything that had happened to my people. And now his attention was on me. I wondered if *he* knew who I was. I'd assassinated six High Elves from his kingdom—men accused of maliciously spreading disease in the Shadow Caverns.

"Revna," he called up to us, his musical voice floating on the icy wind, "have you brought the thief?"

Thief. Not assassin. Good.

"Yes, Father," she said.

"And you have the ring?"

Revna held up the gold ring, which was still covered in my blood.

"Excellent," said the elf king. "The Night Elf has committed theft, murder, and extensive property damage—crimes that must be punished, here, before New Elfheim."

I clenched my jaw, unwilling to show the fear that now welled in my heart. High Elves surrounded me on all sides in seats of stone and ice. They glared at me, their amber eyes eerie in the moonlight.

"Cave scum!" shouted one.

"Throw her into the depths!" screamed another. "We don't want her filthy kind here."

But I was hardly listening as the guard pulled me further down, to the ground floor of the amphitheater itself, below King Gorm's dais. The rope bit into my skin as he pulled me, and I considered calling forth Skalei—but again I hesitated. I'd only have one shot at that.

I gritted my teeth, fighting against the guard with all my might, but he was so much bigger than me, stronger.

Gray granite encircled the black floor, and the guard was careful to stay away from the edge. I stared at the dark expanse now just inches from me, trying to make sense of its strange surface. It looked solid, pitch black and smooth as ice. Some type of volcanic rock, I guessed. Obsidian, maybe. I wondered why the guard seemed so careful not to go near it.

And while it seemed obvious that they planned to kill me—that my execution was the reason they'd all assembled in the middle of the night—there was no gallows, no bloodstained chopping block, no hooded executioner ready to lop off my head.

The king raised his arms, and the crowd quieted. "Are you ready!"

The crowd cheered. They, at least, seemed to know what was going on.

"Opna!" King Gorm shouted.

The obsidian floor shimmered, and my blood froze as I finally understood what I was looking at. What I'd thought to be solid rock was actually a magical illusion. I stood at the edge of a bottomless chasm so deep that even my Night Elf eyes couldn't penetrate its depths.

There was no question in my mind what it was. This had to be the Well of Wyrd—quite literally the edge of the world.

CHAPTER 8

MARROC

I threw myself again and again at the bars of my cell.

The curse burned wildly within me. Infernally hot, it scalded my bones, seared the muscles of my heart. Every nerve ending screamed for me to stop, but I ignored the pain. It couldn't kill me. Not when I was already dead.

I'd seen it happen. The king's daughter had sliced my ring from the Night Elf's finger. And now, I knew what they had planned.

They were about to make a terrible mistake.

So far, I was breaking my body more than the bars. Hot ichor poured from my shoulder, smoking with the curse. But I blocked out the pain, desperate to get to her. No matter what it did to me, I had to break through. My soul depended on it.

My lungs heaved as I threw myself across the cell with all my strength. At last, with a great crack, the bars broke free from their moorings, crashing to the stone floor so hard that the walls shook. I leapt over them, rushing down the hallway like a storm wind.

I knew my way around the place, exactly how to find the stairs that would lead me up to the amphitheater, and I slipped into a narrow spiral stairwell. Inwardly, I cursed the people who'd built this tower a thousand feet high. A wildly impractical testament to ego.

I was taking the stairs two at a time, flying through the darkness. Lucky for me, I no longer felt fatigue, or my muscles burning. I hadn't felt that for eons; I could run forever.

I knew there was only one place they could have taken the Night Elf.

As I ascended, I didn't pause to savor my freedom. There was only one thing on my mind—getting my soul back. In all the time I'd been locked in here, I had never had a reason to break free. Now, it was everything.

No, maybe there were two things driving me. That dull ember in me wanted to keep her safe, too. Even through my curse, the mating bond glowed.

I rushed up the stairs, smoky shadows whipped around me, concealing me. It didn't matter, though. No one was around. They were probably all in the stone seats above, salivating over the thought of watching the death of a Night Elf. Rubbing their hands together with glee at her demise.

Anger coiled through me, and I moved even faster, desperate. Was I too late? This place had too many stairs by about a thousand.

If she died, would I feel it?

At last, at the very top of the tower, I slammed through a wooden door, onto the curving walkway that surrounded the amphitheater.

In the shadows above all the others, I stared out over the crowded stone seats. The last time I was here, I'd lost my soul.

This time, I intended to regain it.

CHAPTER 9

ALI

I stared down at the chasm, certain that I was looking into the Well of Wyrd itself.

The well was one of the few earthly portals to Yggdrasill, the great cosmic tree that bound our world with other realms: those of the elves, the giants, the dwarves, and so on. Only a couple feet of granite and a few inches of stone lip separated me from oblivion.

To fall into the Well of Wyrd would be to fall into an endless void. Eternal isolation. Certain death. Panic slid over my mind. *Now* would be a good time for an escape.

"Skalei!" The dagger appeared tight in my grip.

Revna raised her wand, readying another freezing spell. But this time, I was ready. As the hex hissed toward me, I ducked, jerking hard on my rope. Now it was enough of a surprise that the guard wasn't ready, and he stumbled *right* into the path of the hex.

The spell hit him in the center of his back, and instantly, his body went rigid, hands unclenching from the rope. For a moment, he teetered on the brink of the well, his features fixed in an expression of pure terror. Then he tipped over the edge and disappeared into the depths, silent as the night.

But Revna wasn't silent. No, she was screaming, trying to charge her wand.

And I was free. Already, I'd flipped Skalei around to slice through the ropes on my wrists. Its magical blade cut through them like a hot knife through butter. All around, the crowd began to shout. Were they scared of me?

Revna certainly was. She was backing away from me, heading for the stairs. I followed after her. I wasn't sure what I planned, but I *did* want to take one of her fingers.

But at the bottom of the stairs, I froze. Someone new had arrived—at the top of the amphitheater. There stood the shadowy prisoner, silhouetted against the moon. Ah, so *that* was why they were terrified.

Thick black smoke rose from his body and a low, primal moan emanated from his chest, rumbling over the stone. Screams erupted around us, and the High Elves began surging away from him. Revna ran toward her father. King Gorm drew his wand.

And yet the prisoner's eyes were on me. With magic curling around his beautiful face, he began to move down the steps of the amphitheater. He seemed to be coming for me. Another person who wanted me dead, I thought. I had no idea what he was, only that he scared the living shit out of everyone around me, so I'd best keep my distance.

"Everyone stop moving," King Gorm shouted. "Revna, show him the ring!"

Realization flashed across Revna's face. Dropping her wand, she held up the bloody ring.

"Marroc!" shouted the king. "We have your soul. Another step, and you'll be cursed forever."

The prisoner stopped where he was, midway down the steps. Black magic coiled off him as he stared at King Gorm, his eyes now dark as the Well of Wyrd. He didn't speak, and I had no idea what he wanted... but he seemed intent on me.

It was as if the whole Citadel held its breath, waiting to see what would happen next. No one moved—except me. While they were all staring at the prisoner, I was slipping off my boot. The vergr crystal lay inside it.

Then, silently, the prisoner started moving down the steps once more.

"I'll end this now!" Revna spun and hurled the ring into the Well of Wyrd.

It twirled in the air, gleaming in the moonlight, then plunged into the darkness.

The prisoner was nearly upon me when I reared back and threw my boot with all my might, aiming for the far side of the well. I had good aim and a strong arm, and it landed in the stone seats opposite us.

"Fara!"

A flash of purple light, and I exploded out of my own boot on the far side of the well, bits of shoe leather raining around me. The vergr crystal lay at my feet, and I snatched it up.

In the seats all around the amphitheater, chaos reigned. Around me, High Elves streamed up the stairs, oblivious to my presence, focused only on getting as far from the prisoner as possible. I turned back to look at him—towering over the others like a god of darkness. He picked up a High Elf and threw him into the Well of Wyrd. Then his dark eyes were on me again.

I whirled, racing up the steps of the amphitheater, trailing behind the others. My thighs burned, lungs heaving as I chased the throng of High Elves. No one was looking at me. They were all running for their lives, and I was at the back of the crowd.

What the fuck *was* that guy?

By the time I reached the top of the stairs, my bootless right foot was frozen. But I kept running, turning onto the curving stone walkway. At this point, I was just following the others, racing behind them. I kicked my remaining boot off and ran in my socks, which was cold as shit but less awkward for running.

I was sprinting so fast that I nearly missed the shadow of a moth passing over me. I glanced up just in time to see its rider launch a hex at my head. Diving to the side, I took shelter behind a parapet for a moment. When the spell bounced off the stone, I leapt to my feet again.

The elves ahead of me were running for a door in one of the spires, holding it open for each other. I wasn't exactly sure what I'd do when I got inside, but maybe I'd blend into the chaos, make my escape from the lower floors.

But just as I reached the door, it slammed shut before me. My heart sank as I heard a bolt sliding across.

With my pulse racing out of control, I pulled on the door's handle. Locked up tight.

Could I use the vergr crystal here? I turned, heaving for breath as I peered over the walkway. Clouds puffed around me, and the lights of Boston glimmered welcomingly a thousand feet below.

It was just as I'd thought—far too high to toss the crystal. A vergr crystal might allow me to travel any distance in an instant, but the crystal itself wasn't indestructible. While fifty feet would hardly scratch it, a thousand-foot drop would shatter it to smithereens.

Sadly, traveling to a fragmented crystal was a *very* bad idea. It meant your body would reappear in the same number of pieces as there were fragments of crystal, which was... not ideal.

A shadow swept over me again, and I glanced up at the moth-mounted elf. As he circled above me, swooping lower, my heart hammered against my ribs. I was running out of options *fast.* Any moment now and that elf's wand would be recharged.

I had to find another way out of the Citadel, because I was *deep* in enemy territory.

But when I turned back in the other direction, my stomach fell.

The prisoner was racing for me, dark magic whirling around him. He moved like a phantom—no sound coming from him, shadows coiling off him.

A line of guards trailed behind him even as his gaze bored into me. I could almost smell the High Elves' fear in the air. They were shooting bolts of magic at him, but none seemed to hurt him.

What could I do now? I had no choice but to fight, even if he seemed to scare the crap out of everyone. I gripped Skalei, my legs shaking a little as the prisoner raced along the walkway. I was nimble from my years of assassin training, but he was much, *much* bigger than me.

I widened my stance, ready as I'd ever be. And as he reached me, I sprang forward. My blade plunged into the center of his chest.

Unfortunately, it didn't slow him down a bit. He wrapped his arms around me, then pushed me to ground under him.

The guards were pelting us with hexes now. The air was ablaze with magic, and I could hear the spells hissing and sizzling all around me. Yet, somehow, none hit me. I opened my eyes, daring to look up at this monster.

He crouched over me, shielding me with his massive body. My dagger still protruded from his chest, and the skin on his neck looked burned. So, the hexes had hit him, and yet somehow he was still alive.

The darkness in his eyes faded to ice blue. He pulled Skalei from his chest and tossed it away. Beneath all the dark magic, the man was as beautiful as a god. My breath caught as I looked up at him; I struggled to think of what I needed to do next.

Before I could say a word, he wrapped a powerful arm beneath me and pulled me to him—tight. I was crushed against his iron chest.

As I struggled to break free from him, he lifted me up. The wind whipped over me, and panic climbed up my throat as he leapt on top of the battlements.

Was he going to *jump*? I screamed into his chest, frantic to break free. But he was far too strong for me, his grip like steel.

I looked down at the earth as he leapt off the parapet. For a moment, time seemed to slow down. We hung suspended a thousand feet above Boston.

Then, like a meteor, we began to plummet.

CHAPTER 10

MARROC

We ripped through the sky, a falling star against the darkness of night. And yet even as we plummeted, I felt something I hadn't experienced in a thousand years: ecstasy.

The wind whipped over us. My soul wasn't at the bottom of the Well of Wyrd with the ring—it was inside Ali.

For the first time in a millennium, I could feel it, its power warm within her chest. And with that warmth, the memories of everything I'd forgotten while in prison: sunlight on my face, the gentle breeze through rowan trees. The scent of roses. Now, I could remember the calls of the ravens I'd once kept in my castle, each of them named for a god... That had been before Ragnarok, before the gods had died.

Trapped in a dark prison cell, I'd forgotten the beauty of the world entirely. I'd forgotten how it felt to kiss a woman, and the sweet taste of lingonberry wine—

"What the *fuck*! What the fuck was that!"

My mate's screams interrupted the glorious peace of my

thoughts. Her voice tore through the night sky like a killing hex.

Did she not understand that the guards were going to kill her? That I'd saved her life?

With the curse stealing my voice, I could do nothing to calm her nerves. Her shrieks were grating, like a sword scraping against the inside of my skull. In my cell, I'd grown used to silence. Why couldn't I experience this reunion with my soul in peace?

For the love of the gods, was my mate really this loud?

I tuned her voice out, focusing again on the warmth of my soul as we fell. And yet I still wasn't whole. My soul still wasn't in my chest.

Sadly, it had ended up in the body of this shrieking Night Elf. Had fate, had Wyrd really tied me to a *burglar* like this one? Perhaps fate was punishing me.

And yet perhaps her screaming, given these circumstances, was normal. Trapped in isolation for a thousand years, I thought I'd completely lost my mind. I'd forgotten entirely what it was like to feel *anything*.

It was hard for me to remember normality or what it meant to feel fear. With my soul so close to me, I was catching glimpses of what it meant to be alive, but I couldn't experience it completely. I remembered feeling something like fear…

It was only at this point that it flickered into my mind again—that idea of mortality. The distant memory that when you were alive, death was something to be avoided. The little Night Elf in my arms was terrified because she would not survive this fall, and what the Helheim had I been thinking? I *had* lost my mind.

Worst of all, with my soul now trapped in her body, her death would mean mine as well.

Now, for the first time in a thousand years, I felt it: fear, cold and sharp, like ice exploding in my chest.

My hand whipped out, and I grabbed on to the only thing available to me—a gargoyle's head. Our momentum nearly ripped my arm out of its socket, but I managed to hold on. The problem was that the masonry holding up the gargoyle was cracking, its leering face tilting further down toward the ground. Bits of cement flaked into the air as the masonry crumbled, and the Night Elf's screams rang in my ears.

I had no magic to speak of, only sheer physical strength.

And any moment now, we'd be falling again. She would die.

CHAPTER 11

ALI

I could hardly breathe. That had been the most terrifying few seconds of my life, but somehow, the prisoner hardly seemed fazed.

With one hand, the prisoner pressed me to his muscled chest. With the other, he gripped a gargoyle, which was about to rip from the wall. My heart slammed hard against my ribs as I tried to think clearly. We needed something that would grip the stones, something to stop us from splattering across Boston's streets.

"Skalei." In a moment, the dagger was in my hand again.

Reaching over the prisoner's shoulder, I stabbed the side of the wall, plunging the blade into the cement between the blocks of marble.

But too late. The gargoyle's neck ripped out, and I lost my grip on the hilt. For a split second, we were falling to our deaths again.

Then, like a viper from beneath a rock, the stranger's arm snatched the dagger's hilt, nearly dropping me in the process. I clamped my arms tight around his neck, and for the first time realized I'd tightened my legs around his waist as well.

We were sliding down the wall now, the dagger cutting through the stone. Marble debris cascaded everywhere, but at least our descent was much slower than falling freely through space.

Beneath my panic, though, part of me was already thinking about the amazing story this would make when I told Barthol about it later.

I glanced up at the blade as it carved a straight line down the wall. At least he'd understood what to do with it. He wasn't *completely* insane, even if he couldn't speak and had leapt off the side of a tower.

I looked down and watched as the earth rushed toward us, not a hundred feet away now. As the dagger slid through the stone, we picked up speed, frigid air rushing over us.

This was one of the few moments I wished that Skalei's blade wasn't quite so magical—on one hand, granite was too strong for her, but on the other, she sliced through marble like it was butter. The ground was rushing for me now, only twenty feet away, ten feet—

BOOM!

We slammed into the earth, and I lost my grip on the stranger. For a moment, I lay flat on my back, catching my breath. Then, slowly, I moved my limbs. Pain radiated from my spine, but I didn't think I'd broken anything.

I pushed myself up. When I looked around, I noticed grave markers jutting out of snow. We'd fallen into a cemetery, and if I hadn't had Skalei, I might have plummeted right into my own grave.

Ancient tombstones sprouted from the ground around me like giants' teeth. Above my head, the boughs of an elm reached into the night sky, frozen and twisted like gnarled fingers. An ancient stone chapel—built by humans—lay in ruins.

In a whorl of darkness, the prisoner rose before me like a

ghost. The shadows in his eyes had faded, leaving behind clear blue.

He took a step closer to me, movements smooth and unnerving. Though he shifted like a phantom, his body had been solid as the Citadel walls. Despite his strangeness, there was something oddly seductive in his movements, in the way he moved so assuredly. And his magic... that dark, smoky magic caressed my skin, warm and sensual.

Beneath the shadows, I caught glimpses of tattered gray clothes, threadbare over a muscled physique. Fiery runes glowed on the body of a warrior. The wind whipped at his dark hair. When I looked down, I realized he was barefoot. He must have been freezing, but he didn't seem bothered at all.

I looked down at the vergr stone in my left hand, my stomach churning at the sight of my missing finger. My mouth felt watery, like I was about to throw up.

I could toss the stone across the cemetery yard and try to escape this stranger—but like the High Elves' wands, the stone needed time to recharge its magic. I'd seen how fast this man could move. He'd be on me within moments.

So, I held out my right hand, muttering, "Skalei." When the dagger appeared in my palm, I pointed it at him. "What do you want from me?"

He took another step closer, pale eyes twinkling like I delighted him. But when I spoke, he winced, nearly imperceptibly. I had the sense that he liked how I looked but hated my voice. In any case, my own freezing feet were quickly pulling my attention away from him. I was only wearing socks in the snow.

Even if I could escape, I wanted to find out what the deal was with this guy. Could he help me avenge my people, perhaps?

I lifted the dagger higher. "Stay where you are."

But Skalei, I realized, was a stupid threat. Stabbing him hadn't slowed him down before. The curve of his lips told me he knew this, too. Amusement flickered in his eyes.

He took another step closer.

Blood trickled from where my finger had been severed, staining my palm and wrist. My mind raced, internal alarm bells ringing loudly, telling me to run.

But he'd been protecting me up there, hadn't he? Shielding me from the hexes. Maybe he looked like a god of death, but he'd kept me safe, in his own way.

So far.

If he wanted me alive, maybe that was my leverage. There was only one way to find out. I pressed the edge of the dagger to my wrist. Bluffing, obviously, but I'd see if it worked.

"Don't come any closer," I said. "I want to ask you a question or two, but I want you to stay where you are."

He stopped moving, shadows whipping around him. His body looked tightly coiled, like he was about to leap for me, but he didn't make a sound.

Now, I could hear nothing but the whistle of the wind through the oak that arched over us. When the tendrils of darkness drifted from his face again, it felt like someone squeezing my heart. He really was the most beautiful man I'd ever seen, and yet there was something distinctly *wrong* with him.

Without making a sound, he reached up and snapped a twig off the frozen oak.

I let out a long breath and took a step back. Then I watched as he wrote in the snow, scratching the words *I WILL HELP YOU.*

I lowered the blade from my wrist. "With what? Who are you?"

MARROC, he scrawled in the snow.

It was an old-fashioned name, one from perhaps before Ragnarok. "Your name is Marroc?"

He nodded.

"Why can't you speak?" Immediately, I wondered if it was a rude question, then decided I didn't care.

I'M CURSED, he wrote.

Ah... well, that explained it. The black magic that whirled around him, the fact that he scared the shit out of everyone. Didn't explain his otherworldly speed, though. Didn't explain his interest in me—or what he was.

"Why did you save me?" I asked. "Why did you protect me from the hexes?"

He dropped the branch in the snow and moved for me quickly.

I lifted Skalei, but then I heard the now too-familiar buzz of a spell whistling through the night air. I dove to the side just as the spell hissed into the snow mere inches from where I'd been standing. A shadow passed over the graveyard, and I glanced up to see a moth-mounted elf swooping above.

I was about to throw the vergr stone when Marroc grabbed me, scooping me up in his arms. His wood-smoke scent wrapped around me like a caress.

Then, like an icy night wind through Boston's trees, he ran, holding me tight to his chest. And I let him—because I still had a million questions for him, and I needed answers.

* * *

THE MOTH WAS long behind us, but Marroc clutched me in an iron grip as he raced through the city. Cold air nipped painfully at the nub of my severed finger.

At first, he seemed to move without purpose, needlessly redoubling his tracks as he raced around Beacon Hill, but then I realized it was a stratagem. With his bizarre path, he was making it virtually impossible for the High Elves to track us.

Eventually, he started down Commonwealth Avenue, away from the center of the city. I felt the muscles moving in his chest and shoulders as he ran—it was so strange, the way he didn't breathe or make a noise as he moved. And yet he was so solid, like a marble statue of a god.

"What's the plan, Marroc? Where are we going?" I didn't know why I bothered asking, when it was obvious he couldn't speak.

Without so much as a glance in my direction, he swept past the crumbling brick ruins of Boston University, then crossed over the bridge into Cambridge. With my arms wrapped around his neck, I took a moment to study his face.

It had been harder to see him before, with the cloud of shadows around him, but now I had a close view of his sharp jaw line and cheekbones. Thick, dark, straight eyebrows and eyelashes the color of jet. Skin was pale as ivory, eyes the color of a cloudless sky. His full lips were set in a determined line, and he had a distinct dimple in his chin. His dark hair hung over his shoulders, glossy in the moonlight.

I tore my gaze away from him again, looking over his shoulder. "It's not safe here."

A slow slide of his gaze was the only acknowledgment that I'd spoken. His lip curled a little. Again, I got the impression that he hated it when I spoke. His arms tightened under my legs, and he showed no signs of slowing down.

As we drew closer to Central Square, I spotted the first draugr shuffling out of an apartment building. The undead creature was small, and based on her bleached hair with pink tips, I guessed she'd been a woman, once.

As we raced past, I could have sworn that she clutched an empty wine glass in her emaciated fist.

"This part of the city is infested with draugr," I warned Marroc. "It's not safe."

He only continued on, deeper into the streets of Cambridge.

When I looked over his shoulder again, I saw a group of undead following, shuffling along behind us like drunk college students. Which, really, they could have been a thousand years ago—undead from an ancient era, when nearby Harvard and MIT had still been functioning.

Luckily, my cursed prisoner friend was too fast for them, and he seemed indefatigable. The icy winds kissed my cheeks and whipped my silver hair around me.

We raced down Massachusetts Avenue, past the remains of Cambridge's city hall, into Harvard Square. Snow swept around in squalls, and icicles hung from dormitory windows in Harvard Yard.

But there were even more draugr here, and dread crawled up my neck. They were crawling from shadows around the Harvard campus. Around us, the undead called to each other in low, whispering voices.

Marroc slowed to a stop in front of an impressive building, four stories tall and built of brick. I read its name on the lintel: Sanders Theatre.

Behind us, the draugr closed in, silently wading through the snowdrifts.

Panic made my heart race. "Marroc! We need to keep moving."

He dropped me, and I slid down his enormous body. Then he grabbed the steps of a fire escape bolted to the wall of the theater. With a screech of tearing metal, he ripped the stairs from the side of the building. Before I could move, he had lifted me up by the waist and placed me on the remaining iron platform above him. I was now ten feet above the ground, out of reach of the draugr.

Before I could ask what the plan was, he turned and ran into the darkness. For whatever reason, the draugr weren't interested in him, only in me. And I stood above them like their queen.

On the frigid platform, I leapt to my feet, looking out at the ragged undead army as they spilled into Harvard Yard. The bluish, gnarled bodies of the draugr were everywhere. They moved in the shadows, giving me no free space to throw my vergr stone. Even if there was somewhere I could throw it, they would surround me while I waited for the stone to recharge. From here, I could see no escape routes.

Their rheumy eyes all fixed on my position. A shiver rippled over my body as I searched fruitlessly for a way out.

Nothing.

Why the Helheim had Marroc brought me here only to leave me among the dead?

CHAPTER 12

MARROC

What in the gods' names had become of Midgard while I'd been in prison?

I hadn't expected it to be quite this bad. In Cambridge, there wasn't a single living soul apart from the Night Elf. Only the undead inhabited the streets of the old city.

Now, as I raced down Peabody Street, I thought of her strange silver eyes. I'd never spent any time around her kind. I hadn't even gotten the chance to ask her name yet—or to carve the question in the snow with a stick, as it were.

And there it was again: that unfamiliar feeling, long buried. Fear. It was that ember simmering a little hotter—a need to get back to her.

But first, I needed to retrieve my house key, and I couldn't let the Night Elf see where I'd hidden it.

That was the lie I told myself.

The truth was that she unnerved me on a deep level that I didn't understand, and I wanted to get away from her.

When her silver hair brushed my cheek, a tiny flame flickered in my chest, like I had a heartbeat again. Like I was alive. It was only when she spoke that I wanted the gods to rise again and freeze everything on the earth just so I could have silence.

For a thousand years, I'd heard no one speak but the occasional guard. I'd grown used to the solitude, my stone grave in the Citadel. My world was one of ice and stone. And now I was bound by Wyrd to someone who had questions and screams, and who could break easily.

Mate or not, I wanted to leave her and never return. The dead couldn't actually love, so what did I care?

But she had my soul, and that tied me to her for now.

I tucked my head down as I ran, my dark hair whipping around me in the snow squall. In Harvard Square, the draugr left me alone. They had no interest in someone like me.

And there it was again—fear, like a phantom, creeping up behind me. Would she be all right where I'd left her? I'd thought so at the time, and now I couldn't help but worry.

She had my soul in her body. If she died, my soul died with her.

And the terrible truth was that if she knew who I was, she might want that to happen.

Whatever happened next, I couldn't let her know the truth.

At the iron gates of the Old Burial Ground, I leapt the spiked fence. Snow was thick on the ground of Cambridge's oldest cemetery. Only the tops of the gravestones poked through, black curves in a sea of white. The graves were ancient, some from the days when the humans had hanged witches. I scanned the stones, looking for the familiar tomb.

I'd buried my key among the bones of Reverend Benjamin Wadsworth. I didn't have any particular affinity for the old president of Harvard; it was simply that his grave was tomb-shaped, with a flat capstone atop an open chamber— the perfect place to stash something that needed to remain hidden.

But as I surveyed the cemetery, I couldn't find it.

The last time I'd been amongst these stones was nearly a thousand years ago. Had the tomb disappeared?

Clouds slid over the moon such that I could hardly see. The Night Elf wouldn't have this problem, would she? Her strange silver eyes would be able to pierce this darkness effortlessly.

I ran to a snowdrift, but when I brushed the snow away, it revealed only fallen yew branches. Another drift hid the grave of Washington Allston, whoever the Helheim he was.

A bloodcurdling cry echoed in the distance. I paused, listening. The draugr were calling to each other in their horrible voices. I needed to hurry.

At last, I found the old reverend's tomb, buried under a drift in the shadows of a frozen oak. With a single swipe, I brushed the snow off the lid. I skipped the inscription, instead ripping the ancient slab away. Amongst a frozen pile of bones rested an iron key. My key.

I snatched it from the grave.

In the distance, the draugr howled, and fear trickled over my bones again. She'd be all right, wouldn't she? From what I'd seen, she was fast and cunning, and she had some sort of spell to travel through space in an instant.

I paused as an idea came to me. Quickly, I turned back to the grave, frowning down at the skeleton. After a pause, I snatched up one of Wadsworth's femurs.

With the winter winds whipping over me, I sprinted back toward the theater where I'd left the Night Elf.

As I ran, I tried to remember those buried memories—the flickering images that had come into my mind when I'd been close to my soul. Something with birds, I thought. Ravens.

As a warm spark lit in my frozen chest, a new image flickered.

I needed to get back to her, to that light she held within

her body. I picked up speed until I was faster than the wind, a shadow in the white snow. As I ran to her, dread slid through my blood at the sight of draugr milling around, their eyebrows frosted with snow.

I sniffed the air. There it was, under the scent of the draugr. The faint odor of gasoline.

I turned to a great pile of snow, the remains of an ancient automobile, and punched my fist through it. My hand slammed though snow, then ice, then metal, until it reached the SUV's gas tank. I ripped it out, throwing it on the street in front of me. Thousand-year-old sludge, that once had been gasoline, sloshed on the asphalt. *I hope this is still flammable.*

Ripping a strip of cloth from my shirt, I wrapped it round the end of Reverend Wadsworth's femur, then dipped it into the puddle. I blocked out any worry I had for the Night Elf, raising my hand to trace the rune for fire.

As I moved my finger through the air, the curse kindled. Nearly instantly, my skin felt as if it were on fire—and it had nothing to do with the spell I was trying to cast. I could still use basic magic with my curse, but it meant that I felt as if I were burning alive.

I doubled over, my muscles spasming involuntarily, but I continued to write in the air to form the rune. The skin at my fingertip began to glow.

I touched it to the end of the femur. Instantly, the cloth wrapped around bone burst into flame.

With my macabre torch, I charged up Peabody Street, toward the Night Elf and the sea of draugr surrounding her.

She held my soul and memories in her body. She was my mate, and I hadn't even learned her name yet.

CHAPTER 13

ALI

The draugr circled, closer and closer, staring at me with yellowed eyes. There were hundreds of them now, dark shapes against the icy landscape. Snowflakes drifted down, dusting their upturned faces.

I pulled my hood up, the acrylic fur tickling my cheeks. My feet were painfully frozen in my socks now, the frost creeping over my toes. Any longer out here and they'd be going black with frostbite. The only idea I could come up with was taking off my coat to wrap them in it, but then the rest of me would be cold.

I'd set out to bring back treasure for the Shadow Lords, something that would help free my people. And it seemed I'd be heading to the Shadow Caverns empty-handed, with nothing to show for my adventure but frostbitten feet. If I headed back home at all.

Marroc had ripped away the lower steps of the fire escape, leaving the bottom platform about four feet above the heads of the hungry corpses. He'd left me safe, but trapped.

Before, I'd been sure he was protecting me, but now it looked like I would freeze to death above a throng of draugr.

Right now, I desperately wished I had a way to get a message to Barthol. I breathed out, and mist clouded around me. If I really had to, I could toss the vergr stone over the brick wall to my left, the gate that led into the oldest part of Harvard Yard. But then I'd risk being surrounded by more draugr as soon as I landed.

They were under me now, clawing at the walls. The only thing that kept them from tearing me to pieces was that their gnarled hands couldn't grip the smooth brick. Directly beneath me, a draugr in a tattered miniskirt opened her mouth. She smacked her lips with a pasty tongue.

With a swell of nausea, I realized she was trying to catch the droplets of blood that dripped from the nub of my severed finger. I gaped with morbid fascination as the draugr standing next to her—a blonde—noticed what was happening. She, too, snatched at the blood spatter as it dripped, trying to get a taste.

The first one grabbed the blonde by the head, then twisted it. With a crack that echoed through the courtyard, the blonde's head was gone.

So much for that dye job.

The sound reverberated through the cold air, and the draugr began murmuring to each other again. Then they surged forward, crushing each other in their desperation to get at me. Bony hands reached from below. The headless draugr disappeared under the crowd of undead.

Fear crept up my spine as I realized they were now standing on the bodies of their fallen companions, using the trampled as footstools.

Desperately, I looked at the brick wall to my right. When I saw draugr streaming through the gate, I knew that path was no good either.

I told myself that I'd make it out of this fine, that this would all add to the amazing story I'd tell Barthol over beers later. But my breath was coming in short, sharp bursts, and panic was raking its icy claws up my back.

As I took a step back on the platform, leathery fingers grabbed the metal bars at my feet

Frantic, I stamped on the fingers hard, using the heel of my frozen foot. Only a thin layer of icy sock was between me and the undead, but I gritted my teeth and slammed down on them as hard as possible.

At last, I severed the fingers, but it was too late. Two more draugr were already pulling themselves onto the iron platform. I turned to climb the fire escape, my frozen feet slamming on the metal stairs.

It occurred to me that if I climbed up to the roof, I might be able to find somewhere I could throw the vergr stone. The groan of bending metal rent the air as I raced up the steps, toward the top of the staircase. At the top, I grasped for the handle of a fire door. But when I pulled on it, it didn't open.

Panic snapped through my nerves. Below me, draugr were clambering over the fire escape like deranged kids on a jungle gym.

Freaking out, I gripped the door handle, jamming it up and down. "Let me in!"

This was pointless. No one would answer.

Then, with a tremendous crack, the entire staircase ripped from the wall of the building.

My stomach lurched, and I clung on tight to the door handle, dangling three stories above the ground. "Help!"

My breath froze in my lungs, and I looked out at the sea of draugr. Nowhere to throw my stone…

I closed my eyes, hands slipping on the steel handle. "This will make a great story for Barthol," I whispered to reassure myself, but it was starting to feel like I might not be around to tell it.

The undead churned beneath me in a maelstrom. My frozen feet were blocks of ice against the brick wall. I turned my head the other way, desperately searching for draugr-free snow where I could toss the vergr crystal.

But I saw something perhaps even better—a light shining in the darkness, and a figure sprinting toward me. A tall, broad-shouldered silhouette, dark hair caught in the wind.

Above his head, Marroc held a torch, and he used it to sweep a clear path through the dead.

CHAPTER 14

MARROC

The elf was hanging on to a door handle on the third floor of Sanders Theatre when I reached her. As I looked up at her, a strange feeling pierced my heart, like someone was driving a nail through it. It was an overwhelming urge to get her to safety—an unusual feeling for one of my kind.

Standing below her, I tried to call out to her, to urge her to jump into my arms. But my lack of speech made that a bit difficult.

In the end, it wasn't clear if she dropped into my arms because she trusted me, or because she had lost her grip and had no other choice. Either way, I exhaled with relief as I caught her. Dropping her to the ground, I curled an arm around her shoulders and pulled her tight to me.

With my free arm, I swept the reverend's burning femur through the air. The flames were an arc of light, keeping the dead at bay.

Holding her close, I turned to face the draugr. The beasts had surrounded us, watching my torch with dead eyes. They were afraid of the fire—the only thing that could destroy them. And yet their desire for flesh and blood might be stronger than their fear of burning.

We didn't have much time.

I swung my torch, keeping the monsters at bay. I had the key on me, which meant that all I needed to do was to say the magic word: *Finnask*.

Except—the curse, of course, robbed me of speech.

The draugr moved closer, and I swung the torch to keep them at bay. The Night Elf clung to my side, warm against me. Sunlight flickered in my mind, another memory of rowan trees against a blue sky. A room of stones and vines...

Clutching my mate, I backed against the brick wall of Sanders Theatre.

My instinct was to hold her to me, but she slid away, out of my embrace. I stepped in front of her.

"What's the plan?" she asked in a breathy whisper.

All I needed was for her to speak the magic word for me, to say it out loud, and we'd be free. I glanced behind me, looking for something I could use to write. I didn't have much time, and I couldn't leave her. If the draugr reached her, they'd rip her to pieces and gorge themselves on her flesh. But I had nothing with which to write with...

The draugr must have sensed me hesitating, because one charged, leaping for her throat. I slammed the flaming torch into it so hard that I took off its head. Another draugr lunged, grabbing for my torch, but it missed. If this flame went out, we were fucked.

The Night Elf stayed behind me, pressed tight against the wall. I could feel my own soul radiating from her body. "Marroc!" she shouted.

A draugr's fingers raked along the burning femur, but I was faster. I grabbed the creature by the neck, then threw it into the air. To my surprise, as it arced through the night sky, sparks trailed behind it like the tail of comet.

The draugr landed in a mass of his kind nearly a hundred feet away. For a moment, the dead stilled.

Then the body detonated, like I'd just thrown a bomb.

There it was again—that unfamiliar fear sliding along my bones as the flames spread through the crowd of corpses. All around us, the draugr bodies were igniting. Seemed they were extremely flammable, and the fire was raging closer, putting her in danger.

The Night Elf screamed again, the sound like glass shards in my heart. A strange thought bloomed in my head, a desire to turn into a powerful oak tree that could protect her.

What to write with? How to speak to her?

Fire stained the air with light.

That could be used to write in the air. All I needed was for her to say the word out loud, just once. The pressure to get out of this situation was like a thousand rocks on my chest.

I turned to the Night Elf and pressed my key into her hand. She frowned at it, but wrapped her fingers around it.

I touched her cheek lightly to get her attention. Meeting my gaze, her silver eyes gleamed in the darkness. Her breath was coming in fast bursts. While her gaze was locked on me, I pointed to the torch, trying to signal that she needed to watch it closely.

In the air, I spelled *FINNASK* with the blazing end of the femur.

"Finnask?" she asked.

And that was all we needed to disappear.

CHAPTER 15

ALI

Light flashed, and the grotesque world around me faded away. No longer surrounded by hungry draugr, I was now standing in the center of a beautiful hall. I blinked, hardly daring to believe what I was seeing.

An ivory ceiling arched high above us, with vaults that looked like petals fanning out. The muddy snow had been replaced with a clean marble floor, and the draugr had become towering, peaked windows with moonlight streaming in.

Marroc crouched before a marble fireplace and traced a fire rune in the air. Flames ignited, casting a warm glow over the place. Rising, he gestured to the hearth. Didn't have to ask me twice.

As I warmed my hands, I wanted to ask where we were, but I knew he couldn't answer. Whatever the case, I'd never before been in a place of such opulence. Instead of death, I could smell wood smoke, feel the warmth of fire. Wood chairs with worn embroidery stood before it, but I ignored them, sitting on the hearth to warm my hands and toes.

I stole a glance at Marroc, who stared back at me with an unnerving intensity. Smoky shadows swirled about him like a murmuration of starlings, but I could see his face clearly in here. Shockingly beautiful, he had a sensual mouth, cheekbones sharp enough to cut steel, and eyes the color of pale sapphires. His dark hair draped over his shoulders. Well over six feet tall, he looked like a Greek statue.

He dropped himself into an embroidered armchair before the hearth, looking like he owned the place. And he maybe did. This looked like it could have once been the home of a wealthy human. When he looked at me, the firelight danced in his eyes, and he seemed to soak me in with his gaze.

I still had no idea what he was, or why he was interested in me.

"I'd ask you what the Helheim was going on, but you can't tell me," I said.

His lips quirked for a moment, then he lowered himself to the floor by my side. I frowned at a deep gash on his forearm where a draugr had clawed it, and he touched it with his finger.

"You're hurt." I felt like an idiot for stating the obvious, except as I looked closer, I saw that it wasn't blood. Instead of a normal red, it was a dark blue, and it smoked slightly.

He'd found an old, yellowed piece of paper and a pen. *I'm fine*, he wrote in beautiful, curling script.

"You don't look fine. You look... What are you?"

I can't die. Again.

A chill crawled up my spine. "What do you mean?"

I'm a dark sorcerer. A lich.

My heart skipped a beat, and I leapt to my feet.

"Skalei." The blade was in my hand in an instant, though I clearly couldn't make him more dead than he already was.

Now I knew why the High Elves were so scared of him, and why they'd imprisoned him.

Truth be told, I'd thought liches were mere legends. I hadn't known they were possible. But apparently, they were. And this was bad, bad news, because liches were more dangerous than draugr. They started out alive, but transformed themselves into undead beasts using dark magic. They became immortal.

Like in the human stories of vampires, a lich fed from the living. Constantly hungry, they bit into your skin, drinking your soul through your blood. And also like vampires, they were seductive and cunning, with astounding strength and speed.

Except it wasn't just blood the liches were after. It was souls. Through blood, liches were drawn to life they no longer possessed. To be drained by a lich was to be turned into an empty, walking husk.

"You're a lich?" I repeated, hoping I'd misheard him somehow.

He nodded, blue eyes still fixed on me. Was it just me, or did he have a faint smile on his face, like he found my horror fucking funny?

I pointed the knife at him. "So, you feed on the souls of the living. You want to bite into my neck or some weird shit and drink my soul. Right?"

Marroc merely shrugged, like my words were immaterial. But then his gaze drifted down from my face to my severed finger, and something like anger flashed in his eyes.

"I'm not done with my questions," I said. "I thought liches were driven by an insatiable lust to kill and consume."

He picked up his pen. *That was not a question.*

"Are you going to eat my soul?" I snapped. "Obviously, that's my concern. That's my fucking question."

I'm not hungry. I feel nothing. Then, after a considered pause, he wrote, *Usually.*

"Great. Okay." I lowered my knife. "That's not a ringing endorsement of yourself."

He almost looked perplexed as he wrote, *I won't hurt you.*

So far, he didn't seem as though he wanted to consume my soul. Since I'd encountered him, he'd kept me safe.

As I sheathed my blade, pain shot up my arm, and I winced. The heat of the fire was thawing the stump of my finger, which meant I felt the pain again.

You're still hurt, he wrote.

I looked down at the remains of my ring finger. I felt nauseated every time I looked at it. "Yeah. It's not ideal."

Marroc stood, towering over me, and beckoned me to the door at the end of the hall.

I slipped Skalei into my coat pocket, then followed him into a long hallway of dark wood. We crossed into a room with a large marble table in the center, and I let out a low whistle. I'd read about places like this. *Kitchens*, they'd been called.

I draped my coat over a chair, making myself comfortable.

Back before Ragnarok, when humans had ruled Midgard, they'd devised extraordinary technology that didn't require magic: stoves that heated without fire, insulated cabinets that kept food from rotting, even machines whose sole purpose was to prepare cold drinks. It had always sounded like paradise to me.

And it seemed Marroc, as a former human, had lived in the most luxurious conditions. I wanted to ask him everything about Midgard before the floods and war, about how the humans had once lived. But his lack of speech made that hard.

I was holding my hand at the wrist, as though the pressure would somehow make my finger regenerate. If anything could take my mind off trauma, it was this.

CURSED PRINCE

On a counter, I spotted one of these human devices—a sort of plastic vase with blades on the bottom that rotated. I hopped up to get a closer look, hoping to push all the disturbing thoughts about undead and severed fingers out of my mind. "I've read about these. Is this a blen-door? Gods, Barthol would love this. It crushes up fruit, doesn't it? Mashes it up to make a delicious drink. A *smoothie.* How did you happen across these ancient human contraptions?"

Marroc nodded, that amusement dancing in his eyes again. He slid a piece of paper across the table and wrote, *Wait here, I'll be right back.*

While he was gone, I explored the room, trying to put my mutilated hand out of my mind. I opened the drawers, poked around in the cabinets. I turned on the stove. Just like in the old books, the coils glowed red without fire when I twisted a knob.

When I turned around, I found Marroc writing on the paper, and he handed it to me. *We need to take care of that finger.*

Then he opened a small red bag labeled with a white cross, which I recognized as a medical kit. He unzipped it and removed a syringe along with a clear vial labeled LIDOCAINE.

"Oh, human medicine! I love human medicine." It was what they'd used to heal themselves instead of magic, but most of it had disappeared long ago.

He nodded, then wrote, *This will hurt. But it will help you heal.*

For some reason, I trusted him. Undead or not, he'd clearly been looking out for me so far. It was like something was whispering in the back of my mind that he'd keep me safe, that we had to look out for each other. Although I couldn't explain that at all, given what he was.

Reluctantly, I extended my injured hand to him.

I held my breath as he slowly drew a small quantity of fluid into the syringe, then grabbed the wrist of my injured hand. Before I could say anything, he drove the end of the syringe into the stump of my severed finger.

Something cold and painful slid up my arm, and I clenched my jaw, trying not to scream. I didn't like seeming weak in front of others.

At last, he released my wrist, and I let out a long, slow breath. He snatched the paper and began scribbling on it.

When he flipped the paper around, I read: *The medicine takes the pain away. When your finger is numb, I will stitch the wound shut. From now on, you must understand I am trying to help you. If I wanted you dead, I would have let Gorm throw you down the well.*

"Good." I cradled my numbing hand. "And I want to know why you're so interested in me."

CHAPTER 16

MARROC

I stared at her, heat flickering in my chest again. *Barthol would love this*, she had said.

I found myself wondering who he was. My new rival, perhaps? An icy sort of violence flickered in my veins.

But then—a rival to what? A lich was unable to love. We were driven only by the need to possess. To taste and consume. Even if she was my mate, I'd be an idiot to confuse this with real emotions.

But the drive to taste was real, and it was hard not to stare at her. Under her coat, she'd been wearing black clothes that hugged her delicate curves, and her silver hair draped over her shoulders. Her full lips were pursed a little while she waited for me to speak. But I was used to the silence.

For just a moment, my gaze trailed over her figure, lingering at the curves of her hips. I could almost remember what it was like to have a woman. I would lay her out over the table, slide my hand up her shirt...

Liches were seductive. It was how we got to the blood and souls we desired. For most liches, it came naturally. But I'd been in prison, alone so long that I'd forgotten how to charm someone. Hard to keep sharp on that front with only rats around.

Now, this close to her, the memory of lust gleamed in my mind like a jewel. Even before I'd become a lich, I'd been skilled at seduction. Long ago, if she'd come to my home uninjured, I might have had her on my kitchen table within twenty minutes.

I'd told her that I felt nothing, that I desired nothing. But it seemed that was a lie, because it was rising in me now, a hunger to consume her. I wanted to pull her little body close to mine, to feel our souls mingling. I wanted to hear her gasp as I drank from her.

Already, I knew how I would feel consuming her soul—the pure ecstasy trembling through my body, like light and life warming me from the inside. She was exquisite, and drinking from her would be the greatest pleasure I'd ever experienced. I wanted to press my lips against her neck and rip into her skin. I wanted to taste her, to feel the heat of her body and to soak in her memories.

I could almost feel it now, a thrumming in my chest like a fait heartbeat. Just being near her was making me feel almost alive again.

The lich side of me wanted to possess her completely. To steal her soul and make her mine. And if I weren't careful, I'd give in to my desires and ruin her completely. And while I was at it, I'd destroy my own soul, too.

But just a taste of her…

With her good hand, she drummed her fingertips on the table. "Marroc? Hello? Why the interest in me?"

Her voice snapped me out of my reverie like a slap to my face. So much *talking* with this one.

All liches were cursed in different ways. We were all powerful sorcerers who had trapped our souls within objects. Doing so had given me eternal life, but dark magic always came with a cost—a curse. And mine was twofold. I couldn't speak, and I couldn't use magic without feeling like I was on fire. Strange that she wasn't more afraid of me, this cursed monster before her.

I wrote on the paper, *I will explain later.*

She shook her head. "No. Tell me now."

Let me suture your finger first.

"After you tell me what's going on."

With all due respect, you're bleeding all over my home.

She paused, looking at the bloody stump of her finger. Then, without a word, she walked to the stove.

I realized too late what she planned to do. Even as I grabbed for her, there was a hiss as she pressed her nub of finger against the glowing burner. The scent of scorched skin filled the room.

"There," she said. "I'm not bleeding anymore. You seem nice for an undead creature. But please understand that I can take care of myself, and I do what I need to do to survive. And more than that, I do what I have to do to protect my own people. I've lived without human medicine. I've survived without fancy homes and beautiful six-foot-five knights in shining armor. I don't need your kindness. Just tell me what's going on."

My brain had snagged on the word *beautiful*, and I felt my lips curl into a smile. So, I still radiated beauty. It was startling to find that I really cared what she thought.

Beautiful, I wrote on the paper.

"I'm afraid you missed the point."

It was hard not to fantasize about a version of this elf where she whispered, because hearing so much talking after an eon of silence was jarring. Her voice seemed to echo off the marble kitchen.

Follow me, and I'll show you.

I led her from the kitchen into a stairwell of paneled

mahogany. From there, we crossed into a narrow hall. I could hardly see a thing, but I knew this place like I knew my own body. On the upper floor, I led her into my old bedchamber. I crossed the room, ignoring the oppressive, dusty scent.

Pulling aside the curtains, I showed her the view. The frozen city of Cambridge spread out before us. Snow covered the roofs and red bricks of Harvard's campus, the icy pavement of Cambridge Street. And directly below us, what remained of the draugr horde milled about.

"We're *in* Sanders Theatre?"

I nodded.

"Why haven't the High Elves or the draugr found it?"

I wrote on my piece of paper, *I use magic to conceal it. Like the Well of Wyrd, but better. My key is the only way in.*

"So you've had this place hidden in the center of Cambridge all the time you've been imprisoned?"

I nodded.

She crossed her arms. "You must be quite a powerful sorcerer."

I nodded again.

She pressed her fingers against the glass, staring out at the ruined city. It was nearly five a.m., and while the sun hadn't yet reached the horizon, the early rays illuminated her profile. In this light, I could see that her skin was bejeweled with tiny silver tattoos, and her eyes shone like polished steel.

Gods, I hadn't been alone with a woman in at least a thousand years, and now my *mate* was in my bedchamber. The lust that had been only a flicker before was now kindling to something more. But if I gave in to my desires, I risked losing control and ruining her.

In any case, the spell was broken as soon as she started singing Rick Astley's "Never Gonna Give You Up."

I cleared my throat, desperate for her to stop, and she shot me a glance, looking embarrassed.

"Sorry," she said. "Habit. Anyway, I still don't understand why you're interested in me." She looked back out at the view. "Anyone could have said *Finnask* to get you in here, so it didn't need to be me. Why me?"

I cocked my head, considering how to answer. *This* was dangerous territory. She carried my soul within her, and if she found out who I was, there was a chance she'd kill herself—a sacrifice for her people. She could end both our lives. After seeing her cauterize her own finger, I knew she was capable of that much, at least. *I do what I have to do to protect my own people.*

My mate did not fuck around. And that meant she could never know the truth about me.

I wrote slowly, *You are my prisoner.*

She blinked at me in the rising sun, the rosy morning light gilding her skin. A dark part of me—the lich—quite liked the idea of having this beauty as my prisoner. I imagined how it must feel to be soft, warm, and alive. I was desperate to draw her to me and breathe in her scent. Jasmine and chocolate.

She crossed her arms, fury etched across her features. "You think you can keep me here? I'm a trained assassin."

You can't kill me. I'm already dead.

"Sure. And that's going to prevent me from escaping?"

I ran my finger under the line that read, *You are my prisoner*.

She shook her head, expression darkening. "Bull. Shit." She punctuated her words by poking at my chest. "I need to talk to my brother."

I shook my head.

"Skalei." Her dagger appeared in her hand, and already, she was trying to carve through the window. But even with the magic of her blade, it didn't break. The window was protected by a thousand runes.

Calm down, I tried to say, but the words died in my throat. So instead, I grabbed her by the arms.

Our brief moment of peace had ended, and I found rage in her eyes. *I will do what it takes to defend my people,* she'd said, and I believed her.

She slammed her blade into my chest. Once again, pain exploded within me, and the curse stirred. I grabbed the blade and threw it across the room. Then, before she could call it to her, I pressed my hand over her mouth.

She fought, biting me, but I held her tight as I carried her downstairs and locked her in the guest room.

Once she was safely inside, I leaned against the wall of the hallway. Ichor dripped down my chest, and I closed my eyes.

From the other side of the wall came her voice: "Oh, Marroc! I saw how much you liked my singing. I thought I'd treat you to your own personal show, as long as I'm kept here. I'll sing for you day and night, your own personal chorus, until you set me free."

Then she launched into that infernal song, the sound of it like fingernails dragging against stone. It was that same dreadful tune. A *Rickroll.*

She was doing this to torture me, and it was working. I clenched my fists.

Clearly, keeping her prisoner was going to be more difficult than I'd imagined. And perhaps if she weren't my mate, I'd simply suck out her soul and be done with it. But even undead, I couldn't bring myself to end her life that way. To leave her a walking husk. Plus, I didn't know what that would do to my own soul.

When I realized once more that I still hadn't asked her name, I felt a flicker of self-hatred.

I was a bit of a monster, wasn't I? I had no idea how to

behave normally anymore. I wasn't sure if that was because I was a lich, or because I'd kept company with only rats for the past thousand years. Whatever it was, I'd royally fucked up my introduction to my mate.

Slowly, I straightened. Though my wounds still bled, I didn't return to my chambers. Instead, I headed down to the basement.

It was time to visit my lair and get this curse lifted.

CHAPTER 17

ALI

I hated to admit it, but I was in agony. Marroc had not been lying when he told me the liquid he'd injected into the stub of my finger would numb the pain. What I hadn't counted on was how fast it would wear off. Every time I moved my hand, pure agony shot up my arm like a bolt from Thor's hammer.

Still. I thought I'd made my point effectively. Nothing like burned flesh to underscore a message.

But the worst thing about my situation was being trapped. "One night," I began, "Jeremy the Alcoholic Goat escaped the city farm and found his way into Cambridgeport. How fun it was to dance and cavort among all the stumbling people with blue skin! But the noises they made bothered him, and their staring eyes…" My story faded out. I wasn't as good at Jeremy stories as Barthol was, and it was no fun on my own.

I took in the room around me. It might have been a massive suite, but it was a prison cell nonetheless. Four rooms. A sitting room, a bedroom, a bathroom, and one enormous closet. Nowhere to throw my vergr stone. When I tried the windows, I found them bolted shut with some kind of magic.

Not surprisingly, around the edge of the frames were engraved a multitude of silver runes. I guessed they were designed to keep the draugr from breaking in, but they also did an excellent job of keeping me from breaking out. What I really needed were my anti-magic-hex bolts, but I'd left those in the vault of Silfarson's Bank.

Despite the large number of rooms, Marroc's taste was minimalist. Rosewood furniture, a pair of leather lounge chairs, and a massive platform bed. Long, multi-paned windows reached from the floor to the ceiling.

At this point, it was clear that Marroc *was* a typical lich—one who wanted to keep people as his possessions. At some point, he'd try to drink my soul.

It was a seduction, I thought, with the liches. They lured you in with their porcelain beauty. They drew you closer, made your heart race because theirs couldn't. Death was attracted to life. Liches wanted your blood pumping before they drained you of your memories and soul.

If I let Marroc get too close, I'd lose every memory of Barthol hanging out in our shitty cave, painting the walls with phosphorescence, trying to choreograph dances together. I'd forget the time we'd escaped the Shadow Caverns to an abandoned shopping market and found something called Twinkies. So, I'd stay on my guard. Skalei couldn't kill Marroc, but I'd seen the pain on his features when I'd stabbed him.

I paced in front of the door, the stump of my finger aching. *Think, Ali.*

I tried to break through the doors. Just like with the windows, Skalei did nothing against them. I tapped the walls, looking for weaknesses, but they were all solid stone.

Sighing, I crossed into the bathroom. As I sat on the

porcelain toilet for a quick bathroom break, I looked around the moonlit room. It was magnificent: white marble floors, a giant tub. After peeing, I played around with the faucets, turning them on and off to wash my hands. Was this how the tub worked, too?

I turned to look at it. Held up on brass claws, it was nearly big enough for me to sleep in. Fascinated, I crossed to it and turned it on with my good hand.

Piping-hot water started gushing into the tub. Steam rose invitingly. Prisoner or not, I was not going to pass up the chance for a hot bath. Not after the freezing night I'd endured.

I slipped out of my clothes, wincing as I peeled off my socks. My toes were bright red; the beginnings of frostbite had set in.

It hurt at first, the hot water thawing parts of me I hadn't known were frozen, but soon, I was melting into the steaming liquid. I let out a long, slow shigh. I was in prison, yes. But I was imprisoned in Asgard, the city of the gods.

The heat of the water made my toes sting, but it was good for them. One inch at a time, my body was returning to normal.

I must have drifted off, because a noise made me start—a soft gasp of air that raised the hair on my neck in primal fear. Even as I raised my head, I knew who it was.

Marroc stood in the doorway, ramrod straight, a thick miasma of smoke billowing around him like a shroud. His eyes fixed on me—not blue this time, but a deep, smoldering amber, like fire blazed within him. He wanted my soul, yes, but that wasn't all he wanted. I felt his dark magic tremble over my bare skin, warm and powerful, leaving tingling sensations all over me.

"Do you *mind*?" I shouted.

He ripped his gaze away from me with what looked like considerable effort. Then his body seemed to relax.

But he didn't move from the doorway. Instead, he slowly held a note up in front of his face. In black ink, he'd written three words:

Come with me.

CHAPTER 18

ALI

With Marroc waiting outside, I toweled off, then dressed in my black leather pants and long-sleeved T-shirt.

I couldn't bring myself to put on the icy socks again, so I padded out of the bathroom barefoot. And it seemed Marroc had anticipated my needs, because he'd left out a pair of warm woolen socks for me, along with women's black boots. Only one size too big. I wondered whose they were.

Hugging myself, I crossed into the hall, where Marroc was waiting with my coat. He leaned against the wall, looking totally casual, like he hadn't just walked in on me naked.

No longer dressed in tattered rags, he wore a gray cotton shirt, a pair of black pants, and a black jacket with fur trim. In one hand, he held a small notebook. He beckoned to me, then began to walk down the hall.

I followed at a distance, keeping a good fifteen feet between us. We passed through the entrance hall with the blazing fireplace. Then he led me to a stairwell, and we descended into a musty basement. Soon, we were moving deeper, into old stone tunnels.

At last, Marroc stopped in front of a giant pair of doors. Deeply inlaid with runes and curling lettering, they had clearly been constructed with powerful magic. The doors had no handles, but when Marroc placed his hand on one, it slowly creaked open. He disappeared into a dark interior, and I followed him inside.

As I did, I was grateful for the coat and boots; it was cold as winter in here. Pitch black, too. I was just switching over to night vision when a flame bloomed in the darkness. Marroc slowly lit a candelabrum, and the candles illuminated a room much larger than I'd expected.

Of the four walls, three were encased by ancient mahogany bookshelves, while the fourth was entirely occupied by a massive stone hearth. The floor was bedrock, but much of it was covered with thick Persian carpets. The interior was divided roughly in half with an oak table close to the hearth and a leather couch facing the bookshelves. With the candles lit, it was a cozy place.

I walked to the nearest bookshelf, and my breath caught with excitement. The books were very old, all from the time before Ragnarok. Some, like *Jane Eyre*, I'd heard of, but others were new to me. There was a whole shelf of books written in ancient Norse, and another full of thin envelopes covered in strange pictures.

I started a bit as music suddenly filled the room. When I turned, I found Marroc stepping away from a record player.

I'd heard of such contraptions, but never seen or heard a working one. It was like my little thumb drive, but with a pleasant crackle. From the record player, a man's voice filled the room. Deep and rich, he sang in a language I didn't recognize.

Bottles of amber liquid stood on a mahogany desk, runes

blazing on the glass. Whiskey, I thought. He uncorked one of the bottles, then poured two glasses of whatever it was.

He crossed to me, handing me one of the glasses. When I drank it, it burned my throat. But Marroc seemed to relish it, closing his eyes as he drank like it was the nectar of the gods.

"Do you have any Rick Roll?" I asked. "The music."

Marroc opened his eyes, looking for a moment like I'd ruined his enjoyment. Then he quirked an eyebrow, lip twitching in a slight smile. He leaned over and scribbled in his notebook. *This is Luciano Pavarotti.*

As if that explained everything.

"Okay," I said. "I was asking for Rick Roll."

His lips tightened into a line, and he wrote, *Pavarotti was a classically trained tenor. And I would like to ask that you please never again sing in my presence.*

"Hmm... I guess I'm not inclined to make you comfortable, since I'm your prisoner and you trapped me here. Guess you're stuck with my musical talent till you set me free."

When the first song finished, a woman's voice filled the room. I'd heard plenty of women sing, but the longing in her voice was palpable, like listening to a lovesick nightingale. I'd never heard anything so beautiful.

"Who is she?" I asked.

Maria Callas, wrote Marroc. *La Divina—she had the voice of an angel.*

"What is she singing about?" I plopped down on the couch, wondering why he'd brought me down here.

In this aria, she's singing to the moon. She's asking for peace.

When the song stopped, Marroc turned off the record player. Though I didn't quite see him move away from the shelf, Marroc sat across from me and wrote on his notepad, *I have a few questions.*

"As your prisoner, I don't suppose I can say no, can I?"

First of all, Marroc wrote, *we haven't been properly intro-*

duced. I'm Marroc. And you're? He stopped writing and looked at me.

"I'm Ali," I said. "Short for Astrid. I'm a Night Elf, obviously. One of the Shadow Lord's chief assassins, head of thieves, hider of bodies—"

I need your help, wrote Marroc, cutting me off with his writing.

My eyes narrowed; I sensed a trap.

"You're a lich," I said. "A powerful dark sorcerer with no soul. How could I possibly help you?"

I don't have to stay cursed.

"Your soul is trapped in Helheim. Which seems fair, because the High Elves wouldn't have imprisoned you if you were the law-abiding sort."

They imprisoned you as well.

"I am *definitely* not the law-abiding sort," I said firmly. "I am a thief and an assassin, as I said."

And that is why I need your help. Before I became this—he stopped writing to gesture to himself—*I removed my soul from my body. I hid it in a safe place.*

Now that was interesting. "Where? How?"

I cannot tell you. Just trust me that I know exactly where it is.

"So, what do you want from me?"

I cannot rejoin my soul to my body unless I banish the curse I created.

"Why should I help you do that?"

He leaned back in his chair, looking as though he was in complete control of the situation. *Because you will get to complete the task the Shadow Lords gave you.*

My stomach swooped. He was good at bargaining, truly, but I didn't give him an answer yet.

He started writing again. *What do you think you were sent to steal?*

I stiffened. Thing was that I didn't know what, specifically, the Lords had wanted me to take. "What do you mean?"

Revna cut your finger off. Why?

"The gold ring. She wanted it."

The pieces started to slide together in my mind. She was the daughter of the king. She could buy a gold ring every day for the rest of her life if she wanted. Was that the item that could lead us to Galin—the sorcerer who'd trapped my people in the caves?

"She said Gorm didn't trust anyone but her and Sune. He must have sent her to my cell to retrieve the ring. That's what I was sent to steal, wasn't it? That's the key to freeing the Night Elves. It will help lead us to the sorcerer I need to kill. How would you know that?"

He gave an easy shrug. *And now it's at the bottom of the Well of Wyrd. What do you think your Lords will do to you when they find out you have completely failed to get what they wanted?*

"They'll understand it's not the first time I've messed up an assignment." But that was a lie. The Shadow Lords would send me to hard labor in the Mines of Kolar. And worst of all, the Night Elves would remain imprisoned underground if I didn't complete my task.

You and I both know this wasn't a normal assignment. That the Shadow Lords would throw you in prison.

I had no idea how Marroc knew so much, but he was right. The Lords had been very specific that this one was crucial to the cause. That my life depended on it. I hoped Barthol had been managing to evade them.

"All right. So I'm low on options."

Marroc moved to sit next to me on the couch. He held his notebook in his lap so I could watch him as he wrote. *I can help you get the ring you were tasked to retrieve. But you must promise to help me with my task.*

"What is it exactly that you need to do?"

I want to get rid of this curse. To become alive again.

I pretended to think it over, though obviously I didn't have a choice. Getting the ring was the only way to save my people.

"What's your plan?" I asked. Dread already slid through me.

Because pretty as he was, he was insane, and I already knew his plan would be absolutely bonkers.

And that I would probably agree, because so was I.

CHAPTER 19

MARROC

I wrote in my notebook, wondering if she'd think I was crazy. *We travel to the bottom of the Well of Wyrd, we retrieve the ring, then you help me steal the Levateinn.*

Ali stared at me with an expression that suggested she definitely thought I was insane. "That's impossible," she said slowly.

No, it's not, I wrote, grateful that a defensive tone couldn't come across in writing. *But why would I have suggested it if it were impossible?*

"Levateinn? Loki's wand?" she asked. "It's definitely impossible. For one thing, it probably doesn't exist. For another, if it did, it's supposedly guarded by the goddess Sinmara and stored in a box with nine locks."

And you are a thief, I wrote. *Which is why you're here.* That last part wasn't exactly the whole story.

"I was raised on the stories of the gods, just like every other Night Elf. But the gods are gone. Thor, Odin, Freya, Loki—they've been dead a thousand years. Ragnarok happened, we live in the frozen ashes of the world, and everything is fucked."

If gods are dead, I wrote, *Sinmara won't be guarding Levateinn any longer.*

"But where would we even find it?" she asked, sounding exasperated.

I know where to find it.

She stared at me, unmoving. I hadn't ever spent this much time around a Night Elf, but it seemed she had a way of going very still sometimes, like the night itself. Then, at last, she spoke again. "Where?"

My pen spilled across the page. *At the bottom of the world. The great dragon Nidhogg has it. You said you were the Shadow Lords' chief assassin, head of thieves, hider of bodies. You and I both know you're perfectly suited to help me retrieve it.*

I leaned back, sipping my scotch, and waited for her to answer.

Of course, her criminal predilections weren't the only reason I wanted her to help me. I wanted her with me. I needed to guard her, keep her safe. She had my soul, and she was my mate. The High Elves would be searching the city; if they found her, she'd be dead before night fell again.

She leaned back, drumming her fingertips on the armrest, silver eyes gleaming. "You have magic. Can you get a message out?"

Who? I wrote.

"He's in Night Elf territory. His name is Barthol."

I shook my head, a strange heat permeating my chest. There was that name again. Who the fuck was *Barthol*? A lover? A husband, perhaps?

My face was a mask of composure, eyes sparkling with calm. Inwardly, I seethed. And here I'd always thought myself above jealousy. Never before had I felt envy, and I would not for one moment let myself show it.

Everything about this was mystifying. Alone for a thousand years, I'd stopped feeling anything beyond base desire for souls. Where my heart once beat, I now felt only the need to consume. And then *she* had showed up, smelling of jasmine and dark chocolate, and it had started to stir up the dormant impulses of my kind. She'd arrived, in danger, bleeding before me, and I started to feel something again. But it was all wrong. I couldn't love anymore—I could only want things, and break them.

For a creature like me, feeling anything at all was very, very dangerous. At any moment, I could lose control and find that I'd destroyed her. She wasn't nearly as scared of me as she should be.

No, I wrote calmly. *I'm afraid I have no way to do that. Sleep now, and we'll return to the Citadel at night.* Despite my jealousy, it was the truth. Even if I could send ravens with messages into the Shadow Caverns, it would be too risky. Anyone could intercept them.

Her features hardened again. "Fine. Let's steal the wand of a god, then. It sounds like a fantastic idea."

CHAPTER 20

ALI

We stood at the base of the Citadel's towering white walls. It wasn't that long ago that we'd escaped from here. And now, like a true pair of idiots, we were about to break back in.

I rubbed my eyes, staring up at the walls. I'd hardly slept at all at Marroc's house. I never could sleep when shit was hitting the fan, and shit was definitely hitting the fan.

Everything depended on me getting my hands on that ring. If that was truly the prize I was supposed to return to the Shadow Lords, only then would I be able to free my people. The Night Elves had been imprisoned far too long, and I'd do whatever I could to set them free.

At least I had dry boots and warm socks. In fact, I was dressed in my freshly cleaned assassin's outfit. Back at his mansion, Marroc had shown me a strange pair of devices in his basement he called a *washing machine* and *dryer*. Genius things that had left my clothes softer and fluffier than they'd ever been—and best of all, they'd been *warm* on my body when I first put them on. I'd even thrown my coat in to warm it, although some of the fake fur was a bit melted when I pulled it out.

But now, with the snow rushing around us in whorls, I shivered a little as I looked up at the Citadel.

Still, I had my vergr crystal in my pocket, and Skalei ready if I needed it.

Marroc loomed next to me, wearing a large leather jacket. His magic snaked off him, blending with the shadows.

I took a long sip from the thermos he'd given me. The coffee tasted so delicious that it almost made me forgive him for this whole debacle.

The plan was bonkers, but it was all we had. Scale the wall of the Citadel, sneak over the rooftop, climb into the Well of Wyrd, find my ring. Then we'd travel to whatever world held Levateinn, assuming it existed. Allegedly, Marroc knew where it was, and he'd be able to use the wand to get us home.

Alternately, he was a soulless husk with a mind full of smoke and nonsense, and I was dumb as Helheim for going along with this.

He gently pulled the thermos out of my grasp. He turned, nodding at the Citadel. Seemed it was time to go.

"All right," I whispered. "Let's go."

I stepped behind him, and he crouched down. Climbing onto his enormous back, I wrapped my arms around his neck. As he rose, he drew a pair of daggers. Long and sharp, they glinted in the moonlight, runes shining on their blades.

With me clinging to his back, he leapt into the air. At the top of his jump, he plunged the daggers into the wall of the Citadel. Stone crunched, and gravity jerked us downward, but the daggers held. Then, for what seemed like days, Marroc scaled the wall. Using the daggers like ice picks, he alternated punching them into the stone as he lifted us, hand over hand, up the sheer face of white marble.

The icy wind battered us as he climbed, and I clung tightly to him. Before, his body had felt cold, but now he was growing warmer than the world around me, faintly radiating heat. I could feel the powerful muscles of his back working as he climbed. It was amazing that he never seemed to feel tired.

Around us, snow whipped through the air and gusts of wind rushed over the wall. The cold stung my cheeks even as Marroc's body exuded warmth. While freezing trickles of melted snow dripped down the back of my neck and between my shoulder blades, my breasts and stomach were deliciously warm. I could smell Marroc's scent, a mix of wood smoke and burned sage. Even though we were nearly a thousand feet above the ground, I felt safe.

When we finally reached the edge of the parapet, we paused, hiding behind the crenellations. I hadn't been able to communicate with Marroc the whole time because both his hands had been occupied.

"Do you need to rest?" I asked.

He shook his head.

"You're not tired?"

He took out his pad and pen. *No. My body is untiring. I was giving you time to recover.*

"Well, I'm not tired either," I lied, standing quickly. I wasn't about to admit that my forearms throbbed from simply hanging on to his neck. "Let's get moving."

We crept through the blowing snow, retracing our steps until we reached the Well of Wyrd. This time, the amphitheater was completely deserted. Snowdrifts gathered on the benches and steps. As quickly as we dared, we made our way to the bottom.

Strangely, no snow had accumulated on the top of the well. Like an inky eye, it seemed to stare up into the stormy sky. Suddenly, a voice cut through the storm.

"I thought you might return," shouted King Gorm from the top of the amphitheater, as above us a phalanx of giant moths descended from the clouds. I heard the sound of wands being charged, and moments later, spells began to sizzle into the snow around us. I started to run, but Marroc caught my wrist.

Crouching over me protectively, he reached into the pocket of his jacket and withdrew a small sphere. It gleamed with an unearthly light in the darkness.

"Don't!" I shouted, but he'd already tossed the anti-magic bomb onto the center of the well.

For a moment, it rolled across the glassy surface. Then it detonated with a tremendous explosion. Above us, hexes fizzled and snuffed out in little puffs of light. Elven riders screamed as the magical bindings of their moths snapped and the beasts thrashed wildly under their weight. And, directly in front of us, the magical surface of the well shattered into a million pieces.

Marroc growled. I barely had a chance to brace myself before he grabbed me and leapt into the swirling mix of snow, flailing elven riders, and flapping wings of newly freed moths.

"*No!*" As we arced over the yawning chasm, I realized that our trajectory would not allow us to reach the other side. We were supposed to climb down the wall, not dive straight in. Marroc might survive a gravity-based trip to the bottom, but there was not a chance in Helheim I would. The lich had already gotten me killed.

Then we slammed into a moth. The insect struggled, its wings beating the air frantically, but Marroc clung to it like a limpet. With one hand, he grabbed one of the moth's antennae, forcing the bug into a sharp downward spiral as he pulled himself onto its back. Terrified, I clung to the fur of the moth's body, until Marroc lifted me up so that I sat in front of him.

He gave an unnatural, rasping growl, which I took to be a sort of affirmation. Then he reached over my shoulder and grabbed the moth's other antenna. Gently, he pulled the terrified creature out of its dive.

My stomach clenched. We'd already descended deep into the well. The walls rose around us claustrophobically. Seaweed-green moss clung to the gray stone, and the sound of water dripping came from all angles.

I looked up. The entrance to the well was far above us, a circle of light that grew smaller even as my eyes focused on it. There was no sign of any High Elves. They, at least, had the sense not to descend into the abyss.

The air was cold, and I shivered at the chill. Behind me, Marroc shifted, moving himself closer. Warmth emanated from him, and without thinking, I leaned into his chest. He stiffened for a moment, and I thought I heard a low growl rise in his throat, but it might have just been my imagination. I could smell him again: the faint, strangely comforting scent of wood smoke and sage.

We flew down and down, deeper and deeper into the seemingly bottomless pit. Slowly, the walls narrowed, till after an hour I could almost reach out and touch them. The moss disappeared, replaced first with mushrooms and fungi. Then those too vanished, and we were left with bare stone.

But the rock wasn't endlessly gray. Cutting through it were great veins of quartz, shadowy caves that led into darkness—once, we even passed a massive cavity filled with glowing crystals as tall as men. This was Night Elf territory, though I saw no sign of my kind. It got darker, too, but that wasn't a problem for me. My silver eyes pierced the shadows with ease.

We must have been descending for a least an hour before

I noticed the first root. Initially, I didn't know what it was—a brown serpent that seemed to cling to the rock? But as we continued to descend, they became more and more frequent, and it was obvious they were the woody extremities of trees.

It was strange to see roots this deep in the earth, and I was about to ask Marroc about them when suddenly the walls of the cave disappeared and we passed into an absolutely enormous cavern. The roof was stone, but as far as I could see, there were no walls, just blackness that even my Night Elf eyes couldn't penetrate.

One glance at the cavern's floor answered my questions about the roots I'd seen twisting through the well's walls. It was covered in a massive tangle of them. Giant and tuberous, they wrapped and twined amongst themselves like the entrails of a gutted beast. We flew lower and lower, and I was awestruck by their size. Even the smallest ones were humongous, as tall and wide as houses.

Marroc directed the moth toward a bare spot amongst the roots, and we landed. Stepping off, he offered me his hand, which I took. The moth rose into the air, and the now-familiar flapping of its wings quickly faded into silence. Looking up, I saw that shadows obscured the ceiling. There was no sign of the Well of Wyrd.

"Is this the roots of Yggdrasill?" I whispered. Awe washed over me. It was the cosmic tree that bound the Nine Worlds together.

Marroc's pen scratched for a moment on his notebook. *Yes. Now we must find the great Shore of the Dead, where the dragon Nidhogg dwells.*

I nodded, my skin going cold. "Okay. Sounds like a great time."

I'd do whatever I had to if it meant getting my ring back.

CHAPTER 21

MARROC

I had crossed the northern seas, traveled the astral plane, once visited the mists of Niflheim, but nothing had prepared me for the vastness of Yggdrasill. The power of the cosmos flowed through the intertwining roots, humming up my legs. Even if we failed—if we died and our souls were sent to Helheim—this trip alone would have been worth it. Few elves had visited the place where the gods used to dwell.

"I don't see any sign of the ring." Ali interrupted my thoughts, and I realized I'd forgotten about the ring.

The ring was now worth only the weight of the gold from which it had been cast. The true prize was Ali herself. She was the one who housed my soul. But I couldn't explain that to her; I'd taken her with me under the pretense of finding that ring.

Ignoring my curse, I inscribed *sowilo* in the air, and light bloomed. With a flick of my wrist, I cast up the glowing rune so that it hovered above us, giving me light to search the overgrown floor.

With the glow in the air, I could see that we stood atop a

massive root, wide as a Viking longboat was long. It was nearly black, and slick with water. A few pale mushrooms grew on the bark, dotting it like stars, but I saw no sign of the ring.

"Are those *bones*?" asked Ali.

She was pointing to something on the opposite the side of the root. My eyes followed her finger to what was, in fact, a massive mound of bones. It took me a moment to work out how they'd got there. Piled higher than any of the nearby roots, they made me wonder how many thousands of years the High Elves had been throwing their enemies into the abyss.

And this meant we were likely in the right spot—the place where objects thrown in settled.

"Look." Ali pointed up at the mount of bones, where a fresh body lay high at the top. "That's the prison guard who tried to throw me in the well. The ring might be somewhere near him. I'll climb up to see."

But I held my hand up to stop her. If we did it her way, the search would take forever. The ring could be anywhere in that pile, and we didn't have time to clamber around on it.

What we needed was a location spell. Difficult without the power of speech, but not impossible.

As a lich, I could consume souls. All living things contained magic tied up with their souls. Ali had some—extraordinarily beautiful—magic, the perfect complement to my own. And if I were to drain her soul and her magic, it would be without a doubt the greatest pleasure I'd ever known, pure ecstasy lighting up my body. She'd feel it too: the wild, forbidden pleasure of being drained by a dark sorcerer.

But there was no way in Helheim I was going to disturb her magic or risk killing her.

And besides, another source lay under my feet. Crouching, I pressed my palm against the rough bark of the root. The ancient tree's soul pulsed under the bark, and a strange euphoria spread into my fingertips, racing up my arm. Yggdrasill required enormous amounts of magic to hold the Nine Worlds together.

With a thrill of anticipation, I drew one of my daggers and plunged it into the root. Instantly, a milky, opalescent sap flowed around the blade like liquid pearls.

I withdrew the dagger and pressed my hand to the shining wound. As Yggdrasill's soul poured into me, pure ecstasy raced through my veins, and I shuddered with delight. My gaze flicked to Ali, her body lit up from below by the glow of this pearly sap. Her eyes shone with wonder, and as pleasure filled me, so did an unyielding ache to drain her. How much better would *that* feel? My lips against hers, my tongue against hers, and her soul imbuing me with divine rapture.

I gritted my teeth, mastering control of myself.

When I lifted my hand from the root, I saw that it had healed over where I'd stabbed it.

I rose, my eyes on Ali as I prowled over to her. I'd only drunk a tiny amount of Yggdrasill's soul, but magic was already simmering and crackling in my body. I felt more compelled than ever to pull Ali to me and press my mouth against hers.

Instead, I pulled out my notepad and wrote, *I need your help. I know a spell for finding, but you will have to incant it.*

"Okay. What do I say?"

Carefully, I wrote the words to the spell on the notepad, then continued, *While you incant the words, I'll inscribe the runes.*

Ali nodded, her eyes gleaming like silver coins.

Slowly, she spoke the words, and I began to move my fingers, drawing the shapes of the runes as I'd been taught a thousand years ago. It felt good to be doing magic again: the familiar hum of power building in my veins, the magic between us working together with a delicious thrill. I could sense her soul and mine electrifying each other in her body.

And what was more, the power of Yggdrasill was exceptional. Streams of light trailed behind my fingers, while next to me, Ali carefully read the words on my notepad. As she enunciated the final word of the spell, I drew the final rune. At last, I felt the magic rush out of me and disappear into the darkness. I felt its loss like an ache.

For a long moment, nothing happened. Maybe the magic didn't work between worlds.

But as soon as the thought had entered my mind, light blazed in the darkness. Strong and piercing, it shot straight up, all the way to the cavern's ceiling.

"That's where the ring is?" whispered Ali.

I nodded, a low growl of pleasure rising in my throat. The spell had worked.

Together we clambered over the massive roots toward the magical beacon. When we finally got close, I could see that it was coming from the very top of the pile of bones.

"I can get it," said Ali.

I nodded. She was smaller, lighter, and, as a trained assassin, the obvious choice for this particular task. She hopped down from the root and ran to the base of the pile.

It was huge. Even larger than I'd initially realized, a giant pile of osseous material that towered above Yggdrasill's enormous root system. Ali climbed the pile, pulling herself up even as bones scraped against each other, slipping and tumbling beneath her feet.

She had just reached the top when something large moved in the shadows at the edge of the light. I turned to it, trying to make out what it was. A looming, dark form in the shadows.

Suddenly, it screamed, *"Kuk kuk tztztztztztzzzzzttt!"*

A chittering scream so loud that my entire body vibrated, and I wanted it all to end. It was worse than Ali's singing. While I resisted clamping my hands to my ears, the creature charged toward the bone pile.

Covered in reddish fur, the creature scrambled forward on four massive feet. The thing resembled a cave bear—but much, much larger. No cave bear was two stories tall.

When it reached the bone pile, it sat up on its haunches, and I realized what it was: Ratatoskr, the immortal squirrel compelled to climb up and down Yggdrasill and deliver messages to the gods. With the gods dead, who knew what it did now, but one thing was clear: it was angry. I needed to get it away from Ali.

Ratatoskr chittered again, opening its mouth. I'd expected a pair of giant incisors, but instead, its maw was filled with thousands of tiny, razor-sharp teeth. As the squirrel screamed, its teeth vibrated, clattering against each other.

I didn't care what it was, or what gods it had once served. I'd rip its head from its body if it left so much as a bruise on Ali.

I charged toward the squirrel, smashing through ossified remains like a wrecking ball. I needed to distract it. Get it away from her.

As I moved, I could see the huge shape of the squirrel as it tried to climb the bones, chittering and screeching like a banshee. Panic and rage clutched my heart as I realized the danger Ali was in.

My blood began to steam, and my skin turned fiery. Another effect of the curse: sometimes, powerful emotions made me burn.

But now, I relished the pain, because it cleared my head. I savored the taste of the creosote that filled my mouth, the smoke that rose from my skin. I allowed an uncontrollable rage to take me, because I needed to get to Ali.

I shouted, my ragged vocal cords producing an unearthly scream. In my fists, my daggers glinted like dragon's teeth.

The squirrel whirled to face me, its eyes red—a deep scarlet the color of blood. It chittered again, opening its mouth to reveal the rows and rows of teeth. The teeth spun around in its mouth like mechanical things, and at last, I understood the meaning of its name: Ratatoskr—*drill tooth*.

I only had the pair of daggers, but I held my ground. My only hope was to serve as a distraction. To give Ali time to escape.

When the mammoth squirrel lunged at me, I dodged its mouth, my daggers swiping at its fur. Bones clattered down beneath me. I rolled to my feet, but not before I saw a familiar silver gleam.

From the wreckage of the bone pile, Ali stared at me. Hope thrilled within my cursed heart. She was alive.

Then the squirrel charged, shrieking so loudly I could hardly think. I moved to leap out of its way, but it plowed by me like a bull past a toreador, charging through the bones.

The beast slammed into one of Yggdrasill's roots at full speed. I expected it to fall stunned, but instead, its whirling teeth shredded the wood like a buzz saw. Pearly sap sprayed through the air like rain.

I crouched among the remains of the bone pile and let out a shout. Ready to fight, I watched as Ratatoskr's eyes focused on me.

Good. Now come and get me.

The squirrel charged, head down. But this time, instead of dodging to the side, I leapt straight up, grabbing his ears.

Ratatoskr thrashed beneath me, bucking and scratching, but my grip was solid. I swung my leg over the top of the beast's head, then slid down toward the top of its back, out of reach of its teeth and claws.

After a few minutes of enduring its bucking and thrashing, I attempted to soothe the squirrel a little, petting it behind its ears. Its breathing started to slow. Really, he wasn't vastly different from the rats I'd kept as pets, except he'd still eat us if given the chance.

When I looked behind me, I saw Ali climbing the rump of his fur, moving for me. I reached for her, shifting her into place in front of me.

She'd understood. The only safe place right now—away from this creature's teeth—was on its back.

CHAPTER 22

ALI

Sitting in front of Marroc, I clung to the beast's fur as it bounded between Yggdrasill's roots. With Marroc's steely chest behind me and his arms wrapped around me, I felt strangely secure.

Where the Helheim was this thing bringing us? We'd climbed on it to avoid its gnashing jaws, but now it was taking us on a wild chase over the tree roots.

Despite being as big as a house, the squirrel was surprisingly agile. Even with my magical eyesight, it was hard to see in here. I could just about make out the roots beneath us, but the squirrel leapt from one to another with the ease of a monkey. I was pretty sure we needed to be going down, beneath the roots. Instead, we were on a frantic journey above them.

As the squirrel moved along, I held on tight with my thighs. Slowly, the roots gave way to an enormous tree trunk so wide that I could just barely make out its curvature. Around us, the air warmed, and green light began to filter down from somewhere high above.

Then the situation took a turn for the worse. The squirrel

began to ascend the giant trunk itself—the opposite of where we needed to be going. But he was moving too fast, too high for us to jump off. I slid back further into Marroc, but he held his position steadily, arms locked around me. His body seemed like pure steel against mine.

Even climbing straight up the trunk, the squirrel moved swiftly, its claws digging into the thick bark as it raced toward the light. It climbed until we reached a branch nearly as wide as the Citadel and long enough to taper off into shadows, where I couldn't see the end.

Hardly pausing, the squirrel ran along the branch, and I clutched tight to its fur. I tried not to look at the black abyss below me. Instead, I closed my eyes, thinking of Barthol. *He's never going to believe this.*

When I opened my eyes again, I saw a fork in the bough. The squirrel turned onto a smaller branch, and after a minute or two, massive green leaves began to appear.

It chittered again as it slowed to a stop. Now, we were among a thick clump of leaves, each as large as a small car. Their shape was familiar, and I recognized them after a few moments. Ash leaves. The squirrel's nose twitched with excitement.

Suddenly, it scurried forward and pulled something large from under one of them. A giant seed. The squirrel's mouth buzzed as it began to eat the kernel. From behind me, Marroc touched my shoulder, then nodded at the branch. With the squirrel distracted by its snack, this seemed a good time to make our getaway.

Letting go of the squirrel's fur, I slid down to the branch. Marroc landed behind me while the squirrel ate. At last, it turned and, without even a glance in our direction, sprinted down the branch and into the darkness.

My arms and legs were shaking with fatigue, and I

slumped, cross-legged, down on the branch. Marroc crouched next to me, eyeing me with concern.

"Do you know what that thing was?" I asked.

He pulled out his notebook and began to write. *It's called Ratatoskr. The immortal squirrel of Yggdrasill. Bigger than I imagined.*

"Understatement of the day," I murmured, closing my eyes. My arms throbbed, and I thought there were still bits of bone in my hair.

Marroc touched my shoulder gently.

"Oh, I almost forgot." I opened my hand, showing off the golden ring with a brilliant smile. "I got this."

Happiness streamed over me. This was it. They key to setting the Dokkalfar free forever.

CHAPTER 23

MARROC

I stared at the ring, almost disbelieving that she had it. Through dust, shattered bones, and a very angry squirrel, Ali had somehow managed to find it. On one hand, I was exceptionally impressed, but on the other, I felt a strange twisting feeling in my chest. A lump in my throat. Was this... sadness?

No. *Guilt.*

The problem was that the ring was useless. My soul was no longer within the golden circlet that Ali looked so pleased with herself for finding. It was within her.

And worse, she'd risked her life for a trinket.

If she put together the truth—that she held my soul, and who I truly was—it would all be over for both of us. So, I schooled my features into a charming smile, as though I was happy she'd found this little bit of gold.

"We need to get back down again, don't we?" asked Ali. "The Shore of the Dead is supposed to be at the base of the tree, beyond Yggdrasill's roots."

I nodded. Instead, we'd been carried upward into the tree's canopy.

I was reaching for my notebook when a gust of wind shook the leaves. As it did, the branch trembled violently, and Ali and I both grabbed hold of a leaf to keep from being thrown off.

But as soon as it had come, the gale passed.

"Okay, my dead friend," Ali said. "Let's get down there fast before we're blown out of this tree."

I held the notebook up as I quickly wrote, *We're going to have to keep moving*.

I heard a low rumbling noise, and it took me a moment to recognize what it was, to remember that feeling. Ali clutched her stomach, and it came back to me. *Hunger.* Not for souls, the way I felt it, but for food.

Of course she needed to eat. Even Night Elves needed sustenance. I'd spent so many years undead that I'd nearly forgotten how a normal body worked.

Quickly as I could, I wrote, *I'll find you something to eat.*

She wrinkled her nose. "In the land of the dead? I might wait till we get back to Boston, just grab a muffin or something."

Just then, another gust shook the tree, and we both lurched forward.

CHAPTER 24

ALI

I grasped the stem of a leaf to steady myself, my arms around the base. When the gale finally stopped, I turned to look at Marroc. He was beckoning me toward the main trunk.

As I walked behind him, I looked at the branch under my feet. Here, there were plenty of leaves to grab, but further toward the trunk, there was a long, bare stretch of bough.

"Marroc," I began, "when we get to the bare part of the branch, we won't have anything to hold on to if the wind comes."

He held up his pair of daggers. His meaning was clear: he'd use them to catch hold.

Guess I could do the same. "Skalei." My knife appeared in my hand.

With Marroc in the lead, we walked along the branches, moving back to the main trunk. My muscles were tense, and I was ready to snatch for one of the nearest leaves at any moment. I stayed close to Marroc, too, in case I needed to grab him.

Luckily, we reached the fork without any gales threatening to topple us. And as the branch grew wider, I felt a bit more secure. Nearly as wide as one of Boston's streets, this bough itself was bigger than any tree I'd ever seen.

When we reached the main trunk, Marroc looked at me, his pale eyes gleaming in the darkness like the blades of his daggers. With a seductive smile, he motioned me closer, and I hesitated. The look in his eye was always that of a predator, which made me want to keep my distance. But when he pointed at his shoulder, I understood I was supposed to get on his back again.

"Like at the Citadel?" I asked.

He nodded and crouched, offering me his massive shoulders. I climbed on, wrapping my arms around him from behind. His smoky scent whispered over me.

From there, he took one of his daggers and jabbed it into Yggdrasill's trunk. Then he stabbed the other dagger into the bark. We were still above the main branch here, so I gathered this was some sort of test.

Good thing, too, because after a moment, both daggers tore out, and we slid back to the branch.

Marroc growled with frustration. When he shot me a look, I saw his eyes glowing, and I felt heat emanating from his skin.

Before I could say another word, he leapt up and slammed his daggers into the trunk. We hung for a moment, but again the bark crumbled, and we dropped back to the branch. It was obvious that the bark of the main trunk wouldn't support our weight.

Side by side, we stood on the main branch, peering off into the darkness.

Marroc let out a sigh, then wrote in his notebook, *I'll jump down and find another tool to help us.*

Immediately, I thought of the yawning darkness below us.

"You'd survive a fall that long and be able to get back up again in one piece?"

He looked unconcerned as he shrugged.

"That doesn't instill a lot of confidence. Besides, how are you going to get back up here?"

You need food and water.

I looked at Marroc, my thoughts whirling. "There must be another option. Could you do a spell that would help us float down?"

He shook his head.

I pointed at the tree branch beneath me. "But you have plenty of magic—you can drink magic from the tree, right?"

I've never memorized a levitation spell.

"So, what other options does that leave us? We can't climb down the trunk. We can't climb up the trunk. We could go back out on the branch, but that doesn't lead anywhere, and even if it did, the wind might blow us off."

Marroc took a step closer to the edge of the branch, and my heart sped up. He wore a sly smile, eyes twinkling as he held his notebook up to me. *I will find a way to come back for you.*

"You can't be serious."

He sheathed his daggers. *Falling... the fastest way to the bottom.*

And that gave me an idea.

"Wait!" I shouted, so loud it could wake the dead. "There's another way."

* * *

I HUMMED the Rick Roll song under my breath, walking in front of Marroc. We'd carefully made our way back to the leafy section of the tree. I called Skalei to me as I knelt next to one of the leaves.

"Help me hold on to the leaf," I said.

Marroc arched an eyebrow, looking very doubtful. But still, he gripped the leaf in his massive fist as I began to slice its stem. After I'd cut through, he helped me balance the leaf on a crook of the branch.

I knelt, Skalei in one hand, and pulled the vergr crystal from my pocket. Carefully, I laid it in the center of the leaf. Then, using the edge of Skalei's blade, I sliced strips from the leaf. I used them to lash the crystal to the leaf.

When I was sure that it was secure, I stood back.

"All right," I said. "We can release it anytime. Our homemade airplane."

Marroc arched another quizzical eyebrow—and with that one dubious look, I started to have my doubts. Yes, it was risky. I had no way to control where the leaf drifted. It could get caught up on a lower branch, or wedged in a crack high on the cavern wall. It could even be blown higher by cosmic winds. When I teleported us to it, we could end up appearing in midair. Plummeting to our deaths was a possible scenario.

Before Marroc could hesitate any longer, the air stirred. I instinctively grabbed on to a nearby leaf as a gust shook the branch.

And as the gale blew over us, I watched the leaf with my crystal fall free. It hung for a second as though taking a final look at us, then glided silently into the darkness.

CHAPTER 25

MARROC

*A*li stood by my side. We watched as the leaf drifted off into the shadows.

She had a habit of humming to herself quietly. It had annoyed me at first, but it was starting to grow on me. I found myself wanting to learn things about her. What had led her to become an assassin? How long had she lived in Boston?

And who the fuck was Barthol?

I stopped myself from asking anything. Even if jealousy seared me down to my bones, I'd never allow myself to show it. I had enough pride to hide it.

Also, I couldn't speak, so asking her questions was awkward. I had only my paper and pen.

I slid my hand into my pocket, my fingers grazing an ancient human musical device. Something had compelled me to bring it with me. I supposed I knew Ali would like it, since she'd seemed so enchanted by the old human world, and by music. I wanted to give it to her, but I'd wait for the right time. When she was relaxed, maybe.

As we waited in the dimness, the air was still. A single ray of green light sifted from above us.

We didn't know how far it was to the ground or how long it might take for the leaf to reach it. A few minutes? An hour? Most likely, the leaf was already nestled among the roots below. But it was also possible that it still drifted on the strange cosmic winds. If we teleported too early, we might reappear a thousand feet above the ground and immediately plunge to our deaths.

I looked to Ali, but she didn't look at me. Instead, she stared into the darkness below us. She'd pushed her silver hair behind her ears so that I could see their points. Her expression was pensive—thoughtful, even. If she was worried about falling, she didn't show it.

At last, she turned to me. "All right. I think it's time."

But this plan still unsettled me. Fear tightened my chest—such an unusual feeling for me. It was fear for Ali.

We didn't have another choice, however, and she'd been right that I might not make it back to her even if I survived the fall.

I reached out, then pulled her in to me. She wrapped her arms around my shoulders, and I breathed in her jasmine scent.

With her so close, I felt the warmth of my soul. My mind shimmered with memories of a distant life before Ragnarok... Something I'd forgotten completely. I'd had a pet once: a tamed wolf who'd walked by my side and slept by my bed. I could feel his soft fur.

Then a completely unfamiliar memory: sitting on a sofa before a TV, drinking wine from a box. A man sat across from me—a Night Elf with silver eyes and a mischievous grin.

That wasn't my memory. That was Ali's. And that man who smiled at her—I had a feeling that was Barthol.

I exhaled slowly, forcing the images from my mind. I closed my eyes and wrapped my arms around her shoulders. Gods, I wanted to drink her soul, down to the last drop, and to taste her lips while I was at it. I wanted her vitality...

She seemed oddly trusting of me, even knowing what I was.

With my arms curled around her, she whispered softly. Even through my closed eyelids, I could see a purple flash as we teleported to the vergr crystal.

I waited for the whistle of wind in my ears, the sense of vertigo as we began to free-fall, but instead I found my feet firmly planted on the ground.

I opened my eyes, and at first, I couldn't even comprehend where we were. There was no sign of Yggdrasill's mighty roots, no enveloping darkness. Instead, warm sunlight met my eyes, wind ruffled my hair, and I breathed in the scent of grass and wildflowers.

As my eyes focused, I saw that we stood in a great plain of yellow grass, so tall that it nearly reached my waist. The wind gusted, blowing the grass in undulating waves. The plain spread all the way to the horizon, to where it eventually ended in a range of blue mountains.

It was quiet but for the sound of the wind, and I turned to see Ali standing next to me, her mouth half open. Like myself, she looked out on the vista, almost not comprehending what it was. I closed my eyes, exalting in the feel of sunlight on my skin. When I opened them again, I saw Ali doing the same. A glorious, beaming grin lit up her face, and warmth flickered in my chest. She'd never felt the light of a summer sun.

A bird called. I looked up to see a solitary raven crossing above us in the sepia sky. Thin clouds masked the sun, but even so, golden light filtered down. I realized that, for the first time in my life, I had no idea where I was.

That thought unnerved me, and I scrubbed a hand over my jaw. We were no longer in Yggdrasil's cosmic domain, which meant we'd probably ended up in another one of the Nine Worlds. We weren't in Midgard, since it was perpetually frozen after Ragnarok, but unfortunately, that left eight more.

Next to me, Ali spoke softly—the same question. "Where are we?"

I shook my head and drew out my notebook. *I'm not sure,* I wrote. *I've never seen a place like this.*

Ali looked down at her splayed fingers, tinged with faint gold in the sunlight. "Is this what summer is like?"

I nodded and realized I didn't really care where I was. As the wind ruffled my hair again and I heard insects for the first time in a thousand years, a deep peace settled over me. This place felt primordial—it had clearly escaped the ravages of Ragnarok. It was heaven, and with Ali here, I nearly felt alive again. I had the strongest impulse to give her the gift of music now.

Dust rose in the distance. A chariot pulled by a brace of horses sped toward us. Instinctively, I stepped in front of Ali.

As it neared, I saw that a single figure drove it. A man with thick black hair that flew out behind him like a lion's mane. Not speaking, he drew up the horses twenty yards from us. As the dust settled, I saw that he was shirtless, dressed only in a pair of calfskin trousers. Blue tattoos snaked over his warrior's physique, and his eyes were the color of the deep forest.

He ignored me entirely, his green eyes focused solely on Ali.

Already, I hated him.

And I had no idea what he was. His ears were pointed—an elf of some sort, but I'd never seen one that looked quite like him.

"Who are you?" asked Ali, breaking the silence.

The man smiled, revealing a row of white teeth. "Are you travelers?" he asked, ignoring her question.

"Yes."

The man gestured to the plain. "These are the plains of Vanaheim."

I cursed in my mind. Vanaheim—it made perfect sense now. Home of the Vanir. A growl rose in my throat, and the horses trembled.

The stranger looked at me, and I saw his expression tighten as he recognized what I was. "We don't have *your* kind in our lands very often."

"We arrived by accident," Ali said. "If you can tell us how to return to Yggdrasill, we will be on our way."

The man shook his head. "That, I cannot do. All visitors are required to present themselves to the Emperor. You will follow me."

CHAPTER 26

ALI

I walked next to the stranger's chariot as if in a dream. The air hummed with the buzz of insects, the distant calls of birds, and the scent of wildflowers. We'd lost our way on our journey, but I still felt like I was in paradise, bathing in heavenly sensations I'd never experienced.

I'd been born underground, raised in damp caves and caverns. Sure, I'd spent time above ground. With my vergr stone, I'd been able to cross Galin's wall to visit the world of men. But Midgard was frozen and nearly lifeless. Nothing had prepared me for the feeling of a warm sun on my skin, the wind in my hair, or the gentle brush of grass against my legs.

So *this* was what summer felt like.

And this was what my people had lost. Now I understood the pain of the Shadow Lords, those who'd been born before Ragnarok. They remembered life outside the caverns. They remembered the sound of bees, the sensation of wind, the warmth of the sun.

Maybe I shouldn't have been born a Night Elf. I was made

for the sun. And now, with the golden ring, maybe I had what I needed to free my people.

I ran my hand through the grass. This was something worth fighting for, and I would do anything so the Dokkalfar could see the light again. Even if it was just the winter light of Midgard.

The shirtless newcomer led Marroc and me over the plain and into a long, sloping valley. I couldn't keep the smile from my face, and when I looked over at Marroc, I saw that delight danced in his eyes. How old was he, anyway? Liches didn't die.

"Have you felt this before?" I asked. "Did you ever know summer?"

As his smile faded, sadness flickered in his eyes. So, he was over a thousand years old. What had happened to him? Maybe he'd just wanted immortality and had given up his soul to live forever.

As we walked, I felt my cheeks flush, and a trickle of sweat ran down my neck. I pulled my coat off, tucking it under my arm, and took in the scene around us. Horses roamed in the fields. White, gray, roan, and bay, there were hundreds of them grazing on the golden hillsides. They watched us with curious eyes, and our guide rolled on in his chariot to our right.

I was deliriously happy.

Marroc touched my arm. He was holding a little white square out to me, with two pieces of string attached to what looked like beads.

Confused, I took it from his hand, frowning at it. It looked human, but I didn't know what it was. What was I supposed to do with this?

Then he popped one bead in each of my ears.

"What are you doing?" I asked.

He leaned over me and pushed a button on the little

square. A single word flitted across the screen.

Beyoncé.

And with it, music began to play. My grin widened at the sound of the music—the most glorious sound I'd ever heard filled my ears.

Beyoncé, whomever she might have been, was a genius. A goddess of music.

Here, I had sunlight, I had music, and almost nothing could be more perfect.

Marroc was watching me listen to the music, mischief twinkling in his eyes as I smiled at him. Here in the bright daylight, I could truly see his beauty. Before he'd been in prison, I imagined he'd broken a million hearts. And this, the music—it was almost a *romantic* gesture.

Still, only an idiot could let herself get charmed by a lich. Because charming was what they did: luring you close, letting you feel safe before they drew blood.

So, I'd enjoy the music, and I'd enjoy the sun.

But I could never forget what Marroc was.

* * *

I GLIDED ALONG, hardly noticing the scenery as Beyoncé sang into my ears. I'd never heard anything quite like her before. Maria Callas might have been the closest, but she didn't sing in a language I understood.

At this point, we'd walked to the bottom of the valley. A few yards away, a wide river flowed. Clean and clear, it ran swiftly between large boulders. As soon as I saw it, I realized how thirsty I was. It looked amazing.

The charioteer led his horses to the bank to drink, and I followed. I crouched down, cupping my hands to lift icy water to my lips.

"How far do we have to travel?" I asked the guide once I finished.

"Not far." His dark hair lifted in a breeze, and he turned away from me to direct the horses onto a dirt path wending alongside the river.

I slipped the little music beads back into my ears, but this time made sure to pay attention to our surroundings. We walked as the sun slid lower in the sky, staining the grass with peach hues. Grasses glowed more golden than I ever could have imagined. Only then did it occur to me that time was different here—daylight where it was night in Midgard.

At last, we turned away from the river, moving toward a high bluff. As we approached it, my breath caught at the view. Below us, hundreds of buildings ringed an ancient temple, all made of gleaming sandstone.

"What is this place?" I asked.

Our ebony-haired guide stood tall. "Njord's Hall."

"And the Emperor is down there?"

Our guide nodded, turning the chariot toward a path down the side of the bluff.

I was getting annoyed at the dust it kicked up, which stuck to my damp skin, and the fact that he hadn't asked us to join him on the chariot.

But soon, we merged with a larger road that led into the city, and we began to pass more people. Gleaming stone buildings stood on either side of us, with wispy curtains caught in the wind. Like our guide, everyone around us had dark hair and green eyes. Even stranger, they all seemed to be men. Nearly as beautiful as Marroc, muscular and tattooed—all of them intent on me. If I stuck around here too long, I'd get a bit of an ego.

I saw their eyes widen with surprise as we passed.

"Are there women here?" I asked.

Our guide didn't answer.

The sun had nearly set, casting long shadows over the city, when we finally reached the center. A massive temple stood before us. Built of enormous blocks of tan sandstone, it towered over the dwellings around it, its great columns spearing the sky. Unlike the Citadel, this building was half in ruins. Chunks of rock had crumbled away, and most of the roof had fallen in.

We passed through a broad gate flanked by guards wearing breastplates and golden helms. Our guide dismounted from his chariot and turned to face us.

His eyes never left me as he spoke. "This is where I leave you."

When I turned, I saw the guards circling behind. It seemed like they were blocking our exit, and it took all my willpower not to call Skalei to me.

A new guard dressed in silver armor led us into a large hall, where thick animal hides covered the floor and golden tapestries hung on the walls. Embroidered with blue and purple threads, they depicted herds of horses, forests and stags, and great battalions of dark-haired soldiers. In here, the air was cool and dry, and light streamed in from an oculus high above.

"Welcome to my kingdom," came a voice from the far end of the hall.

I turned and saw a tall man striding toward us. Like the rest of the men we'd seen, he had ebony hair and green eyes, but he wore a small gold circlet on his head.

So, this was the Emperor.

"Come closer, travelers." As he walked closer, his voice boomed off the walls, and the guards led us toward him.

When we were about fifteen feet from him, the Emperor held up his hand for us to stop.

"Who are you?" he asked. Softer now, his voice a gentle tenor.

"I am Ali, daughter of Volundar." I decided it was best not to mention that I was a trained assassin.

"A Night Elf? With a lich?"

"Yes."

"Is it true you were found on the high plains?"

"Yes." I wasn't sure how much information to offer.

"What brings you to our kingdom?"

"The wind blew us here."

For an instant, confusion flickered over the Emperor's features, and he frowned slightly. "From where was that?"

"Yggdrasill."

The Emperor's frown deepened. It was obvious that he wanted to question us, but also clear that he didn't want to give up his position of passive authority. "Your kind does not travel along the roots of the Great Tree."

I cast a quick glance at Marroc, but he didn't look worried. "Not often."

The Emperor stared at me. His green eyes roamed over my body, and I tried not to imagine how I must look covered in a thick layer of bone dust and squirrel fur.

Seemingly satisfied with what he saw, his gaze flicked to Marroc. "Who is the lich?"

Marroc met the Emperor's eyes, which were beginning to glow in the dim light of the temple. *The lich* looked annoyed, and I thought he probably didn't like how he was being addressed.

"His name is Marroc," I said.

The Emperor's gaze flicked back to me. "Is he your lover?" he asked smoothly.

CHAPTER 27

MARROC

I'd been growing increasingly irritated with the Emperor, but this question delighted me, particularly since Ali's cheeks were flushing.

"No," she said, clearly caught completely off guard. "He's not my lover. We just came here by accident, really. And we are trying to get back to Yggdrasill."

My fingers twitched as I realized the Emperor was still staring at Ali with an expression that I understood perfectly. Even covered in grime, with her silver hair snarled and matted with dirt, her beauty shone through. Anyone could see that. And based on how the Emperor's eyes moved over her body, he could see as well as anyone.

Already, I sensed that he wanted to keep her here, which made me consider ripping his throat out and sucking his soul out from his body.

Though that might cause political problems, so I'd avoid it if possible.

And I needed his help to get out of here.

What I needed was leverage—a weakness to exploit—and I tried to remember what I knew of the Vanir. They were a race of warriors. Thousands of years before my birth, they'd fought the High Elves to a draw before retreating into their kingdom. Since then, nothing had been heard from them. They were also said to be followers of Freya, wife of Odin, goddess of love and witchcraft.

The Emperor was staring at Ali now with an intensity that made my muscles tense.

"It is my pleasure to have you here," he continued. "It is not often that our kingdom gets visitors. Tonight, we must host a feast."

Ali rubbed her forehead. "We really just want to get back to the tree."

His eyes flicked to his guards, imparting some information I did not understand, before he turned back to Ali. "Is there anything that you require for your stay here?"

"The way out?"

He smiled placidly. "We'll get to that in time. But for now, let me offer you full use of my chambers. You appear to have had a long journey."

* * *

THE EMPEROR'S chambers were sumptuous, spread out with golden carpets, ottomans, and daybeds. A warm breeze whispered in through large windows that overlooked a city of sandstone. Bamboo canary cages and pedestals holding bowls of fruit stood around the room. Ali seemed delighted by the fruit, and was exploring the place with a half-eaten apple in her hand.

It reminded me of the splendor I'd grown accustomed to when I was young. And yet none of this was getting me to Loki's wand any faster.

Apparently, we were supposed to wait here and "refresh ourselves" until dinner. I didn't know what the Emperor's game was, but I suspected he had designs to keep Ali here. I wouldn't let him get anywhere close to her.

"Marroc!"

I turned to see Ali standing by the entrance to a large balcony, as she finished the last bite of her apple. As I approached, I saw what she was looking at: a marble-lined pool below, filled with clear water. The late-afternoon wind gently rippled its surface.

She turned to me, smiling. "Do you think it's for swimming?"

I nodded, my chest warming at the look of delight in her eyes.

"I haven't been swimming since I was a kid. We don't have water like this in the Shadow Caverns." I could hear the longing in her voice. She wanted to jump in, didn't she? "It's all gray and murky subterranean lakes. And there are things that live in the deep caverns, creatures that feast on the flesh of elves, and worse."

I smiled slyly at her. Maybe a little detour wasn't the worst thing in the world. At that moment, I wanted nothing more than to swim with her. Could I convince her to join me, even without the ability to speak?

I pulled off my coat and draped it over the balcony. Then I started to unbutton my shirt.

Ali shot a glance at me. "What are you doing?"

With a slight smile, I nodded at the pool.

I didn't miss the fact that her eyes were lingering on me, though she tore them away fast when I started to take off my trousers.

Once I was undressed, I climbed over the balcony and leapt in.

She stared down at me, drumming her fingertips on the stone ledge. I could see how much she wanted to join me, though, like any sensible person, she was wary of me.

I lay back in the water, swimming backward. I closed my eyes to show her how much I enjoyed it. The water rippled around me, enveloping me in a cool embrace.

When I opened my eyes again, I saw her pulling off her shirt. And as I watched her slide off her leather trousers, my body felt completely electrified. Under her clothes, she wore a simple white bra and underwear. She was beautiful, and she was mine. Gods, I wanted to sink my teeth into her neck and taste her soul...

I swam away from her, mastering control of myself. But when I heard the splash of water, I turned to see her in at the other end of the pool.

She grinned at me, the water rippling around her perfect shoulders. "The water *is* amazing. This was a truly good idea."

My gaze drifted lower, to her neck and the faint heartbeat under the skin. With her eyes locked on me, she moved closer in the water. My seductive aura was drawing her in. Water trickled between her breasts in little rivulets, entrancing me.

When she was only a few feet from me, I breathed in her scent. I imagined how she would tilt back her head, opening her throat to me. I'd trace my fingers over her waist; my lips would graze her skin.

With a jolt of horror, I realized I needed to pull myself away from her before I ruined everything. Before I ripped out her soul and mine and destroyed them both.

I turned abruptly. Climbing from the pool, I headed back up to the Emperor's chambers.

* * *

AFTER DRYING MYSELF OFF, I dressed on the balcony again. When I turned around, I saw Ali, her damp silver hair draped over a black shirt. She held a notepad and pen out to me. Somehow, I could tell what she was about to say next was important to her.

"Can I ask *you* something?"

I nodded.

She took a deep breath. "When the High Elves caught me, I wasn't alone. I'd been working with someone named Barthol. I haven't seen him since. Do you think they could have put him somewhere else in the Citadel?"

Barthol. That name again.

The unspoken subtext of her question was clear. She desperately wanted to know if this friend of hers was alive. Unfortunately, I didn't have much of an answer for her.

I'm sure he is fine, I wrote, my fingers tense with irritation. I half hoped he wasn't fine. *If the High Elves had caught or killed him, King Gorm would have brought him or his body out to throw into the Well of Wyrd along with you.*

She smiled. "You think so?"

I nodded.

"I have another question."

I didn't respond, but Ali plowed ahead anyway.

"How did you become a lich?"

I tensed. This was dangerous territory. *I was cursed. And now I'm alive, but only in a manner of speaking. Obviously, I'm dangerous.*

I wasn't sure why I wanted to emphasize that last part. Maybe it was that I'd let her get too close to me.

She crossed her arms, curiosity lighting up her eyes. "But what was your life like when you were human? Your home looks like you were rich."

Ahh... she'd assumed I was human. It certainly would have been better if she continued to think that, but... *Not human*, I wrote.

Ali's eyes narrowed. "What do you mean? I thought liches were always former humans. So, what were you?"

Ice chilled my veins. I'd hoped to avoid this conversation. *Elf.*

Her entire body went tense. "What kind of elf?"

A High Elf.

"What? I didn't even know elves could become liches. Why didn't you tell me this before?"

She stepped closer. Her fingers twitched like she was thinking about calling forth that magical knife of hers.

"The High Elves have imprisoned the Dokkalfar for a thousand years. Ever since Ragnarok, we've been trapped in caves underground. I didn't see the horizon or the sunlight until I was sent on this mission to retrieve the gold ring. So, who were you, Marroc? I already know you're old as Helheim. You were around then, weren't you? You were alive when the High Elves sent the Night Elves into the caves, locking us underground."

Dread crept over me slowly like an afternoon shadow. She was getting too close to learning the truth. For the first time in the past thousand years, I was grateful I couldn't speak.

I only shrugged, and I could feel her fury rising. The hatred in her eyes burned so sharp and bright that I wondered what horrors she'd experienced under the ground. A shard of sadness split me open.

She took another step closer, eyes sharp and narrow, and poked me in the chest. "I told you I'd do anything I could to protect my people. My whole life, I've had nothing to keep me warm but my family, and my dreams of revenge. So, I have some questions for you, Marroc. I want to know who you knew, exactly. Before Ragnarok."

Gods, she was breathtaking. The sheer audacity to give

commands to an ancient lich, to launch into an interrogation...

She jabbed my chest again. "Do you know where I'd find Galin? The sorcerer who imprisoned us? He worked for the king."

Darkness clouded my mind.

She folded her arms imperiously. "Suddenly can't find your pen and paper?"

Now, she hardly trusted me at all. That was good. Because if I lost control around her, my world would end.

But her interrogation was interrupted by the sound of footfalls, and I turned. The Emperor and a pair of guards stood in the doorway, their eyes fixed on Ali.

"Once you are ready," said the Emperor, his voice husky, "we will leave for dinner."

CHAPTER 28

ALI

Night had fallen, and Marroc and I walked together through a primeval forest. The trunks of ancient pines stood around us, like the columns of a cathedral, while above us the tree's canopy was so thick that it blocked out the sky. The air was damp and heavy, fragrant with the scent of the pine trees. A perfumed wind kissed my skin.

I stole a glance at him. Once a High Elf, was he? As soon as we got away from these guards, I wanted to know everything he knew.

My mind whirred with the tasks ahead of me. First, we'd get Loki's wand so we could return to Midgard—and he could get his soul back, supposedly. Then I'd take the golden ring back to the Shadow Lords. With their help, I'd free my people.

I'd always believed my mother, and soon, I'd finally prove her right.

All I had to do was help kill the dark wizard who'd locked us in there. And if Marroc was right, the ring in my pocket was just what I needed to find the sorcerer. He was the one who'd imprisoned the Night Elves in the Shadow Caverns after Ragnarok. Only his death would free us.

I stole a glance at Marroc. What I really wanted was to question him about where to find the dark sorcerer, but I couldn't do it with other people around.

After living underground so long, after watching my friends and family die in subterranean darkness, I wanted nothing more than to drive my blade through Galin's throat, but I'd have to be patient.

Under the ancient pine trees, we were led by a pair of guards, who carried torches that cast shadows over the mossy forest floor. It was quiet but for the whisper of a breeze circling between the trunks. All around us, tiny lights flickered between the boughs and branches.

Despite my dreams of revenge, I couldn't help but smile. This was the first time I'd ever seen fireflies. For a few minutes, I forgot about Skalei slicing open the throats of the High Elves.

And now that Marroc had reassured me about Barthol, I could actually enjoy this beauty a little before we returned to Midgard.

Despite my blood-soaked revenge fantasies, things were looking up. Granted, Midgard was still freezing, but at least we'd be aboveground. I shoved my hand into my pocket, sliding the ring onto my finger. I couldn't enjoy this place too much. I had to get this thing back to the Shadow Lords before anything got in my way.

Soon, brighter lights appeared ahead of us, and I sucked in a breath as we stepped into a large clearing. A circle of giant stones stood round a blazing bonfire. From between them, the Emperor walked, arms outstretched.

He grinned jovially, white teeth flashing in the firelight. "Welcome, welcome."

"Thank you," I said. "What is this place?"

"This is the one of Vanaheim's most sacred groves."

"You eat dinner here?"

"Yes, yes," he said. "You'll see why soon. This grove provides entertainment you can get nowhere else."

"And over dinner you'll tell us how to get out of here, right?"

The Emperor didn't answer, and I didn't have time to ask what this *entertainment* might be before he turned to lead us toward the fire.

As we passed between the mammoth stones, a rush of darkness curled off Marroc, licking at my skin. Something had unnerved him, and I could guess what. Stone circles were places of powerful magic. Everything about this was super weird.

Within the circle, a small feast had been arranged on wooden tables. There were roast chickens, turkeys, and even a suckling pig with an apple in its mouth. There were also loaves of bread, platters of steaming vegetables, and even a few pies. Enough to feed a large party of people.

I looked around, but other than the guards and a few servants, we seemed to be the only guests. My hackles rose. Why so much food, then?

The Emperor gestured to a long wooden table set with earthenware plates and bowls and pewter goblets. "Come, sit with me."

"Are we the only people eating tonight?" I asked, suspicious.

"For now," said the Emperor, indicating that Marroc and I should sit on either side of him.

As soon as I took my seat, the servants began to bring us food. The meal looked delicious, and not just because I'd been literally starving. I was served chicken roasted with sage, slathered in butter. My mouth watered, and *gods*, I wanted to eat it. But this Emperor was weird as shit, and I didn't trust him at all. This could be dosed with anything.

The Emperor filled my glass with wine. Even thirsty as I was, I wouldn't drink it.

"Why are we eating here?" I asked. "Why not dine in your palace?"

"As I said, this is one of my kingdom's most sacred places. The stones have been here for thousands of years. I bring all my honored guests." He nodded at my plate. "Not hungry?"

"Right, but we're just travelers, passing through." I tried not to sound impatient. "And you were going to tell us how to get out of here, so we can return home."

"Oh, but you're so much more than that. You're a Night Elf, and he's"—the Emperor inclined his head toward Marroc without directly looking at him—"he's a *lich*. I don't believe we've had either of your kind visit for at least a thousand years. It's only appropriate to show you the utmost hospitality."

Marroc didn't appear to have any interest in his food, which was either a lich thing or the same sense of caution that I had.

The Emperor took a long sip of his wine. Then, standing, he asked, "Well, if you're not hungry, are you ready for the entertainment?"

Before I could ask what the entertainment was, the Emperor turned to face the forest. He lifted his hands to the night sky.

"Spirits of the forest," he said in a clear voice. "I have brought a feast. Come and sup with me and my guests."

My muscles were completely tense, hair standing on end. For a long moment, nothing happened. The forest remained dark and still, like a great beast holding its breath. Then, deep within it, I saw a light shine, then another.

Were these the fireflies I'd seen earlier? As I watched, more and more lights appeared.

"Come, my children," called the Emperor. "Come and feast with me."

I gasped as the first fairy stepped from the trees. No larger than a sparrow, she floated towards us on gossamer wings. As I stared, another appeared. In seconds, hundreds were gliding between the stones, floating on the breeze like dandelion seeds.

"Eat and be merry," said the Emperor. The fairies swarmed the feast, and the food disappeared in a haze of glowing light. As they finished eating, they began to spiral around the stones. They spun and swirled like a flock of birds.

They were, I had to admit, absolutely transfixing.

"They're beautiful," I whispered. I glanced at Marroc, who looked as enchanted as I was. But when he licked his teeth with a hungry look in his eyes, I realized he probably just wanted to drain their souls.

The Emperor smiled. "Listen," he said, holding a finger to his lips.

I strained my ears until I heard a low humming that rose and fell. As the fairies danced around and around within the circle, the humming grew louder.

"They're singing," I whispered.

My worries seemed to fade away now. The song grew louder, and a smile spread across my face.

"Oh my gods. I recognize that song. It's 'Halo'—they're singing Beyoncé! I heard it on the way over." Baffled, I turned to the Emperor. "How do they know Beyoncé?"

He grinned. "They're magic; they can sing what you desire to hear. You just have to know the song, to love it, and they'll sing it. Now do you see why I brought you here?"

I listened as the fairies danced, twisting and twirling their tiny bodies in time with the music. I knew there was something I had to be doing now—something about a ring, saving the world, assassinating the High Elf royalty, blah, blah. But dancing... now *that* would be amazing. To simply let go of my worries, to release all the pressure on me. To twirl and sing like the fairies.

Only then did I realize I already *was* dancing, hands over my head, hips swaying.

Marroc was looking at me with sharp eyes, like he was ready to pounce and bite into my neck. But the dead were no fun, were they? Spoilsports.

Now, I found my legs carrying me toward the fire, and I stepped into the swirling cloud of tiny spirits. Laughing, I spun around as thousands of fairies swarmed about me like moths. Their wings fluttered, gently stroking my skin, and they kept singing.

"Can you do—" I thought for a second, trying to remember the name of the song. "Can you do 'Single Ladies'?"

CHAPTER 29

MARROC

I watched as Ali danced, spinning round and round, surrounded by the glittering fairies.

Part of me wanted this to be real. I'd never seen her like this. Relaxed and happy, an expression of joy spread across her face. Drinking her would be pure light, pure beauty—the most exquisite rush.

In the firelight, her silver hair flowed around her shoulders like a waterfall, her eyes glittered like jewels, and she laughed.

But this was not real joy, no.

This was an enchantment, and I had to stop it. I turned to the Emperor. I'd slaughter him if I had to. But as I tried to stand, I found I couldn't move, that something held me to my chair.

When I looked down, I saw that threads and cords stretched over my legs and arms. They bound me to my seat like the filaments of a spider's web. Dark rage poured through me like billowing smoke.

Little creatures moved at my feet. From under tiny mops of black hair, the pointed faces of pixies grinned at me.

My lip curled as I looked back up at the Emperor. I wanted to explain to him that as soon as I freed myself, I'd be draining him of blood and life, but the words wouldn't come. Icy wrath flooded my body. I tried to stand again, but if anything, the pixies' bindings seemed tighter.

The Emperor was staring at me, his lips curled up in a half-smile. Then he leaned forward, just out of reach of my teeth.

His whisper was so quiet, only I could hear. "She's mine now."

CHAPTER 30

ALI

I danced, spinning and spinning, twirling and twirling, the fairies flying around me like tiny stars. It was a perfect rush of joy, excitement, and freedom. While I danced, the fairies sang "Single Ladies" not once, not twice, but three times, and I never wanted it to end. I was about to ask for it a fourth time when they suddenly stopped, falling silent.

They drifted around me like motes of dust in a sunbeam. Their bodies were still, their voices silent. Only their wings moved, faintly fluttering, just enough to keep themselves from falling to the ground.

"Keep singing," I heard myself say, pleading. "Keep singing."

But they'd stopped listening to me. They'd turned away, and I saw they were looking at the Emperor. He stood before me, illuminated by moonlight. His dark hair fell to his neck, his green eyes on me.

Was he beautiful? I hadn't noticed it before. Had I been with someone more beautiful…? I couldn't remember his name now. He wasn't important.

"Emperor," I heard myself shout as though from a distance, "make the fairies sing again!"

"May I dance with you?"

I smiled. "As much as you'd like."

Was I flirting with him? I didn't know. I didn't care. I just wanted to keep dancing. To listen to the fairy song.

The Emperor moved across the circle as if in slow motion, never taking his eyes off me. Now, the fairies swirled around him like a beautiful, glowing, glistening cloak.

In seconds, he was by my side, his hand at my waist. At that moment, my legs gave way, and I sank into him. The fairies surrounded us.

I could hear them whispering, "You've won the Emperor. You've won the Emperor."

I was victorious!

They begin to sing again, a new song I didn't know, but it was beautiful, and the Emperor spun me around as we danced, his hand firm on my hip. He was grinning at me like the cat who got the cream. But I'd won him, hadn't I?

And he was… I wanted him.

No. No, not him.

There was something… something rotten about this.

The fairy singing grew louder, until it drowned out my own thoughts. The Emperor gripped me by the waist and pressed himself to me. I could feel his firm grip on my lower back, his hips moving against me.

My heart was beating fast, but he was the wrong one.

Insistent, the music throbbed. The wings of a thousand tiny fairies, beating in unison.

I turned, and then I saw him. The right one—Marroc. His name came back to me, and he stared at me with ice-blue eyes. Even from here, I felt the pulse of his seductive magic rippling over my skin. *That* one. He might be a lich, but I was

CURSED PRINCE

safe with him, and his beauty was like a blade right to my heart.

"Help me," I tried to say, but no words came out. I couldn't speak. I could only sing with the fairies.

The Emperor swung me around the fire toward the table. It was empty of food now—the fairies had consumed every morsel, every bite of sustenance. Only bones remained.

Then he pushed them aside, pressing me onto the wood. His breath was hot on my neck. He licked my cheek, whispering, "You will be the mother of my children."

Nausea rose in my gut. "No!" I tried to fight him, but my body was not my own, and I was compliant in his hands.

Marroc's eyes were fixed on mine, burning with rage. It wouldn't kill him to step in here, would it?

Then I saw the dozens of cords binding him. Ahh...

Well, I was the North Star, and I could find a way to save myself. I'd bring Skalei through this man's neck.

I just needed to think clearly under this haze of music and dancing and confusion.

"You are mine," whispered the Emperor in my ear. "I will never let you go."

Oh, I would enjoy killing him.

But with that phrase, those words, a distant memory sparked in my mind. Something important.

Never let you go.

Tiny fairies bobbed and weaved and danced around us, singing the Emperor's song. Vainly, I tried to struggle, but his grip was like iron.

And as the look of rage on Marroc's features faded, he looked like he was weakening somehow. He was under an enchantment of his own.

"I will never let you go," said the Emperor again, his voice raspy with desire. His hand was on my thigh, pushing up my dress.

And then I remembered. It was like that song that Marroc hated.

In my mind, I implored the fairies, *Sing Rick Roll.*

CHAPTER 31

MARROC

Through the fire and smoke, Ali stared at me, her expression fierce. But she seemed so distant, and fog clouded my mind. I'd wanted to get up and rip off the Emperor's head, but the ropes were enchanted with a magic too powerful even for me. And worse, they weakened me.

At my feet, the pixies danced, even as they tossed more of their magical cords over me, binding me tighter and tighter. The bonds wrapped around me like a cocoon. A magical sleep crept over my mind like a blanket of night.

Distantly, I could hear the voices of the fairies, but they were fading. Quiet and pleasant. And even as I closed my eyes, I knew there was nothing I could do. The Emperor had won.

But then the fairies launched into a new song, a tune that cut through my mind like a sword dipped in acid. No, it was worse than that. This was like claws on stone, like a perpetually squealing tire.

Who in their right mind would tell the fairies to sing Rick Astley?

And then my mind cleared. The spell of sleep had

shattered.

My eyes focused, but the pixie ropes still bound me. I strained against them, but they were strong as steel.

I snarled with rage at the sight of the Emperor pressing Ali to the wooden dining table. His head turned slowly toward me, his lips curled into a broad smile.

Incandescent rage coursed through me.

Because of the curse, when my emotions got out of control, I burned. My body turned hot and fiery. And right now, I was incendiary. Fiery hot, the curse poured into me like molten steel from a crucible, ten thousand degrees boiling and incandescent like the surface of the sun. I was burning—but so were the ropes.

Freed, I burst into the air. The Emperor's hand was at his belt.

Howling with rage, I charged through the bonfire as if it were only a guttering candle. With one hand, I tore him off Ali. I lifted him into the air by the throat. I'd be ripping that open in a moment.

Gasping, eyes wild, he stared at me, skin blistering under the heat of my grip.

A strangled shout: "Help!"

Hunger tore through me. How would the soul of an Emperor taste? I brought him closer, ready to plunge my teeth into his skin.

But, like a lightning bolt, Ali streaked past me. Her dagger was in the Emperor's heart before I got the chance to taste him.

I spun, hurling his body into the bonfire.

Vanir warriors charged from the forest, pointing wands at us.

Hearing a warning shout from Ali, I spun round as spells whipped through the air. Driven by instinct, I covered her body with mine.

CHAPTER 32

ALI

Marroc crouched over me as spells and hexes whizzed through the darkness. The fairies scattered, and I curled in on myself, pulling my knees to my chest. Marroc's massive frame absorbed the damage, and after what seemed like an eternity, the guards' wands ran low and the spells stopped.

Marroc rose above me like a conquering god, soaked in an Emperor's blood. Still clutching Skalei, I stood next to him. Before I could say a word, he wrapped his arms around me, his body still warm. He lifted me, and I clung to his neck. As he broke into a run, the piney air whipped over us.

Part of me hated the thought of being carried by a High Elf—like I was a damsel in distress. But the other knew he was far faster than me, and this was the smartest option.

He ran nearly as fast as the hexes, but a spell arced toward us. Marroc dodged away from it, picking up speed as he raced past the Vanir warriors, beyond the stone circle, and into the forest.

Moving like smoke in a storm, we raced between the trees. Despite his speed, his movements were smooth. A welcoming darkness closed around us as we wove between the trunks of the primordial trees, great boughs hiding the moon.

Exhausted, I closed my eyes, pressing my face closer to Marroc's chest. He ran like a stag, untiring, his legs flying over the thick carpet of pine needles and brushing past ferns.

Then, distantly, I heard a sound that chilled me to my core. Far away, but clear nonetheless, an eerie keening rose. It sounded like hounds. The Emperor's men were hunting us—and we still didn't know how to get out of here.

I felt Marroc's muscles tense, and he rushed faster through the forest, but the dogs kept calling for us as they followed our scent.

"Marroc," I said, "we need to find a stream. We can use water to hide our scent."

But it seemed like he already knew what I had in mind, and he began heading downhill, to a low-lying area. The forest thickened; the tree trunks grew larger than I'd imagined. Still, Marroc dodged effortlessly between them. I kept my arms tight around his neck, breathing in the scent of wood smoke and sage.

Now, he wasn't hot at all. He was nearly cool to the touch, his breath coming smoothly and rhythmically. When I first heard his feet slosh in water, I nearly cried out with joy, but the crying of the hounds, closer than before, silenced me.

We were running through the center of a brook. Bows and branches slapped into my exposed back. I had hoped the water would confuse the hounds, but they kept coming, growing steadily louder. Clearly, there must be some sort of magic at play.

We ran for what seemed like miles.

At last, the rays of dawn began to break through the trees. Holy smokes. How long had I been dancing for?

Around us, the forest was thinning. And beyond it, Vanaheim's golden plains stretched like an endless sea.

"We can't go out there," I whispered to Marroc. "They'll be able to see us. We'll be visible for miles."

The stream followed the edge of the forest for a few more miles, then spilled out onto the plain. There wasn't any other choice, and yet this seemed like death.

We plunged into the ocean of golden grass. Marroc ran yard after yard, his breath even. He crossed the stream a few more times, trying to confuse the dogs.

Lifting my head from his chest, I looked over his shoulder to the edge of the forest. Dread gripped me as huge beasts emerged from the trees. Not hounds, but boars nearly the size of horses—with black fur.

They could see us now, squealing and crying. Vanir warriors mounted on horseback moved among them.

"Marroc, where are we going? How do we get out of here?"

Of course, he couldn't answer. He turned sharply back toward the water. I glanced over my shoulder and saw that the stream had widened into a small river.

We charged into it, water spraying around us, and Marroc let me go. We both started to swim in the cool water, though I still had no idea what the end game was. Only that the giant boars now lined the riverbanks. They tracked us, calling for the horsemen.

In the water, I heard a new sound I couldn't place, a distant roar like unending thunder.

The first spell hit a wave next to us with a sharp, sizzling pop. Instantly, Marroc grabbed me by the shoulder, pulling me under. Above me, through the swirling water, I could see the distorted shapes of the dogs and horses, and on them the dark shapes of men, wands raised.

Their spells fizzled against the water's surface like mighty raindrops. I tried to stay underwater as long as possible as the river began to churn with killing hexes. But my lungs burned; pain spread through my chest.

Death below and death above. I was going to drown if I didn't get a breath.

I rose above the surface to gasp for air, and a spell burned my cheek. I plunged under again, desperate for more air.

But the water was rushing now, and we twisted and tumbled like flotsam in a storm.

Again, my head broke free. The boars and horsemen were gone, replaced by rocky cliffs and the thunderous roar of what I now understood was a waterfall.

CHAPTER 33

MARROC

When I spotted the sharp cliff and the waterfall before us, fear speared my chest. The river was raging out of control, the waters carrying us along and spinning us around. I kicked my legs, fighting against the currents, but they were supernaturally strong.

Whatever happened, I didn't want to lose Ali. I grabbed her to me, pulling her close with one arm.

A rock rose in front of us, large as an elephant. We slammed into it, but before I could grab it, we'd already bounced off. We spun again, and I saw another boulder. This time, I was able to hold on to it, but only for an instant. Slick with mud, my hands slid off. With water rushing around us, the waves swept us back into the seething river, churning us under this time.

And through it all, I felt her soul next to mine—a golden ray of light beaming from her body. It was like some of her memories were spilling into me: Ali as a child, painting on the walls of a dark cavern by the light of candles. A female Night Elf spun a lantern carved with animal shapes, her eyes bright as she told a story. She looked like Ali. Her mother, maybe.

Then Ali stood by the bed of the same woman, but the woman's eyes were no longer bright. Now, her face was gaunt, lips dry and blistered. She whispered something, and it sounded like *leidarstjarna*—the North Star. The lodestar and the guiding light. But the air smelled of illness, and blood spattered the sheets where she'd been coughing. And I felt the heartbreak, felt it shattering...

How could I feel these things again?

The dead couldn't truly care for anyone.

The visions faded, and I was back in the currents, clinging to Ali. Using all the strength in my body, I kicked to the surface. Around us, the river had turned into white foam. No up and no down. Just spinning, just froth.

It was too late.

No matter what I did, we were going to go over the edge. I felt Ali's fingers tighten on mine, and I wrapped my arm more tightly around her. The sound of the water and the sound of thunderclaps deafened me as we were swept over the lip and dropped into an abyss.

Something like fear hammered on the inside of my skull.

Weightless, I couldn't see anything but bubbles as we twisted around and around, falling. I gripped Ali as tightly as she was holding me.

We plunged faster through the water until we hit the bottom in a deafening crush of spray and churning water.

The impact was bruising. We were immediately thrust under, darkness closing around us. I spun upside down, disoriented, kicking and fighting, trying to make my way to the surface.

At last, I broke free, but the river had torn Ali from my grasp.

My thoughts went nearly blank with panic, and I craned

my neck to look for her silver hair. But I saw only churning foam, and the river was still carrying me. Slick stone arched above me as the current pulled me into a cavern. Narrowing rapidly, the river became a thunderous torrent.

I tried to call Ali to me, forgetting for a moment that I had no voice.

Worse came as the cave walls closed in and darkness descended. I could barely tell up from down, much less left from right. Kicking and thrashing took all my energy as I fought to stay at the surface.

It was only when the water began to slow that I could swim out of the main current, and found myself drifting in an eddy. I dove under the water again, kicking my legs, swimming toward what I hoped was a shallower part of the underground river.

It was pitch black. I growled in frustration, and the noise echoed eerily in the darkness.

At last, my foot touched the bottom. Slimy river stones. I tried to stand, nearly slipping. I growled again, louder this time, but I heard no answer.

A sharp ache was splitting my chest open, but I wouldn't admit to myself that I'd lost her.

And yet, apart from the sound of lapping water, only silence greeted me.

CHAPTER 34

ALI

I floated in the darkness, my Night Elf eyes adjusting. The rapids had slowed, and the water expanded into an underground lake. Here, a gray stone ceiling arched twenty feet above my head. Pockmarked with dark holes and crevices, it looked like the moon seen from Earth. I wondered what sort of geologic processes had created its strange appearance.

I shivered in the icy water, my teeth chattering. I needed to find some place warm and dry. Fatigue seared my muscles.

As if on cue, I spotted a dark shape a hundred yards away, sitting on a rocky island in the cavern. As I swam toward it, I smelled the familiar scent of sage and wood smoke. Relief flooded me. Marroc was alive, which meant we could find a way out of here together.

"Marroc?" I called out. "I'm over here!"

I swam as fast as my aching muscles would allow. As I neared the island, I saw him standing on the shoreline. Tall, with his impossibly broad shoulders, he stood silhouetted against the inky darkness of the shadowy cavern. Despite his distinctly large shape, immediately I knew it wasn't Marroc. The scent of wood smoke had faded now.

My stomach clenched. This man had the golden hair of a High Elf.

"Who are you?" I asked, swimming in place.

He crossed to the water, almost gliding over the stones. He was beautiful. Honeyed hair, golden, luminous skin, and eyes as blue as shadows in an ice cave. His body seemed to emit light. "I'm here for you, Ali."

"Who are you? How do you know my name?"

He didn't answer that question.

Why would a High Elf be here? He didn't look wet, his hair drifting gently in a subterranean breeze.

"What are you doing here?" I asked.

"You must be freezing." He held out a hand to me. "Come join me. I have dry clothes. I can warm you up."

He looked familiar, I realized. The golden hair, the luminous skin, the long silver robes. I'd seen him before. At first, I thought it must have been at the Citadel. Was he one of the elves who'd shown up for the spectacle of my execution?

Then I realized it was far, far worse than that. *He* was the one I needed to kill.

He was Galin. The sorcerer. The one who'd imprisoned the Night Elves under the ground. The one I'd sworn to kill. The one I hated with every fiber of my being.

"You're Galin." I did my best to keep my voice smooth, though my emotions were trembling through my body.

This man before me was why Mom and Dad had died of the cave sickness, their bodies racked by fevers, skin dappled with sores. This man was why none of us ever saw the sun or the horizon, why we starved under the earth.

I thought of calling Skalei to me, but it was too early. He couldn't see me as a threat.

The faintest hint of a smile flicked over the High Elf's face as he took a step closer to the edge of the rocky shore. "I am whatever you desired me to be."

My body shook with rage, but I tried to keep a level head so I didn't fuck this up. This was the man who'd brought a thousand years of suffering to my people, the man I'd vowed every day of my life to kill. He looked remorseless, smug. And I needed him to keep his guard down before I slit his throat.

"Why are you here?" I asked again. I tried to keep my voice light and calm to mask the rage. Let him think I was harmless.

"Waiting for you," he said, his voice melodic.

What the fuck?

Well, I wasn't going to sit here chatting with him any longer. This was the time. I rushed forward. The water was at my knees now.

But something was holding me back—that question niggled in the back of my mind. *Why is Galin here in this dark, wet, subterranean lake?*

I didn't want to kill him till I understood what was happening.

"Are you real?" A little anger tinged my voice, and I marshaled a sense of calm. An assassin was supposed to stay in control, to master her feelings. I took a long, slow breath.

Galin smiled. "Yes. I have always been here for you, Ali. I have been waiting for you for a very long time."

His eyes swept over me. There was a fierce desire in them. And something else—a different emotion. Hunger.

I stopped walking, the lake water lapping at my ankles.

None of this made sense. I waited, ready to call Skalei at any moment. Icy rivulets dripped down my body, and my muscles shook with fatigue, but I was focused only on him.

"Waiting for me?" I successfully kept my voice light this

time, and I even managed what I thought was a genuine smile.

The High Elf was only feet from me. He was extraordinarily beautiful. His golden hair floated around his head like a halo, and his pale eyes twinkled, a sly smile on his lips. He looked relaxed, amused. "None of that is important, Ali. And I don't mind dying."

"Skalei," I whispered.

But just then, something brushed my leg. Something cold, slimy, and covered in translucent suckers. Something that felt toxic. I whirled, slashing it with Skalei.

Then Galin *screamed.*

CHAPTER 35

MARROC

I peered into the darkness, straining my eyes, but it was futile. I couldn't see through the inky blackness. I'd just finished tracing the rune for sun when a small hand touched my shoulder.

"Marroc, are you okay?" Ali's voice brought a smile to my face.

I turned to her, and she beamed at me, eyes shining. Her silver hair hung in wet waves to her shoulders. As my gaze went lower, my breath caught.

Just like at the pool before, she wore only her white underwear. The sun rune illuminated her transparent bra, nipples straining against it. A long-forgotten desire stirred in my body; I wanted to claim her right there. I wanted to taste her skin, her neck. I wanted to feel her against me.

She hugged herself. "I'm cold," she whispered. "I lost my clothes in the rapids."

With one hand around her neck, the other on her hip, I was now pressing her against a boulder. I let my body warm the air, heat pulsing off me. A sly smile curled my lips. So, I hadn't lost the ability to seduce, even after all that time in prison.

I looked deep into those silver eyes. I was boxing her in, but the look on her face told me she liked it. As I leaned in closer, I could smell her delicious scent, so perfectly mine. Her neck was arching. Inviting me.

"Everything is going to be fine now," she said softly. "You're making me warmer."

Water dripped from her hair, along the curves of her shoulders, her skin puckered with goosebumps. Her nipples were hard in the cool air, her mouth half open with desire.

So tempting to just grab her, to take her up against the stone, my mouth on her throat. But I'd take my time with her. When I touched her shoulder, I found her body ice-cold to the touch.

I pressed in closer, sliding my hand up her back, into her hair. I pulled her head back and leaned down to brush my lips over her throat. She wrapped her arms around my neck, pulling me to her. I could hear her breathing quickening, and I was enjoying having her here in my thrall.

I could feel it now—my heart beating. Life pulsing within me. I kissed her neck, tasting her. My tongue swirled over her skin, my thoughts becoming muddled. I was fighting the urge to break the skin, to release her blood...

I pulled away a little bit, leashing myself to stay in control. Then I slowly trailed kisses down her throat. I could hear her heart beating, feel her pulse throbbing beneath her skin.

I was battling a ferocious need to possess her completely, to make her mine, body and soul. I skimmed my teeth over her throat. My eyes slid over her body once more, and I fought the overwhelming need to rip off those damp pieces of white cloth. She smiled at me, hips moving closer to me. My blood roared in my ears like I was alive again.

I traced my fingertips down, from her shoulders to her wrists. I watched her shiver as I touched her, like her body was exquisitely sensitive. Normally, she seemed so fierce, but now she was helpless before me, desperate to be touched.

My assassin—tamed.

I gripped her wrists and pinned them above her head. I leaned down, pressing my lips to hers, kissing her deeply. A low growl rose from me, and I was dangerously close to losing control. I felt her damp body against mine, her soft breasts brushing my chest. I wanted to fill her. When she moaned a little, fire shot through me.

As my mouth claimed hers, I felt like I could see into her soul again—to the first time she saw the sunlight, her eyes dazzled. I wanted to keep her in the light, always. As we kissed, it was like we became one, souls twined together. I pulled away from the kiss with a nip of her lower lip.

When I ran my hands slowly down her arms, I heard her gasp. Gods, I wanted her naked, but I was staying in control. My heart was beating now, strong in my chest.

I lifted my gaze to hers. Even when I was alive, I had never desired a woman more than at this very moment.

With a light touch, I stroked my fingers up her body—then my palms grazed her breasts, and she gasped again.

She whispered my name—*"Marroc"*—and the word froze me in place.

Because that wasn't my name, and at some point, she'd learn the truth.

The betrayal would rip us apart.

CHAPTER 36

ALI

Galin screamed, reaching for me. His face shimmered like rippling water—one moment elven, the next a twisting mass of gelatinous flesh. What the fuck?

A tentacle wrapped around my leg. One slash from Skalei cleaved it in two, and gray pus squirted from the severed end.

Galin continued to scream, but his voice was changing. No longer the singsong High Elf dialect, it had turned phlegmy, like he was trying to speak with a mouth full of goo. I leapt away from him, feet splashing in the water. My blood pounded loud in my ears.

So, this wasn't Galin. Of course I wouldn't be so lucky as to just run into him here in the middle of a dark cave.

"Come back to me, Ali," he commanded. "I *will* protect you."

Sure you will. I took another step back, and another tentacle reached for me, sliding over my skin. I severed it, then dove back into the frigid lake. I swam underwater, away from the island, until my lungs burned and my body began to convulse.

When I surfaced, the creature was howling with rage. Not Galin—a grotesque monster that hung from one of the ceiling's cavities. A giant mollusk—a gelatinous body thick as a tree trunk, but with tentacles writhing around its mouth.

It called me again in a gurgling voice. "Ali, I will protect you!"

I swam toward deeper water. I knew what this creature was now: a *nokk*. One of the most dangerous subterranean animals. Many a Night Elf had been lured to their death by their telepathic magic.

The nokk's method was simple. They strung out a net of tentacles, then waited for their prey to approach. If one of their tentacles touched you, they would project images into your mind, drawing you closer and closer with the promise of your deepest desires. If I hadn't sliced that tentacle away, the creature would have consumed me.

I watched the nokk twist and turn above the island like a slimy pendulum. I'd thought it would try to chase me, but it didn't seem able or willing to move from its spot. I was trying to decide where I should swim next, when a familiar growl pierced the darkness. *Marroc.*

I searched for him. Where was he? He growled again, and fear snaked through me. Either it was the nokk calling me again with another illusion, or Marroc was actually nearby.

Cautiously, I swam toward the sound of his voice. I needed his help if I was to return to Midgard. If the nokk had him, I might be stuck in these depths forever. And worse, though I was loath to admit it, I owed him for his help. He'd helped me get the ring I needed, and I needed to help him find Loki's wand so he could get his soul back. Or at least *try* to help him. I doubted we'd actually get it.

I hoped that Marroc might simply be calling out to me, but when I finally saw him, my worst fears were realized. He hung ten feet in the air, gray tentacles coiled around him like snakes. His eyes were closed, but he struggled in the nokk's grasp.

I needed to free him.

"Skalei."

I stood slowly in chest-deep water. The stones under my feet were slick with river slime. I tried not to think about what sorts of animals lived in an environment that was completely dark.

Fake Galin appeared again on the lakeshore. "Ali, you've returned to me?" he called from the darkness.

I tensed. The only way a nokk could project an illusion into my brain was if one of its tentacles was touching me. I spotted one floating in the water near my thigh. I sliced through it, and Galin disappeared again.

I probably only had a few seconds until the creature sent another tentacle reaching for me, so I threw Skalei as hard as I could. Spinning end over end, my blade was aimed right for the nokk, until it twitched rapidly. There was a metallic clank as the hilt bounced off the thing and hit the ceiling, then splashed into the lake.

Balls. I missed.

Galin reappeared on the shore. "Ali," he called. "Ignore the lich—focus your anger on me. I'm the one you want to kill."

I was about to call Skalei to me, but stopped. Something had moved in the darkness beyond the nokk. Slowly, the gray body of a second nokk slid from a hole in the rock. Its tentacles twisted frantically, sensing the air. I guessed it was trying to determine where the clank from my dagger had come from.

"Oh, crap," I said under my breath. "Skalei."

The nokk gripping Marroc looked like it was about to crush him. I didn't have much time.

Holding Skalei, I estimated I was forty feet from the nokk. At this distance, the knife would rotate between two and three times. I was pretty sure I hadn't thrown it quite hard enough last time.

I reared back and hurled the blade. It spun through the darkness. With a *thunk*, it sank into Marroc's arm.

I grimaced.

Marroc didn't move, didn't so much as twitch. Whatever the nokk was doing to his mind, it was effective. But now, the second nokk was twisting toward the sound, tentacles twitching excitedly.

I gritted my teeth. "Skalei." The blade returned to my hand, wet with ichor.

I knew I had the velocity right—I just needed to improve my aim. This time, I visualized the blade sinking into the nokk's gelatinous body. I threw it again.

It spun end over end, and with a squelching smack, it sank into the nokk's flesh. The blade was a tiny speck against the trunk-like body, but I'd made a successful strike nonetheless.

I grinned, waiting for it to drop Marroc.

Instead, it only squeezed harder. My heart slammed against my ribs.

This was pointless. Skalei might be lethal in my hands against an elf, but against a massive nokk, it was like trying to kill an elephant with a toothpick. I needed a different approach—

Then the nokk screamed: a high, piercing sound that slid through my bones. Its tentacles spasmed, reaching frantically for Skalei to pull the knife free.

My lips twitched in a smile. The beast might be big, but its skin was sensitive.

No—wait. It wasn't Skalei that was upsetting it. A tentacle from the second nokk had wrapped around the base of the first nokk's body.

The nokk holding Marroc thrashed back and forth, slamming itself against the rocks as more tentacles latched on to it. Marroc swung in its grasp.

"Drop him, drop him," I whispered under my breath.

The second nokk lunged. Its snout split open like a pair of pliers, revealing rows of yellow teeth. With a slobbery crunch, it bit into the first nokk's side.

The first nokk screamed again, its tentacles lashing its attacker. Nokk screams and howls echoed in the dark cavern. Marroc swayed to and fro, then, finally, he slipped from the nokk's grasp and dropped into the lake with a splash. The nokks ignored him as they fought. The cavern filled with their primordial cries; gray nokk blood fell like rain.

I swam toward Marroc's body as fast as I dared. He was floating on his back when I reached him, his eyes closed. Still and beautiful.

"Marroc," I whispered. "Wake up."

But the lich didn't move. What had happened to him? He couldn't die if he was already dead. Whatever the nokk had done to him had left him completely unconscious.

Grabbing hold of his shirt, I pulled him away from the fighting nokk, though his weight made me groan. I scanned the darkness as I pulled him into deeper water. Something moved, and my stomach clenched. Above us, more nokks began to poke their heads from holes in the rock, their tentacles twitching in the direction of the two fighting each other.

I had to get Marroc out of here now. If we stayed here, I was certain we'd be eaten.

CHAPTER 37

MARROC

Whack.
A wet slap against my cheek.
Whack.
I groaned, trying to move my head out of the way.
Whack. Whack.
"Marroc, wake up." I recognized Ali's voice.
Whack.
I opened my eyes a sliver, just in time to see a delicate hand fly into view. Immediately followed by a painful smack against the side of my cheek.
"Mhhggghh," I half groaned, half growled.
I opened my eyes wider. I could see. It was no longer pitch dark. Pale light filtered through a gray mist.
Ali crouched beside me. She leaned close, her silver hair damp against my neck. She was clothed now, but the memory of her kiss still burned on my lips.
She raised her hand to hit me again, but this time, I caught her wrist.
Now this is an interesting kink. I was about to pull her to me, to feel her body against mine, but she glared at me and

tried to wrench her hand away. Why so shy now? She'd been trembling against me only moments ago.

"Marroc," she whispered sharply, "are you all right?"

Why was she asking me this? I was completely satiated, of course. And why was she suddenly so shy? She should be straddling me.

She interrupted my thoughts: "Marroc, we need to get moving. We can't stay here. I don't think it's safe."

I sat up, confused. Last I remembered, before I'd fallen asleep in Ali's arms, we'd been on our own private island. I'd taken her hard up against a boulder.

Yet it appeared Ali was right. We *were* sitting on a dirty bank. At my feet, brown water rushed over gray stones. The scent of death hung in the air. *What was going on?* I reached for my pen and notebook, but I found no sign of it. Just as well. The paper would be soaked.

"I don't know where your notebook is," said Ali. "I think it must have been lost in the river."

I wrote in the dirt with my finger. *How did you get your clothes back?*

Ali looked confused. "What? I never lost my clothes."

Then, as she stared at my dirty scribble, her mouth slowly fell open.

"Marroc," she finally said, speaking slowly, "after we went over the waterfall, we were swept into an underground cavern. A great subterranean lake. We were separated. I swam to an island. There was a nokk. It almost caught me, but I was able to slice off its tentacles."

I stared. A nokk? Ah... They were supposed to have extraordinary powers of illusion and mind control.

Ali continued, "But you were caught by the nokk."

I growled, and a pang of disappointment clenched my chest. No matter. I'd seduce her later.

"After the nokk released you, I had to drag you back into the current. You've been unconscious for hours."

She reached for me, then pulled my shirt open to reveal the rows of red welts that crisscrossed my chest. The marks of the nokk's suckers.

Ali crossed her arms. "You had a vision of me without clothes?"

I gave her a sly smile, then shrugged. *What illusion did you see?* I wrote.

Her expression went cold as ice. "It was the strangest thing. At first, I thought it was you, but then I saw Galin. Did you know him, Marroc? Before Ragnarok?" She looked fierce, sparks flashing in her steel-gray eyes. "The nokk tried to lure me onto the island to kill him."

Somehow, I managed to keep my face neutral, but I could feel the dark, heated magic pulsing off me.

"Did you know him?" A barely controlled fury laced her voice.

This time, I lied. I shook my head slowly. It felt wrong lying to her. Immoral, even. How long had it been since I'd cared about that?

Her eyes were still narrowed as she looked at me. "But you were a High Elf. You were alive before Ragnarok. Did you know who he was?"

This time, the truth. I nodded.

"And he didn't die in the chaos after Ragnarok, right? No one has seen him for a thousand years, but the Lords said he still breathed."

I went still as a marble statue, and she leaned closer. Her eyes blazed with ferocity.

"He's still alive, right?" she said. "Because if he isn't, then you dragged me here on a wild goose chase after a ring that serves no purpose."

I shrugged. I had, after all, been in prison a thousand

years. There was no reason for her to think I'd know what happened to Galin during that time.

She pulled out the golden ring to show it to me. "When we get out of here, I might need your help. I want to find him among the High Elves. You know more about them than I do, of course. Will you help me do that?"

I nodded again, wishing the nokk would attack us again and end this conversation.

"It didn't make sense that he'd be living on an island in the dark for the last thousand years." Her fingers curled as though she was thinking of calling her blade to her. "I've been waiting for you to wake up. Something seems off about this place."

With a dawning horror, it occurred to me that my mate had saved my unconscious body from a monster, and she'd been waiting over me as I slept. I felt I needed to reassert some sense of strength and masculinity.

Slowly, I stood and dusted off my clothes. My body was tired, low on energy. I needed to devour a soul if I wanted to replenish myself. That always made me feel better.

I'm going to investigate. Wait here.

Then, before Ali could protest or ask to come along, I brushed off the last of the dirt and climbed up the side of the riverbank. At the top, the ground was broken up by small tufts of gray grass. A thick fog had descended, and with it, the heavy stench of death.

In the misty distance, I saw a shadow move. I stiffened, motioning for Ali to stay before I began creeping forward. More shapes moved in front of me—the silhouettes of people. A smile crept over my lips. What I needed was a bit of feasting. To rip someone's neck out, to regain some energy.

I growled softly, a sound that usually lured a person to me.

I crept closer. The silhouettes of men and women moved along a raised platform, maybe two feet above the muddy plain. An ancient road. I sucked in a short breath as I realized why they hadn't noticed my growl.

Their skin was pale, eyes glazed. They trudged forward in a silent march, their gazes locked on the stones at their feet. Their bodies glimmered faintly with light.

I couldn't eat a single one of them.

They were dead, and I knew then exactly where we were. My disappointment at not getting to feed was soon replaced by joy.

I turned back to Ali, then crossed down to write in the dirt. *It's the road to Helheim.*

"You're certain?"

I nodded.

Ali's lip curled. "So that smell is… corpses?"

I nodded again. This road—Helvegen—would lead us straight to the Shore of the Dead. Leaning over, I wrote in the dirt, *Our journey is almost over.*

CHAPTER 38

ALI

Marroc and I had been walking for hours. My throat was parched, and my stomach grumbled. I tried to remember what I'd eaten today, but all I could recall was the apple in the Emperor's chambers. What I would do for a bite of it now. There was water in the marsh beside the road—dark pools hidden behind bunches of gray reeds—but I was afraid to drink from them.

All around us, the dead shuffled forward, eyes dull and mouths hanging open.

At first, they'd had me completely on edge. Though their bodies looked intact, they moved like the draugr. But I quickly learned they had no interest in the living. Or anyone else, for that matter. They all walked north, toward what I could only assume was Helheim itself. The only sound was the soft shuffling of feet over ancient cobblestones.

Marroc kept close to me, watchful and silent. Wisps of smoke drifted off his skin. He was the one beacon of beauty in this parade of the dead.

I wished I could listen to the little device he had given me, but it was waterlogged and wouldn't start. I'd tried humming a few bars of music, but it just didn't feel right walking amongst the corpses.

Eventually, Marroc touched my arm, and I turned to see that in front of us, the dead were slowing. The dark form of a building rose from the mist. Something else was different, too. A new sound joined the noise of shuffling feet. The roar of rushing water.

The dead slowed nearly to a halt as they began to discard their clothes and belongings, dropping them in piles and heaps on the road. Marroc crossed to a pile and rummaged around until he found an old book, then kept searching, presumably for a pencil. While he did that, I sifted through the shirts and jeans until I found a bag.

Resupplied, we pushed forward among the dead. Eventually, the mist parted, and I saw that the dark shape was a narrow bridge that spanned a roaring river. The bridge was only large enough for one person, but opulent, made of crystals and gold.

We weren't in Hel—not yet. Helheim was a walled realm. But we were getting close.

By the bridge's entrance stood a towering woman, at least ten feet tall. Dressed in iron armor, she balanced a long sword in front of her and stared out onto the road. Not dead, but not really seeing, either. I realized I knew her name. This was Modgud, the furious battler, the giantess who guarded the river Gjoll. Her glimmering blond hair draped over her armor.

As we approached the bridge, the dead funneled into a narrow path so that only one could cross at a time. Slowly, they shambled over the bridge, and we moved behind them.

When we got to the entrance, Marroc started to cross, and I wondered if the giantess would notice. But she didn't move a muscle. Her eyes remained straight ahead.

As soon as I took a step onto the bridge, however, her sword shattered stones at my feet.

"What brings the living to my bridge?" she growled, fixing me with black eyes. "Why do you wish to cross these waters?"

"I—" My mouth opened and closed. I couldn't explain to her that I wanted to steal Loki's wand, could I? I'd keep it simple. "I am traveling to the Nastrand—the Shore of the Dead."

The giantess didn't move, and her sword continued to block my path. "You must pay the toll. The dead don't need to pay. Only the living."

I opened my palms. "You want money? Because I don't have any."

"What would I do with money?" growled the giantess. "Your kind pay the toll in *blood*. Wet my blade and you may pass."

It took a moment for her intention to sink in. "You want me to cut myself on your sword?"

"Either you do it yourself or I'll do it for you." Her muscular forearm flexed, and the sword shifted toward me.

I looked at the blade, then at my hand and missing finger. Couldn't be as bad as that. "All right."

I gripped the sword, then slid my palm down fast, cutting into the skin—but not too deep. All the same, pain lanced up my arm. It hurt more than I'd expected.

"Is that enough?" I said, pointing to the smear of blood I'd left on the giantess's blade.

Modgud raised her sword and licked it clean with a pale tongue. My lip curled.

She didn't look at me as she spoke. "You have paid the toll. You may pass."

I stepped onto the bridge. It was constructed of clear crystal, and I could see straight through to the river. Water rushed between massive boulders. A feeling of vertigo washed over me, and I made my first mistake. I grabbed hold of the guard rails to steady myself, nearly falling anyway as searing pain blurred my vision. I'd pressed the wound on my hand directly onto the edge of sharp crystal.

Slowly, I moved forward, gripping my injured hand. Blood dripped from my palm onto the crystal bridge. When I reached the middle of the bridge, I paused. This was when I made my second mistake. I looked down.

Trapped between the stones were thousands of silver sticks. I paused, squinting. No, not sticks—swords. Thousands upon thousands of razor-sharp blades stuck out from between the rocks. A cold wind stung my cheeks.

As I looked down, the bridge started swaying precariously, like the thing wanted to throw me off just for being alive. I started forward again, trying to stay upright as I rushed toward the end of the bridge.

As I stepped onto the land, I gripped my injured hand, wincing.

Modgud's deep voice called out to me. "Living elf, you have crossed into the land of the dead. Your fate is sealed. Understand that you cannot leave by this path."

Marroc was already ripping off a piece of cloth from the bottom of his shirt. Now that it was ragged and torn, I could clearly see the rippling muscles of his abdomen underneath it.

"Is that true?" I asked Marroc with a growing sense of panic. "I'm trapped here now?"

He grunted, pulling me closer to him, binding the cut in my palm. While he was doing that, of course, he couldn't answer.

As soon as he'd bandaged it up tightly, I asked again. "Marroc. What does she mean? I can't leave here?"

He flipped open his book and scribbled something on the first blank page. *You cannot leave by this path.*

A bolt of anger shot through me. He *knew*? "Why didn't you tell me before I crossed?"

He gave a slow shrug, like he had not a care in the world. *Loki's wand will allow us to escape.*

But the wand was *bullshit*. Probably. "What if you're wrong about it being here? What if we don't find it? What if I'm not able to steal it?" Panic was rising in my chest. "My entire life depends on a legend. An unproven rumor that *you* believe."

We will not fail. I will not allow it.

"Oh, really? You won't allow it. Because you control everything." Rage was rising in me, and my fingers twitched. "Mom always told me what your kind was like. The High Elves. That you were self-serving, never to be trusted. You look out for your own kind, don't you? That's why you threw us in the caves. You all blamed us for Ragnarok. And now you're willing to risk my life for your own goals."

Marroc had gone very still, his dark hair caught in the wind.

"Guess Mom was right," I said.

CHAPTER 39

MARROC

On this side of the river, the mist thinned. An icy breeze stirred the air, revealing muddy plains on either side of the road.

Ali walked in front of me, her back stiff, eyes fixed straight ahead. Blood from her palm soaked the strip of my shirt I'd given her. I wished I'd been able to clean it.

Without the power of speech, it was hard to explain my certainty to her. I knew the wand was here, because I could feel it. It was like the thing had been calling to me. And here, in the world of the dead, it was growing stronger, its power like a gleaming beacon drawing me ever closer.

Soon, I'd have my soul back. I'd be alive again, for the first time since Ragnarok. Since floods had drowned the world, since disease had spread and the gods had slaughtered each other. The deaths of the gods had been Fate... Wyrd.

And now, Fate was telling me to get the wand.

I'd bet my life on it. But I didn't suppose Ali would be swayed by a feeling.

Seemed I should have told her in advance the entire story, but I'd forgotten how to deal with people long ago. The thousand years in prison had robbed me of all ability to work with other elves. The lack of a soul didn't help, either.

Once it was returned to my body, I'd remember.

As we followed the road, figures started to move father out in the plains, slipping in and out of the fog. The longer we walked, the more numerous they became. Soon, I heard the clash of steel and the clink of armor rising around us.

With the pounding of hooves, a warhorse charged out of the mist. The rider waved a banner, his mouth open in a silent scream, and a legion of the gleaming dead raced behind him. The hooves were the only sound the entire horde made, and as they rushed around us, I pulled Ali in close.

With glimmering dust clouding around us, the soldiers split into two factions, one on either side of the road. Ali pulled away from me, still looking furious.

We walked slowly, now, as a great battle raged on either side of the road. Dead men fought in complete silence, even as they stabbed each other with spears. Dead warriors lopped limbs with swords and bashed in skulls with battleaxes. The mud ran thick with their blood, but they rose again and pieced their bodies back together like grisly jigsaw puzzles.

But they wouldn't bother us.

Ali was as silent as the dead warriors, and I knew she was seething like the mists around us.

When we'd finally moved past the silent battle, the fog thinned a little, and I could see a dark line rising from the fog, stretching out on either side. As we approached, it grew larger and larger until it was as taller than the highest skyscrapers in Boston. Taller even than the Citadel on Beacon Hill.

Before us loomed a massive iron wall extending in either direction as far as the eye could see. Great streaks of rust stained the wall, like giant smears of blood. Lines of dead shuffled toward it.

This was the wall surrounding Helheim itself. Not a defensive structure, but one meant to keep the souls of the dead trapped inside.

We followed the road north until a pair of towers came into view, jutting from the wall, flanking an entrance. Almost all the dead streamed into it, but a few turned to the right or left, ambling along.

The gate to Helheim.

When we were a hundred and fifty yards away, I stopped and pulled out my book—which I now realized was an old romance set in a time of pandemic, called *Quarantined with a Bad Boy*. I grimaced at the cover, then flipped it open to a mostly blank page.

I wrote, *Let me go in to explore. I'm already dead, and it's better that I go on my own. You're mortal. I can't die.*

She nodded, still barely meeting my gaze.

I turned to see a shambling legion of the dead moving toward the gates. I blended into the crowd, walking among them until I was maybe a hundred yards from the entrance. I tried to look inside, but it was filled with a shimmering mist. From the other side of the gate, I could hear disquieting noises—howls, shrieks, and a low, unending ululation.

From the stories and legends, I knew that visitors to Helheim didn't pass through the entrance with the rest of the dead, but I didn't know why. I guessed that since my body was already dead, I was unlikely to be affected by any magic that might be in play here. Still, I had to be careful. I crept up closer.

I watched as a dead man with a white beard approached the gate, his body gleaming. He trundled forward, one foot in front of the other—but when he reached the swirling mist, he stopped, and his body seemed to freeze in place. With a gust of wind, his skin crumbled into dust. In the flickering instant as his body disintegrated, I saw a shadow pass into the opalescent mist.

This was why the other travelers in the stories had found alternate entrances. The main gate stripped a man's body from his soul.

And since I had no soul, I'd become nothing but dust.

With rising frustration, I turned back to Ali.

CHAPTER 40

ALI

Marroc and I walked along the base of the soaring iron wall, close enough that I could reach out and touch it. My feet sank into the mud, and it pulled at my shoes, squelching with every step. At least we'd moved away from the unseeing eyes of the dead.

Water dripped down the wall in rivulets, streaking it with rust. The wall wasn't entirely smooth. Strange bumps—rivets, maybe—marred its surface. I guessed it was attached to some sort of structure on the other side, but it was impossible to tell. And what I couldn't understand was how, if it kept the dead in, we were going to be able to breach it.

Curious, I reached out to touch the wall, but Marroc pulled my hand away.

Probably for the best. I had no idea what sort of magic was at play in this place.

I stared up at it as we walked, dread rising in my chest. Was Mom in there? And Dad? My mouth went dry, and I swallowed hard. I didn't want to think of them dead. I didn't like thinking of Mom sick, wasting away in her bed. I wanted to remember her like she was when she was healthy, braiding my hair and telling me how Ragnarok had unfolded all those years ago—it had started with a flood all over the world, and the disease set in. Then the battles between the gods and the giants that had left nearly all of them dead. Mom called it *Twilight of the Gods.*

She'd told me stories of the world of Midgard even before that, before humans thought it could end, when everything was light. When they'd danced to music in nightclubs. The way Mom spun a tale always lit my mind on fire. She was a fleck of light in a world of darkness.

And if I could see her again…

Marroc turned to face me. Pale smoke drifted off his skin, though it was hard to tell where the smoke ended and the mist began. He was writing in the romance book, which, quite frankly, I wanted to read later.

He showed me his note. *I think the best thing will be for me to climb over and then for you to join me.*

I pointed at the wall. "I can climb, too. There are divots between the sheets of iron where I could fit my fingers." Even with my injured hand, climbing it would be a breeze.

He nodded. *Going up will be easy. The going down will be more difficult. We don't know what's on the other side, and it's easy to slip when climbing down. If I fall, I won't die.*

I arched an eyebrow. I'd spent years scaling slick black rockface in the underground Shadow Caverns, but whatever. I was too tired to argue.

We kept moving until we reached a long seam between two sheets of iron. It looked like it ran all the way to the top.

I'll need your crystal, wrote Marroc.

It took me a moment to realize that he was referring to my vergr crystal.

The crystal.

For a few terrifying seconds, I thought I might have lost it in the river, but then I found it deep in one of my pockets. "Why do you need it?"

Marroc wrote, *I'll climb the wall. When I reach the other side, I'll bang on it three times with all my strength. Then you travel to the crystal, and we continue.*

It wasn't the *worst* idea.

I handed him the crystal. "Don't break it. And don't keep it in your pants or something when you call me, because I'll come bursting out of them. It would be awkward for us both."

With a ghost of a smile, he slid the crystal into his pocket. Then he started to climb, latching his fingers into the crack between the sheets of iron.

I watched him climb until he was a tiny black speck high up on the wall.

Most magical creatures were repelled by iron, but elves were like humans. We had iron in our blood. Still, that was probably why it was built of iron. Maybe it repelled the spirits. Helped keep them in.

Marroc had disappeared into the mist high above. I glanced across the field toward the road leading up to the gate, where the dead kept shuffling, an endless procession.

Mist roiled over the mud, and I shivered. My stomach rumbled, and I closed my eyes, envisioning the roast chicken I'd refused to eat before. What the Helheim had I been thinking?

Surely Marroc would be at the bottom by now? I listened for any sounds of knocking, but when I moved closer to the wall, all I could hear was the faint gurgle of water trickling down the side of the wall. Strangely relaxing. I plopped down on the ground and rested my face in my hands.

In the distance, through my fingers, the dead moved slowly, inching forward like ants through molasses. The mist shifted, but I still heard no knocks from Marroc.

I didn't know if it was the hypnotic effect of the mist or simply extreme exhaustion and hunger that caused me to close my eyes. I drifted off, dreaming of Mom and Dad and Barthol, their faces shining over the birthday cake they'd made for me. Ten candles gleaming like stars. A tradition left over from the humans. Barthol and Mom looked so much alike—same pointed chins and delicate features. Same cupid's-bow lips.

In my dream, Mom leaned over my cake, and the candles warmed her features.

"Avenge me, Ali," she whispered.

CHAPTER 41

MARROC

I straddled the wall as I got my first look into Helheim itself. Unfortunately, there wasn't much to see.

Like the gateway, the surface of Helheim was entirely obscured by fog. Sooty clouds pressed low to the ground and roiled in unnatural twists and swirls. Behind me, a plain of brown mud and mist stretched out as far as I could see. Only the dark curve of the road, like the back of a giant serpent, interrupted it.

I looked straight down the wall. My eyes followed the crack, but I couldn't see Ali from here. I didn't like the idea of her alone so near the road of dead. I wanted her close to me.

Best get this over with fast, then. I rolled my shoulders.

Time to get moving. I turned and jammed my hand into the crack on the Helheim side of the wall. Then, drawing in a deep breath, I began to descend. The crack cut clear through the wall, so climbing down was only a matter of locking and unlocking my fingers. As I slowly lowered myself, mist began to surround me.

With a creeping sense of dread, I quickly realized it was

more than mist. Much thicker and darker, it wrapped around me like a funeral shroud. In moments, I could barely see my hands where they touched the wall.

Though I'd seen the stygian fog moving from my perch on the top of the wall, now that I was within it, the air felt oppressively still, like a creature holding its breath.

I continued climbing downward, one hand at a time. Everything was going smoothly until the crack stopped. I paused, confused. I couldn't see a thing; the crack had just disappeared.

Hanging by one hand, I pulled myself close to the wall.

A low growl rose in my throat. The crack was there, but it had been welded shut. I drew one of my daggers and scratched at it, but it wasn't doing much good.

How high was I in the air?

Maybe I could just drop and deal with the pain of bones shattering. I'd recover. Eventually.

As I was steeling my resolve to let go, the fog grew even thicker, until it had a wet texture over my skin. The temperature dropped.

Worse, my skin prickled with the sensation that I was being watched. Suddenly, a dark shadow passed above me, and I realized something was in the fog with me.

I growled softly, more a warning than a threat as I craned my head around, trying to see what it was. But the shadow had disappeared. The chill deepened.

What the Helheim was it?

Suddenly, something ice cold wrenched my hand from the wall, and dread clamped a hand around my heart. In the next moment, I was falling.

I hit the ground with a smack. Mud sprayed around me, thick and black as tar. Pain shot through my limbs, but there was no cracking of bone. I wasn't seriously injured.

I lay on my back for a moment, then crawled to my feet, holding my daggers in front of me.

I could see nothing beyond the ends of my blades in the fog. Silent as a grave, here.

Frowning, I tried to brush some of the mud off myself.

As the temperature dropped even further, a chill washed over me. Condensation on my skin froze. Ice formed on the tips of my daggers. A shape flickered in the periphery of my vision, and I spun, trying to see what it was. In the swirling fog, it was gone.

And there was that sense of eyes on me.

Then the fog began to thin around me, revealing a shadowy figure hovering at the edge of the fog, tall and thin like a scarecrow. It stayed just out of sight.

I knew what it was now—a shade—a soul of one in Helheim. They weren't necessarily good or evil, but they always told the truth.

I raised my blade as more shades appeared around me. One stepped forward, out of the swirling vapor. It was completely black, but its outline continually shifted as though stirred by an invisible hand. I couldn't quite focus my eyes on it.

"It is sacrilege for an earthly body to cross into our lands," said the shade. Its voice sounded muffled, as though it was shouting from a great distance.

I began to write in my book, to explain that I was on my way to the Shore of the Dead, but the shade glided closer. Close up, I could see its pale white eyes gleaming at me.

I tried to lift my book but couldn't. My arm was frozen. A growl rose in my chest. It cut short as the air in my lungs filled with ice.

"Do not challenge me," it whispered. "The dead rule this realm. You're in our domain."

CHAPTER 42

ALI

When I woke, I felt a pang in my chest. That happened sometimes, like I'd lost Mom all over again every time I woke up.

Rubbing sleep from my eyes, I saw that the slow procession of dead continued to inch forward. Shit. I hadn't slept through the banging, had I? I had no idea how much time had passed. There was no sun here, just an unwavering gray light sifting through the mist.

I stood slowly, my limbs stiff and cold. I shook my hands and rolled my shoulders. Turning to the wall, I traced my fingers along its cold, pitted surface.

What had happened to Marroc?

I started pacing, the worry now making me alert. Should I go to him now? If I opened my mouth to say *Fara* and jumped to the crystal, I had no way of knowing where it was. I could end up reappearing in the stomach of a giant beast, in the midst of a battle, or trapped in a prison.

Luckily, I had another option. I could climb this wall. I peeked under the makeshift bandage, checking the wound on my hand. Already, it had scabbed over.

I started to pull myself up and stopped. A new idea occurred to me: what if I could talk to Marroc? Raising my knuckles, I rapped on the wall as hard as I could.

Thunk, thunk, thunk.

I didn't know if the sound traveled through the metal. It was so thick, so ancient. I had the sense it was reverberating, but I still waited to hear if there was an answering series of taps. Only silence greeted me.

Okay, then. Climbing was my only option, unless I wanted to starve to death and enter Helheim that way.

I latched my fingers into the gap and leaned back so that my weight held my grip in place. Then, slowly, I began to climb, one hand over another. Just like I'd done in the Shadow Caverns. Locking my fingers, moving my feet. Unlocking the fingers of one hand, reaching higher up, locking my fingers again. Slow going, but I was moving steadily up.

After about twenty feet, the crack widened, and I could wedge my feet inside, climbing more easily. It felt good to move again, to be in control.

I just had no fucking idea what I'd find on the other side.

CHAPTER 43

MARROC

I didn't know how long I'd been walking. The fog hung close, and the landscape had no features except mud. All around me, the dark forms of the shades glided through the fog, silently watching me.

Right now, the shades controlled my body, forcing my feet to move one in front of the other in a perpetual march. I couldn't raise my arms, turn my head, or even lift a finger. Ice filled my veins. It was so frustrating to be around creatures I couldn't kill. What did I have to threaten them with?

The only thing I could control was my mind, but that was its own torture, because it was screaming with questions: what had happened to Ali? Was she still waiting for me to knock on the wall? Would she still jump to the vergr crystal?

If she tried to climb it, it would be a disaster. But I had to count on the fact that she'd figure it out and wait till she heard my signal. I'd find a way to get out of this.

I could feel the stone's weight in my pocket. If Ali appeared next to me, the shades would surround her in an instant. She wasn't dead, so maybe they wouldn't be able to control her as well. But still, the presence of a living person here would enrage them.

Beneath my feet, the mud grew drier until it turned into soft soil. The fog thinned. Around me, the shades floated, their dark forms tracking me like a murder of crows.

Slowly, the ground began to rise, and the soil hardened into a path. Now, from out of the corners of my eyes, I saw something unexpected—I appeared to be walking on a floating island above a sea of fog. Mist rolled all around the island like the waters of a river.

Ahead of me, the path joined an old cobblestone road, the stones coated in a thin layer of grime. No one had walked on them in a while.

Before me rose an escarpment, a black cliff nearly as tall as the wall I'd climbed. The road led straight toward it, but it was only when we were a few hundred yards away that I glimpsed the yawning crack in the cliff face. With the shades surrounding me, I passed once again into darkness.

As I entered the crevasse, the jagged rock quickly gave way to stone walls, constructed of boulders and carved into interlocking shapes like pieces of a jigsaw puzzle. The smallest boulders were twice as tall as a man. Every few yards, small alcoves had been carved into the stone. Within them flickered faint blue flames. Some sort of death magic, I guessed.

The shades floated along next to me, silent as ever. The only sound was the quiet footsteps of my feet on the stone. We walked along this stone pathway until it expanded into a massive hall.

I found the dimly lit hall empty. As the shades led me forward, my footsteps echoed in the vast space, and a faint whispering fluttered around me, growing louder and louder the deeper we moved. Through the corners of my eyes, I searched for some way out of this, some key to breaking the spell over me.

At last, we reached the end of the hall. It was empty but for a massive throne. Completely black, it appeared to be constructed entirely of obsidian. A giant form slumped over in it, and a shadow crept over my heart.

I knew who this creature was—or had been. One half of her body was a deep indigo, the other the color of weathered bone. Her hair hung limp over sunken cheeks. She wore a long gray robe covered in a thin layer of dust, and her eyes were closed. A gnawing terror filled my chest as I looked at her, like I was trespassing on something I was never meant to see.

Before me was the corpse of the goddess Hela herself. This was the mummified body of the queen of Helheim, Loki's daughter. There was no question the goddess was dead, so I had no idea why they'd led me to her.

Under the control of the shades, I walked up to the throne. Slowly, they forced me to kneel.

A shade swept before me. "Why have you trespassed within our realm?"

I shook my head, pointing to my throat. He'd be waiting for an answer for a long time, since I couldn't speak.

The shade's eyes flickered. Suddenly, its inky arm thrust out and down my throat. My vision flashed white with pain. Then the shade's fingers retracted, and it spoke again.

"Answer," said the shade. "Now, you can speak. Tell us the truth. Why do you trespass on our lands?"

CHAPTER 44

ALI

I straddled the top of the wall, gazing at the vast expanse of Helheim. Beneath me, soot-colored clouds hid the ground. I hesitated as cold fear crawled up my spine. Whatever was down there, it didn't want to be seen.

I desperately wished I could wait a little longer, but I knew that wasn't an option. I hadn't eaten a meal in days, and I was becoming dangerously dehydrated. I had to go down there, had to find Marroc. He was my ride home, my way back to Midgard.

Assuming we found Loki's freaking magic wand.

Whatever it took, I had to find my way back to my people, with the golden ring in my hand.

I looked once again toward the road of the dead. Then I took a deep breath and jammed my fingers into the crack between the iron plates. Slowly, I began to descend, hand over hand.

As I inched my way down the wall, my shoulders and forearms throbbed with exertion. Slowly, I passed into the dirty clouds. A thick fog surrounded me, cold and oppressive. The iron became slick with condensation. Then the temperature dropped sharply.

Something brushed past me. A dark shape that seemed to fill my veins with ice. Frost spread across the iron like icy spider webs. Unease rose in my chest, and I clutched the wall tight. Whatever that was, it was bad.

I looked down, hoping to see the ground beneath me, but I saw only mist and fog. Fighting my instinct to cling to the wall, I unlatched one of my hands.

I was reaching down when a shadow appeared above my head. I looked up in time to see an inky hand reach for mine. The instant its fingers touched me, my hand spasmed. I lost my grip and fell.

I tumbled, spinning. Sooty fog rushed past me, and panic snapped through my nerves.

My mind raced. *This* had been a bad idea. If I didn't do something fast, I was going to die.

There was only one thing I could do.

"Fara!" I yelled.

I disappeared in a purple flash of light. An instant later I reappeared, flat on my back, bits of cloth in my hair, skidding fast across a stone floor.

Smack! I slammed into something solid. My vision flashed, and the air rushed from my lungs.

When I opened them, a dark shape hovered over me—gray shadows and beaming white eyes.

"One of the living trespasses in our realm." His hollow voice rang in my mind.

I groaned, pushing myself off the floor. I was in a large hall, though shadows covered most of it. It felt almost like one of the Shadow Caverns where I'd grown up, but those caves had signs of life. This felt like a mausoleum.

Above me, silhouettes hung in the air as though suspended from invisible threads. I stiffened. They looked like the creature that had pried me off the wall. It took me a moment to recognize them for what they were—shades.

When I looked beyond them, my mouth went dry and my legs trembled. The corpse of a giant woman rested in a black throne, and Marroc knelt before her, ignoring me. She was the goddess Hela, I thought—one of the gods who'd died in Ragnarok. It felt *wrong* to see her resting place, her body slumped in gray robes.

Was this what Marroc was really after? Did liches worship the goddess of the dead?

Marroc must have sensed my presence, because slowly, he turned to look at me. His pants were torn, but he didn't seem to notice. Instead, his eyes locked on mine.

Slowly his lips parted, and he spoke. "Ali, are you all right?" His deep voice shivered over my skin.

CHAPTER 45

MARROC

Ali stared at me, open-mouthed.

"Marroc." Confusion furrowed her brow. "You can talk?"

I nodded.

She frowned. "Then why are you nodding?"

"I'm out of practice." My voice sounded the same as it always had, though I was out of the habit of speaking. "It's been nearly a thousand years since I last said a word."

As I talked, the leader of the shades glided between us. His pale eyes glowed in the dim light. "Tell us why you are here," he whispered.

Considering they had the power to control me, I had to give them a reason. I just wouldn't give them the *whole* reason.

I flashed an easy smile. "We are on our way to the Nastrand. The Shore of the Dead. We have business with the dragon Nidhogg. The pale wyrm." I shrugged. "Just an ordinary Saturday."

The shade's eyes flickered. "What sort of business? This realm is for the dead alone, not the living."

I relaxed my shoulders. I wouldn't show any unease. "I am dead, as you can see."

"Your kind is an abomination," growled the shade. "Cheating death with black magic."

"What business is it of yours what I've done with my soul?" I asked. "That happened in Midgard. It's none of your concern."

The shade swept around me. "We have desires that extend beyond the walls that imprison us." He turned from me, eyes fixed on Ali. "Night Elf, tell us why *you're* here."

Ali stood still as a statue. I couldn't tell if she was afraid, or angry, or whether the shade had managed to fix her body in that position.

"I am here as Marroc's—the lich's—companion."

Good. Ali wasn't a puppet, and she knew better than to tell them too much.

"What have you to gain from such a vile union?" said the shade.

"The lich is helping me find Galin." She held up her hand with the missing finger. "He has already helped me locate the sorcerer's ring."

Fear coursed through me like a sharpened blade, and the air seemed too thin. The shade's pale eyes didn't move.

"Galin is dead," whispered the shade. "The lich is lying. Galin was—"

Panic crept up my throat. I had to stop this before they ruined everything.

"We are here to retrieve Loki's wand," I cut in.

But Ali was more focused on the shade. "Wait. What did you say about Galin?"

The shade had spun to face me, its eyes shining like stars. "You have come to steal the Levateinn?"

Good. That got his attention. I kept a pleasant expression on my face. "Yes."

"Why?"

I arched an eyebrow. "To return my soul to my body, of course. And to bring myself back from the dead."

I could tell by the tensing of Ali's muscles that she was about to lose it. That she wanted to call Skalei and start stabbing. "Are you saying Galin is here in Hel?" she asked.

"Quiet, mortal," said the shade.

All around us, the shades had gone completely still. They hung in the air limply, like black rags on a clothesline. Only their pale eyes moved, fixed on me, and they listened to every word. The lead shade turned back to me. "You can raise the dead?"

"Loki's wand can transmute any form. It can change a fish to bird, a man to a woman, the old to the young. Of course, it can also transform the dead into the living."

The shade looked to the throne, to Hela's mummified form, and my heart sank as I realized my mistake. "What about a goddess?"

I felt the shade once again send ice into my veins, and my body went rigid.

He whooshed closer to me, eyes gleaming. "The entrance to the Shore of the Dead is within our realm. We will not allow you to travel to its bloody sands, to parley with the pale wyrm, if you don't agree to our demands."

"Hela is dead," I stammered. "All the gods are dead. Ragnarok cannot be undone."

"Everything can change. You just told us the wand can transmute any form," said the shade. "Listen... do you hear her? Even in death, our queen calls to us. She asks to be woken, to once again rule over her domain. We are but her servants."

"Your queen is dead. You are masters of your own destinies now."

"False," growled the shade. "We are prisoners in iron

walls, forced to dwell in muck and darkness. Hela says she will free us. Our queen has not forsaken us, even in death."

But this wasn't possible. What they asked would destroy us all. "But that is not meant to be, I'm afraid. Ragnarok is known as the Twilight of the Gods. To raise one again would be a crime against Wyrd. Endless destruction would follow."

"You *will* help us." The shade moved close to me, and the chill of death surrounded me. "I saw how you looked at the Night Elf. If you do not raise our queen from her throne, your woman will remain within our walls forever. She will be ours to torment."

Volcanic wrath poured through me, but I kept my mask of calm—the diplomatic expression of a prince—even as something like panic was rising in my mind. "May I remind you that you have no claim to the living. She has made you no sacrifice—"

I stopped right there as I realized what Modgud had required with her sword.

The shade's eyes flickered. "Modgud gathered the mortal's blood with the steel of her blade. She made a sacrifice to enter here."

Ali looked like she wanted to murder everyone here, but she couldn't.

"Skalei." The blade was in her hand.

The shade spun, pale eyes blazing. "Do not challenge us," it whispered savagely.

Fast as a viper, he lunged at Ali and pressed an inky palm to her chest. She fell to the floor immediately, her eyes rolling up into her skull. Her body began to twitch.

The shade was killing her. Shock ripped my mind apart.

"Stop!" I shouted. I wanted to threaten them—like I had with the guards for the last thousand years. *I'll drain your blood. I'll rip out your throat.*

None of that would work here.

The shade released Ali, turning again to me. "Have you changed your mind?"

I felt like someone had ripped out my lungs. There was no way I could actually help bring back the goddess of the dead, not when it would corrupt Wyrd and destroy the world. But there was *absolutely* no way I was going to let Ali die, to let the shades claim her soul. Right now, her chest was still rising and falling. I prayed she'd only have a terrible headache when she woke, that she'd still recover easily.

"Yes," I said finally, "I will help you revive your goddess. On one condition."

The shade's eyes narrowed. "What is that?"

I pointed at Ali. "I'll need her blood. Release her from your bondage."

"No," said the shade. "If we release her, what will prevent you from simply reneging on your offer?"

He might be dead, but he wasn't stupid.

My mind raced as I frantically tried to piece together how to fix this. I wished I'd never brought her here. "I will take her place in Hel."

"You are already dead."

I pointed to Ali's unconscious form. "She is only a Night Elf, while I am so much more than that. Once I have Levateinn in my possession, I'll become a mortal god. I will be able to raise Hela and bring down the walls that surround your kingdom."

Lies, of course.

I was worried I was laying it on a little thick, but all the shades watched intently, their eyes glowing with excitement. *This* was what they wanted, and their desire clouded their judgment.

I raised my palm to my mouth, biting into the skin so it

broke. Then I squeezed it hard, and hot, steaming ichor dripped on the floor. "There is my oblation. When I succeed in securing Loki's wand, my bondage will be complete. My soul will be yours until Hela is raised. Is that good enough?"

All the shades spoke in unison. "Yes."

CHAPTER 46

ALI

I opened my eyes, and my head throbbed.

Marroc crouched over me, his blue eyes flickering. He looked worried. "Are you okay?"

I sat up, rubbing my temples. But the problem wasn't my body. The problem was that I'd failed.

I felt like my ribs were hollowed out with sadness. So much for the *North Star* nonsense. All this time, I had thought that what I needed to do was kill Galin. That if the sorcerer was dead, the Night Elves would go free. Turned out, he was already dead, and my people were still stuck in the disease-ridden caves. Why had Marroc seemed so certain I needed to come here and get the ring? And why had the Shadow Lords sent me after it, for that matter?

The shades always told the truth, and they'd told me my mission had been a complete waste. That I'd failed.

The disappointment pierced me. "They said Galin is dead. That means there was no point to any of this. The whole purpose of getting the ring was so I could find him and kill him. I didn't know how the ring would lead to him, but it seems it would never work anyway."

The shades hovered around us, quiet but watching intently. It almost seemed as though they enjoyed my suffering, which made me even angrier. Marroc leaned close and whispered in my ear. "I can bring him back to life, and he can tell you how to lift the curse himself."

A chill rippled over my skin. "Are you sure?"

"Yes. Once we steal Loki's wand, I will be able to raise the dead—Galin included. And you will get what your heart has always desired, Ali."

Now that he could speak, I could hear the sensual timbre of his voice, and the little hint of sharp steel underneath it. His physical beauty was distracting enough. But his voice? That was a whole new matter altogether.

"You always seem very certain of yourself," I said. "Too certain."

"I have had hundreds of years to think this over before I even met you," he murmured. "The wand can raise the dead. Is that not the purpose of this mission? Raising the dead? Me included."

I turned to the shades. "Is that true? Can he raise Galin?"

"The lich speaks truth," said the shade softly. "If you help him, Galin can be raised. We can all get what we want."

So, he was speaking the truth.

But I knew there was a *lot* he wasn't telling me. Even if he now had the power of speech.

* * *

THE SHADES KEPT CLOSE to us all the way from Hela's tomb, leading us through mud and darkness, across fields of black muck shrouded in mist, until finally they stopped at a massive sinkhole.

It reminded me a bit of a children's toy—the one with the plastic funnel and marbles that circle until they fall through the hole in the bottom. Only here, the marbles had been replaced by black sludge, and the hole at the bottom smelled of death.

A sinkhole we had to enter.

"The entrance to the Nastrand," the lead shade whispered.

The specter immediately started downward, gliding over the path. We moved more slowly. The sides of the sinkhole were so slick and so steep that one slip would send us sliding all the way to the bottom.

We trod carefully, avoiding the heaviest streams of muck and keeping one hand on the slope above us at all times so we didn't slip. When we reached the bottom, I stopped at the edge of the opening, but Marroc simply jumped in.

I peered over the edge into the darkness, and he called up to me. "You can toss me the crystal if you want," he said, voice echoing. I still wasn't used to the sound of him—a masculine voice, but one smooth as cream.

I chose to climb down the side instead.

When I reached the bottom, the shades led us into a labyrinthine sewer system full of dark side passages. Even I couldn't see in here.

At last, we reached a set of thick iron doors that completely blocked the tunnel. Streaked with rust, they seemed to have been made by the same hand as the wall that encircled Helheim itself. It was hard to tell if they were designed to keep something in or out.

It was quiet except for the sound of dripping water. Marroc stood next to me, and the shades hovered around him.

"The Nastrand is on the other side," said the lead shade. "This is where we leave you."

As the shades slid back into the darkness, Marroc put his shoulder against the door. With a rusty groan, it creaked open.

CHAPTER 47

MARROC

I pushed open the doors to the Nastrand. Though few had ever visited the place, I knew from the stories what to expect. The Corpse Shore was a series of beaches that bordered an ocean of blood. It was where the worst of the dead were sent to suffer. And, most importantly, it was where the serpent Nidhogg swam.

So, I'd expected darkness and screams of agony, but instead, we were met by sunlight and a gentle breeze. Great dunes spread out until they reached a sparkling sea. The sun shone in a scarlet sky.

When I glanced at Ali, I saw the sun gleaming in her eyes. I'd been lying to her, again. But everything I did, I did for a reason.

My magic had told me that Wyrd decreed this path—that I must find the great wyrm, and I would get my soul back. And I had complete faith in fate to set me on the right course. It might seem insane, but fate had brought us to this terrible place. And spells for divining the true course of fate had never been wrong before.

"You see?" I pointed to the beach, and Ali's silver gaze

followed. "Nastrand, the Shore of the Dead. Where murderers, adulterers, and oath-breakers go after they die. Don't say I never took you anywhere nice."

She arched an eyebrow at me, seemingly surprised that I'd made a joke. Actually, it had surprised me, too. It wasn't like I'd joked with anyone in the past thousand years. I'd just eaten them.

I stepped onto a path of white cobblestones, into the new realm. On either side rose enormous piles of red sand.

I'd only gone a few steps when I heard Ali say, "Oh." She stood stock-still staring at the white cobblestones.

"What's wrong?"

"We're walking on—skulls."

I looked down. Sure enough, what had appeared to be white stone was actually bleached bone. "Ah. Now, look at that. And here I was, hoping we'd find a romantic setting by the Corpse Shore."

She met my gaze. "Right. Nothing sexier than the bones of the dead."

Was that a dig at me? Unnecessary. "I can tell you're annoyed. Just because I dragged you into Helheim and it turned out you might be trapped here forever."

"You convinced me to join you on a pointless mission to kill a dead man. Maybe you can raise him from the dead, but I'm not sure I trust your judgment at this point."

"You got the ring you needed, didn't you?"

Except she didn't need it—not at all. Perhaps I should stop lying to her. When I got my soul back, I might feel bad about things, though I wasn't entirely sure.

I could remember facts from my past. I could remember people and events. But my own life? That was as illusory as smoke. I had glimpses of memories, but no idea what kind of person I'd been. Any real facts I knew about my life before this had been told to me by the guards.

Only when I was close to Ali could I get glimpses of the past—the flashes of ravens I'd kept. But soon enough, I'd know it all.

I walked slowly along the bone-cobbled path as it wound between the dunes in the direction of the shore. A thin wind blew the sand off the tops of the dunes. Otherwise, it was deathly quiet. Between the dunes, I could see the winding and undulating roots of Yggdrasill. The cosmic tree drank its nourishment from the water in which Nidhogg swam.

Ali walked by my side, and we stopped when we reached the last dune. On the beach below us, a cluster of people swarmed. Instinctively, I crouched. *Draugr.*

"Get down," I whispered sharply.

Ali knelt to me, hair shining like quicksilver. "Marroc?" Her gaze was behind me, body tense.

I spun, but it was too late. A second group of draugr had crept up behind us—gray skin and empty eyes. In front stood a large man with lank white hair.

"Don't move—" I started.

The white-haired draugr raised a bony hand. "Do not," said draugr slowly, "attack."

They'd surrounded us now. I was on my feet, daggers out, steel flashing in the crimson sunlight.

"Tell us why you are here," said the white-haired corpse, "and we will not hurt you."

I hesitated. I'd never heard a draugr speak before. Usually, their consciousness was the first thing to go.

"Why should we trust you? The dead feast on the living."

"We are not hungry." The corpse raised his hand higher to point at the blood-red sea. "We have plenty to drink."

"What are you doing here?" asked Ali.

"We are all murderers," said the lank-haired corpse.

Next to him, a corpse dressed in rusty armor spoke. "I slew a man with a sword."

Another dressed in a thick gray sweater and hiking boots added eagerly, "I killed my family with a hatchet."

"I killed a man with my bare hands!" shouted a very large corpse dressed in a wrestling singlet and a bright blue luchador mask.

A small draugr jumped forward. She wore a bloodstained chef's apron and was grinning excitedly. "I gutted my husband with a breadknife. Then I plucked out his eyes and ate them."

The corpses turned to stare at her, mouths hanging open.

"You ate his eyeballs?" said the white-haired corpse. His face had twisted into a look of disgust. "While he was still alive?"

The little corpse glared. "The sound of his chewing bothered me. Especially when he ate chicken wings."

They all nodded, satisfied with this reasonable answer.

The lank-haired draugr edged closer. "Why are you here?"

Perhaps they could help. "We are here to find Nidhogg. Where do we find her?"

A low murmur rose among the draugr. "They come for the pale serpent!" shouted the white-haired corpse. "Our great foe, the night ravager, the bone breaker, the curse striker. We *hate* the wyrm."

A bit dramatic.

The lank-haired corpse suddenly leaned forward. "Are you a friend of the wyrm?"

"No."

"Then why do you want to see her?"

I sighed. "She has something I want. That's all."

"They wish to hurt the wyrm. I'm sure of it." The white-haired draugr clapped excitedly. "We loathe her. We will help you. Follow us; we will take you to her."

The draugr closed in behind Ali and me, and they

motioned for us to walk toward the sea of blood. I kept close to Ali as they mumbled in their broken voices.

We walked along the shore. Apart from a dry breeze blowing in from the water, it was eerily quiet. The usual sounds of the sea were absent—no gulls called; no buoy bells tolled. Even the waves lapped soundlessly on the shore. Junk littered the sand: rusted cars, electronics parts, even bags of old potato chips.

Ali pointed at the water. "What happened to those corpses?"

I followed her finger and saw the pale, glowing bodies of the dead bobbing in the sea.

"They are fed to the wyrm," said the white-haired draugr matter-of-factly. "The wyrm demands sacrifice."

"Right," said Ali. "Of course."

The white-haired draugr's expression became deadly serious, "Only the oath-breakers. The vilest among us. They count as nothing. The wyrm's metabolism is slow, but still, she must be fed."

I felt a chill crawl up my neck.

The oath-breakers. The liars.

That would be me.

As we walked, the draugr kept clear of the water, sticking close to the dunes. We picked our way between the rusted cars and climbed over Yggdrasill's tree roots.

We'd just clambered up a particularly massive root, when the lank-haired draugr raised a rotting arm. "Welcome to our mead hall."

I looked around, confused. I didn't see anything that resembled a mead hall. Just a massive root and a large pile of garbage.

The draugr began walking toward the garbage pile. "This way."

I squinted. What I'd first taken as a random pile of trash

appeared to be some sort of dwelling. It looked like something a desert island castaway might construct from whale skeletons. Pieces of tan fabric were strung between bleached bones. The walls were constructed of rusted metal.

"What kinds of bones are those?" asked Ali.

"Nidhogg's children," said the draugr. "The wyrm reproduces on her own, without a mate."

I stared at the bones. They were large, at least ten feet tall.

"How *big* are Nidhogg's children?" asked Ali.

"Big."

"And you kill them?"

"No, Nidhogg does. She's not much into maternal care."

"You know a lot about her."

"Before I died," the draugr leader said, "I was a professor of herpetology. Specialized in reptiles. Turns out that knowledge of snakes is a valued skill down here. When we found you, we were looking for wyrm eggs. But before we talk more of Nidhogg and her progeny, let me show you some hospitality."

Within the skeletal structure, the draugr led us through a corridor. Here, the rust-colored walls were old car parts, but the roof was covered in a translucent, plastic-like substance I didn't recognize.

"What is that?" I asked.

The lank-haired corpse laughed. "Snakeskin. When Nidhogg sheds, we collect the skin as it washes up on the shore. Makes a nearly waterproof roofing material."

"And this is how we get to the wyrm?" asked Ali, looking uneasy.

The draugr shrugged. "Well, not exactly. We just wanted to show off a bit. We don't get many visitors."

Now, I was growing impatient, desperate to get to Loki's wand. I could almost feel the magic from here, tingling over my skin. And I was starting to wonder if these draugr had any designs on eating Ali.

We crossed through an arch of interlocking vertebrae and into the hall. A table constructed from a long piece of driftwood ran down the middle of the room. Above the table hung chandeliers made from the skulls of massive snakes, presumably also Nidhogg's children.

Soon, the draugr's large mugs filled with red liquid—blood, by the smell of it. When all the stools were filled, their lank-haired leader stood.

"A toast to our new companions!" he shouted.

The draugr raised their mugs in a great gurgling cheer, then slammed them down.

Ali stiffened.

"Don't worry, don't worry," he said. "I promise no one will lay a finger on you. Especially now that we've drunk. Is that not right, my dead brothers and sisters?"

"Where's Nidhogg?" I asked, impatience roiling in my blood.

The draugr sighed. "She lives in the sea." He gestured in the direction of the sea. "Where the water is deepest."

"I don't suppose you have a boat?" asked Ali.

"I do, as it happens."

A plan began to form in my mind. "You said you sacrifice some of your kind to her?"

He nodded cheerfully. "Yes, at night we push them into the sea. In the morning, they are nothing but gnawed bones."

"Perfect," I said.

CHAPTER 48

ALI

The draugr leader led us along the beach again, and we walked silently under a sky that had turned dark.

I shivered, but not from cold. The draugr unnerved me. Not breathing, their eyes unblinking, quiet as ghosts. Even though I'd seen them drink blood, and their leader had promised they wouldn't harm me, their dead eyes followed my every step. They still hungered for my flesh; I was certain of it.

They'd given Marroc a large rucksack, which he now wore slung over one shoulder. It bore the logo of an old human sports team—the New York Jets. It smelled terrible, but he refused to tell me what was inside of it.

We kept away from the sea, walking high on the shoreline. Though they hadn't specifically stated it, I assumed the draugr were worried Nidhogg might come lunging up from the red water and drag them into the depths.

In front of me, smoke drifted off Marroc's skin. His gaze was straight ahead.

The dunes rose higher, and Yggdrasill's roots became

more numerous. The draugr became ever more vigilant, and the smoke thickened over Marroc's shoulders. I called Skalei to me.

"What is it?" I whispered to a gray-faced draugr walking next to me.

"We are near the home of the—"

The draugr never finished her sentence; we were interrupted by shrieking cries that sent a chill through my blood. I whirled, my knife ready. From the dunes, a mass of draugr charged toward us, screaming like banshees. Unlike our cohort in tattered clothes, these draugr wore slacks, leather shoes, and oxford shirts.

"Oath-breakers!" one of our draugr friend shouted. "Keep away from her!" He spun to face me. "You need to hurry. We won't feast on your flesh, but the oath-breakers will. The boat is just over there. We'll hold them off."

He pointed at a Viking longboat with a single sail, the color of bone. Marroc and I broke into a run. My feet pounded the rocky ground as I sprinted toward it. We were almost at the boat—almost to the wooden dock that led out to it. By the sinuous twists of the dock's wood, it looked like it was made out of Yggdrasill's roots.

Marroc reached it first, and I followed close behind him, climbing onto the roots. They stretched out into the red sea, fifty meters away.

Marroc leapt onto the ship, and I followed. My lungs burned.

"Help me cast off," Marroc shouted. He pointed at a line in the front of the boat. The bow, I thought. I hustled over to the rope.

But the sound of moans turned my head. Just behind us were two hungry draugr, rushing for us.

I untied the rope and threw it onto the dock. "I'm clear," I shouted, turning back to Marroc.

He was at the other end of the boat, still working his way through the rope.

A sinewy draugr wearing a barrister's wig charged for me. Instinctively, I called Skalei. I threw the blade. The steel flashed in in the air, and I hit my mark. The dagger hit the corpse's stomach with a *thud.* He fell into the bloody water.

"Skalei," I said, and the hilt returned to my palm.

The second draugr was reaching for me, but my blade stopped him. It plunged into his neck, and he fell backward off the roots.

Not terrible. But there were more draugr where those came from.

I turned to see Marroc tossing the line onto the dock, and we were free.

"Let's go!" I shouted.

Except... the boat wasn't moving. There was no freaking wind here.

I gripped the sides. "We need a motor. The oars and the sail won't get us moving fast enough."

"Help push!" shouted Marroc, leaping onto the dock, and I figured out what his plan might be. Give it a strong shove, then leap in.

I leapt over the side, mirroring Marroc's position on the dock. I shoved with all my strength. Slowly, the boat began to move, and Marroc hoisted himself back up into the boat. Before I could join him, a bony hand started digging into my flesh.

I whirled to find a draugr bellowing in a British accent, "You have committed an offense against my person when you threw your knife into my stomach!"

With my nerves sparking, I punched the draugr in the jaw so hard his neck bent back at a ninety-degree angle. He fell backward into the red sea.

When I turned to look at Marroc, he stood at the edge of

the boat, and it had drifted away from me. *Dammit.* Black smoke swirled around him like a maelstrom. His eyes glowed like embers.

My stomach clenched. The boat was now nearly thirty feet from the dock. Safe from the draugr, but too far for me to jump to him. I was on my own.

Then, from the bloody sea below me, a pair of sinewy draugr arms clutched at my elbow. The draugr in the barrister's wig rose from the sea. "Maritime salvage law is clear. You have injured me; I am entitled to fair compensation in the form of your flesh."

"Skalei!" This time, I slashed at his neck so hard I nearly severed his head. "I can do this all day, bitch."

Problem was that he didn't stay dead.

I kicked him hard in the chest, and he sank under the surface once more. Then I reached for the vergr stone in my pocket and turned to Marroc.

"Catch!" I shouted, tossing the crystal toward the boat.

It sparkled in the dim light before landing gently in Marroc's hands.

"Fara!" I shouted.

CHAPTER 49

MARROC

I was still holding Ali's crystal when she teleported, so instead of reappearing next to me, she popped into existence with her feet at about shoulder level. She started to fall, but I caught her, wrapping my arms around her waist and legs.

I stabilized the rocking boat with my feet and breathed in her scent. "Are you all right?"

"I'm fine," she said.

She pushed away from me, and I realized I'd been holding her tightly. Slowly, she slid down my body, standing in the boat. Her stomach grumbled, and the sound made my gut clench. I needed to get her out of here, back home as soon as possible.

"I'll get you home soon," I promised. "Once we get the wand from Nidhogg."

I glanced around, thinking of the mission. While the boat was clear of the dock, it was simply drifting. If we didn't get moving, the waves would push us back onto the beach.

"We need to get this boat moving," I said. "Have you ever sailed before?"

Ali shook her head. "I grew up in a cave, remember?"

"Not a problem. Before Ragnarok, I used to sail in Boston Harbor."

"That was a thousand years ago. You might be a bit rusty."

"It's like riding a bike," I said, turning to study the boat. Built like a traditional Viking longship, it had a single mast, wooden oarlocks along the side, and rows of oars. Both ends were pointed and carved in the shape of bird beaks. Rows of circular shields lined each side. It looked ready to ferry a Viking raiding party across the North Sea.

There was only one thing that seemed out of place. The hull wasn't built of wood. Instead, it appeared to be constructed from a plastic-like material.

"What is this thing made of?" said Ali, as if reading my mind.

I bent down to inspect the hull. It was rougher than I'd expected. As I ran my hand along the side, little pieces flaked off under my fingers. I blew out a long breath as I realized what the boat was.

"This isn't just any boat, Ali. This was Loki's ship, the *Naglfar*."

Ali grimaced, pulling her hand quickly away from the hull. "The one that was built from the fingernails of the dead?"

"Yes."

Ali hopped up onto one of the wooden seats, looking disturbed. "I've heard the story about how when a person dies, their fingernails keep growing. And that you should cut them, unless you want them to end up on the Naglfar... but I never thought it was real."

"I think that a lot of things we believe are legends have a foundation in truth."

Already, we'd drifted closer to the beach, and I sat down to grip a pair of oars.

"I don't want us to run aground," I said. "I'm going to row a bit."

"I'll help." Ali sat in front of me, gripping another pair of oars. Her silver hair draped down her back, and I realized it was almost gleaming in the moonlight. We rowed in tandem, and I watched the muscles in her back move under her black shirt.

All remained silent around us.

Our oars cut into the sea like knives, and slowly, the boat began to move until it was picking up speed. I watched with a growing sense of relief as the dock grew small in the distance.

Already, I could feel that we were closing in on Nidhogg's domain, where the water was deepest.

CHAPTER 50

ALI

I stole a glance behind me at Marroc, at his shirt sleeves rolled up to the elbows, showing off his muscular forearms. White had not been the best choice for this journey, as the shirt was now streaked in mud.

Wisps of smoke rose off his skin as he rowed. He gripped the oars tightly, and with each stroke, his shoulders squared. He might be dead, but he nevertheless exuded a powerful masculinity. His wood-smoke scent curled around me.

"You can stop rowing if you like," he said as he pulled on the oars in an even rhythm. "I'm not even remotely tired."

Right, of course. I'd forgotten how he was basically indefatigable. I put down my oars and turned to face him.

Beneath us, the longboat cut through the waves. As he rowed, he studied me. In the darkness, his eyes were a deep indigo color, like sapphires held up against a night sky. Fiery runes gleamed on his chest, visible through the open collar of his shirt.

"So, how are we going to find Nidhogg?" I asked.

"Bait," Marroc said as he prepared to take another stroke.

I frowned. "With what?"

"We'll use that." He nodded at the rucksack he'd been carrying since we left the hall. "And now that you mention it," he continued, "can you open it for me?"

I poked the bag with my foot instead. "Tell me what's inside it."

"Well, I wanted a bull's head, but they didn't have one. This is something that washed up on the beach. The draugr leader thought it would work."

I poked the bag with my foot again but didn't open it.

"Look, you're going to have to open it." He pulled on the oars. "My hands are occupied."

Slowly I unzipped the bag. Inside were three human heads. Nausea rose in my throat. "Nope, no thanks. These are the bait?"

Marroc let the boat coast again as he spoke. "Once, when Thor fought Nidhogg, he used the head of a bull tied to a rope to lure in the wyrm. Except we didn't have a bull, so we have to use humans."

He reached into the bag and pulled out one of the heads, then grabbed the end of an unused rope lying on the floor of the boat, tied it tightly around the head, and tossed it over the side. It bobbed for a moment before sinking out of sight.

* * *

I'D IMAGINED that Nidhogg would come roaring up from the deep, hungry and vicious, ready to ravage our boat as soon as Marroc tossed in the "bait," but instead, nothing had happened.

A deep calm settled over the sea. Waves lapped quietly against the hull. There was no wind, and the dark sky stretched over us. I watched out the portside, while Marroc looked the other way.

I leaned over the gunnel and stared into the water.

Nothing moved in the depths. I could see only an impenetrable darkness, nearly as black as the sky above us.

"I don't think Nidhogg is here," I said quietly.

"I think you might be right, Ali. We should head for deeper water."

Once more, we were rowing, and a gentle breeze washed over us. Marroc jerked hard on the oars, and I tried to match his pace. Soon, he had the boat surging over the sea.

My job now was to dangle the bait. On the list of things I'd wanted to do before I died, fishing with a human head in the world of the dead was pretty low.

Then something glimmered down deep, at the very edge of my eyesight. As I watched, it grew larger—a pale green glowing light. Then, next to it, another one blinked into existence.

"Marroc?" I said in a sharp whisper. "There's something down there."

Marroc stopped rowing. "What is it?"

"I don't know. I think it might be a pair of eyes—"

But as I spoke, a third light blinked on, then another.

"No," I said. "Not eyes. Too many—"

He leaned forward, shoulder brushing mine, and I felt the heat of his body as he crouched next to me. "Where is it?" he asked, his voice rumbling deep in his chest.

I pointed into the water at the largest glowing light. "Do you see it?"

Marroc started to shake his head, then he stopped. "Okay, I see it."

"There's more than one." The lights grew bigger and brighter as they rose out of the depths. "Do you know what they are?"

I felt Marroc's shoulder move as he shook his head. Then he whispered, "Ali," as he wrapped an arm around my hips and pulled me away from the gunnel. "Look."

All around us, the sea glowed a pale green, lights floating under the waves. They appeared nearly stationary, drifting at the same speed as the longboat.

"What are they?" I asked.

"I think they might be jellyfish. Glowing ones." He prepared another line of bait on the rope and tossed it into the sea.

I was just pulling away when, suddenly, like a switch turning off, all the lights in the water went out. Behind me, Marroc stiffened.

"What the Hel?" I whispered.

The sea was pitch black, the sky just as dark. Looking toward the horizon, it was impossible to tell were one ended and the other began.

"Can you see anything?" Marroc asked.

"Not a thing. I'm not sure I ever experienced this before."

Then the bait line jerked so hard in my hand that I would have been pulled over the side and into the sea if Marroc hadn't grabbed me tight around my waist. The whole boat listed hard to port, the gunnel nearly slipping under the water. We were going to get pulled into the water.

"Let go of the rope," he said.

Then I saw it. A huge form rising in the darkness behind us, nearly as thick and as large as Yggdrasill's trunk. Pale as bone and covered in opalescent scales, it was unquestionably the coil of a massive serpent.

"Ah," I said, letting go of the rope. "Nidhogg is here."

CHAPTER 51

MARROC

Nidhogg's huge shadow passed over the boat, and I turned to face her. The air vibrated as the wyrm spoke in a deep voice. "Who has sailed the *Naglfar* into my domain?"

"I'm known as Marroc," I said.

The beast was impossibly massive, her head longer and wider than our boat. Behind it, a giant body looped and twisted. The coils were so large that, had I not known they were part of the wyrm, I would have mistaken them for islands.

The serpent's head lowered until it was level with the longboat. "Marroc?" she said. She inhaled, and as she did, her breath sucked the *Naglfar* closer. "But I don't sense a soul in you."

Slowly, her head turned so that a massive yellow eye fixed on me. A long pink tongue, thick as a tree trunk, flicked out. "But I smell warm flesh. You have brought me a living elf?"

"I have," I said slowly, my entire body tensing.

"I haven't tasted fresh blood since Loki and Thor last sailed these waters. I accept your offering."

"The elf is not an offering."

Nidhogg's tongue flicked out again, and a deep hiss shook the boat. "She is not? Why bring her to me, then?"

"She's a warrior, and she is helping me on my journey."

Another hiss, followed by another. The *Naglfar* tossed and bounced. It took me a moment to realize the wyrm was laughing.

"A lich has help from another? A compatriot? No, no. Do not think I am so gullible. A lich serves only himself. A lich does nothing without a purpose for himself. If you told me she was your mistress, I might believe you."

The wyrm drew in another great breath. Her giant yellow eye remained fixed on me, glistening with red seawater.

"Oh, I see." She breathed out in a low hiss. "I see now. That's a complicated position you've found yourself in, isn't it, lich?"

"What is she talking about?" whispered Ali.

I shrugged, pretending that I didn't know, though I was pretty sure the beast had sensed the pair of souls within Ali.

My voice boomed over the sea as I said, "I am here for the wand."

The serpent paused. Her yellow eye studied me. "The wand?"

"Loki's wand, the Levateinn. You have it."

Slowly, the giant wyrm's head moved. "I have no such thing. I defeated Loki nearly a thousand years ago. The god is long dead."

"That's not possible," I said. The spell I'd conducted had been very clear. The wyrm had the wand. There was nowhere else it could be.

Nidhogg gave a great, thundering laugh. "I remember it like it was yesterday. Loki, the fool, tried to fight me. He lost, of course. Not even a god is a match for me. I ate him in one bite." Her head moved closer, her shadow once again falling over the bow of the ship. "Give me the elf now. My stomach churns with hunger. I haven't had fresh meat in a thousand years."

Doubt flickered within me. Had my spell, the one through which I'd divined this was where the wand was, been wrong?

I'd never been wrong before.

"No," I said. "My magic was—"

But before I could finish speaking, the beast struck. The hull shattered beneath my feet as the serpent's jaw tore through it. Pain erupted in my stomach, and I looked down to see a venomous fang protruding from the center of my gut.

CHAPTER 52

ALI

For an impossibly long moment, which couldn't have been much more than a second or two, Marroc struggled in Nidhogg's maw. Then the wyrm's jaws slammed shut, and Marroc and half of the *Naglfar* disappeared into its mouth.

I screamed as a wave slammed into me. I slid toward the sanguineous sea, fingers scraping along the hull. For a moment my mind was blank with panic before I remembered Skalei.

With a shout, I called the blade to me, then drove it into the side of the boat. The dagger punched through the hull and, like a mountain climber's axe, arrested my descent.

I looked around. The front half of the boat was missing, and the stern, where I hung, was slowly lifting into the air. Beneath my feet, red seawater bubbled and churned as the ship sank.

The wyrm's voice boomed from somewhere in the darkness. "Where are you, elf?"

I clung to the hilt of the dagger, hardly daring to breathe.

I peered over my shoulder. I couldn't see Nidhogg's head anymore, but the sea writhed with her massive coils.

I tried to think of a plan. A way out. But all I could think of was Marroc. I'd just seen him impaled and devoured, and I wanted to cry. Surely that would kill even a lich.

My heart ached, and the boat shuddered, sinking fast. There wasn't time to think about Marroc. I needed a plan. *A life raft.*

The boat lurched. The sea of blood rushed up until it was only inches from my feet.

"There you are," said Nidhogg.

The wyrm's massive head hovered over me. Her tongue flicked out, nearly a meter in diameter and split at the end like a snake's.

"What do you want?" I cried out.

"You. Two souls for the price of one." The serpent's tongue brushed my cheek, slimy and cold.

I yanked myself up, lunging for the gunnel. My fingers had just brushed the edge when the wyrm's tongue wrapped round my stomach.

She jerked her head and tossed me high into the air. I spun, twisting awkwardly. I flung out my arms, trying to steady myself. Below me, Nidhogg tore through the remains of the long boat. Pale skin, eyes, and fangs long as lances. She lunged for me.

Everything seemed to move in slow motion. The wyrm's mouth gaped so wide that I could practically see down its throat. Her fangs flashed, coated with green venom. This was it. The end of my life. Swallowed by a giant snake.

And then I knew where to find Levateinn. At the moment of my demise, I knew I'd discovered the final resting place of Loki's wand.

There was only one thing to do. The wyrm's jaws

snapped shut, closing around me, ready to cut me in two, but I was gone—vanished in a flash of purple light.

CHAPTER 53

MARROC

A burning pain overpowered my senses. It grew hotter and hotter, like a fire poker piercing my stomach. I could feel my skin burning, my viscera scorching. It felt like my curse had been condensed and focused on just one part of my body.

I *would* get out of this. Wyrd had decreed it. My magic had never been wrong before.

Blocking out the pain, I reached down, fingers gliding over the wound in my stomach—a six-inch hole punched clean through me. Pain lanced up from my fingertips as venom burned them.

It all came flooding back in an instant: the ship, the wyrm, the fang that had impaled me, the final moments as Nidhogg's jaws snapped shut. The end of everything. My magic had failed, and I'd failed Ali.

Guilt spread through me, burning hotter than the poison.

I opened my eyes. I saw only darkness. I closed them and reopened them. Still darkness.

I tried to inscribe *sowilo*, to shine light in this infernal darkness, but nothing happened. I tried again—still nothing. My body didn't work. I had no magic.

Fear rose within me. That could only mean one thing. I was dead. *Actually* dead. Sent back to Helheim for the shades to collect their debt. Beneath me, a thick mud oozed. The shades would be on me in minutes.

I'd promised them I'd raise their queen. Clearly, I'd failed, and they would want vengeance. My chance at regaining my soul was gone. Lost. The shades would not be kind.

I considered standing, trying to run, but there was no point. Even if I made it as far as the iron wall, I'd already confirmed that it was impenetrable. This was one prison from which I couldn't escape. Besides, I deserved what I had coming.

I lay in the mud, my eyes closed, and silence pressed down on me.

Ali...

Her face came to me behind my shuttered lids. I'd failed to protect her. Left her to die in the sea of the dead. Nidhogg would tear her to shreds. This was the worst possible outcome—and it was all because of my unwavering belief in my own magic.

Why had I been so certain of myself that I'd led her into the very depths of Helheim?

She was my perfect counterpart. I wished to be near her now. To hear her voice. To see her. To smell her. I should have left her in Boston, safe in my home, and visited the Nastrand on my own—even if my magic had told me otherwise.

So why was it that I could still feel the wand, its magic like a shimmering balm over my skin?

A faint voice came from the darkness. "Marroc?"

The shades were coming. I was ready for their punishment. I certainly deserved it.

"Here," I gasped.

"Marroc?" The voice again, louder. I lifted my head from the mud, and the ooze trickled from my ears. Something wasn't right. This shade's voice was clear.

"Marroc?"

My entire body stiffened. Pain erupted from the wound in my gut. But now, I recognized the voice.

"Ali? What are you doing here?"

CHAPTER 54

ALI

I reappeared in darkness on my hands and knees and felt for my vergr crystal. My fingers wrapped around the stone, and I slid it into my pocket.

I stood slowly as my eyes adjusted to the gloom. I was in a narrow corridor. It was hot in here, and wet. It smelled terrible. There was no question where I was now. Nidhogg's stomach. Exactly where I'd intended to go.

"Marroc?"

My voice echoed faintly in the cavern, but there was no answer. I peered around, looking for his massive form, but all I could see was glistening stomach lining.

"Marroc?" I called again.

Then I saw him. Lying on his back, his eyes staring blindly. It took a second for me to realize why. He couldn't see in the darkness. He just didn't have Night Elf vision like I did.

"Marroc," I said, hurrying to his side. "Are you okay?"

"Ali?" He reached out for me. "I'm sorry. I failed."

"You need to get up."

"No. When the shades come, they'll destroy me. They'll probably condemn you, too. They know that you're my—"

"Marroc," I said, "how do we find the wand?"

He stared at me, eyes wide and unseeing. "What do you mean? We lost. Nidhogg won. The wand wasn't with her."

"No, I'm certain it's close by. And you're not dead. We're inside Nidhogg. And we need to get out of here, fast."

"That explains why I can still feel the wand's presence." Marroc paused. "We're *inside* Nidhogg?"

"Don't say I never took you anywhere nice. And do you remember when she said she'd eaten Thor and Loki? They must have brought the wand in with them. That would explain why your spell said the wand was with Nidhogg."

Finally, I saw hope return to Marroc's face. "Brilliant. So my spell *was* correct."

"Let's cut down on the gloating and get moving. I can show you where to walk."

Marroc slowly got to his feet. The way he stood, I could see he was in serious pain.

"Will that get better?" I asked, pointing to the wound in his abdomen.

"It's taking longer than usual. Maybe it's because the fang severed my spine..." He paused, obviously frustrated. "You go on ahead; I'll walk more slowly behind you."

I shook my head, forgetting that Marroc couldn't see me. "I'm not leaving you here. We can both go slowly."

He walked behind me until the stomach walls expanded into a large chamber, then closed off. I stopped, sucking in a short breath.

"What is it?" Marroc asked, sensing my hesitation.

"The stomach stops here." My breath started coming fast, and panic was about to overtake my mind. I'd grown up in dark spaces, but they had been nothing like this. We were inside the gut of a monster, and I felt like the walls were closing in around me.

Marroc frowned. "I can sense it here, but not its exact location. If I travel to the astral plane, I should be able to sense the wand and home in on it better."

I could hardly parse his words; the sense of claustrophobia was suffocating. Was there enough air in here? If we couldn't find the wand, how long would it take to suffocate?

He closed his eyes. For a long moment, he stood perfectly still. And as he did, it was like all the darkness and filth around us faded away, and there was only Marroc. Slowly, I started to feel like I could breathe again, like there was air fresh around me.

With his arms out to the side, his body glowed with a pale light, his hair lifting and whirling around his head. Blue light carved the masculine planes of his face and streamed from his body. The light shifted in hues, like sun rays through a stained-glass window. I'd seen so little beauty in the past few days that I didn't want it to stop.

I looked down at myself, watching as the light streamed over me and cleaned the filth from my body, from my clothes.

The stomach walls around us transformed, now shimmering with white light. A faint music filled the air—like I'd never heard before, so beautiful it could have been written by the greatest of the gods' bards, Bragi, when he'd been alive.

The gods were dead, but right now, Marroc seemed a lot like one. I wanted to know what wonders he was seeing in the astral realm. I envied his ability to transport himself to faraway places.

Then his eyes flashed open, and the light faded. The music fell to silence. I regretted the loss of that beauty for a moment. The claustrophobia started to return, my breath quickening, heart rate speeding up.

"It's close by." He pointed at one of the walls.

"Skalei." My dagger appeared, and I turned, slashing downward and carving through Nidhogg's flesh.

Instantly, the wyrm's stomach muscles contracted, and we were thrown upside down. Somehow, I managed to hang on to Marroc's waist. But even as Nidhogg thrashed with pain, I didn't hesitate. With one hand, I gripped the edge of the wound, and with the other, I hacked at it. With each slice, I carved deeper and deeper into the stomach lining.

I felt its power, even from here. I reached inside, my fingers tightened around a smooth surface, and I pulled out a gleaming silver wand. My breath caught in my throat at its beauty, so stunning that I was sure it was never meant for mortal eyes. I didn't want to hand it over to him, but this was why we'd come here.

I held it out to him. "I hope I can trust you with this kind of power."

CHAPTER 55

MARROC

The power of Levateinn flowed into me. I closed my eyes as a thick metallic taste filled my mouth. It was a magic like I'd never experienced, smooth and silent. Quicksilver, I realized, was its basis. This, I knew intuitively, was the wand's innate power of transformation.

The wand's energy continued to thrum in my fingers. My senses expanded. I could hear the movement of Nidhogg's blood, feel the flex of her massive muscles as she swam. I could even sense the movements of jellyfish floating in the sea.

My perception narrowed. From here, I could feel Ali's beating heart. I could sense her mixed emotions, her fear and excitement at being so close to this relic of the vanquished gods. And in the center of everything, I could feel her soul and mine. Entwined together. A perfect pair.

At that moment, I had but one desire: keep Ali safe. I drew magic from the wand. While my magic was powerful, it was nothing compared to Levateinn. Ancient and primordial, the wand was a direct conduit to the power of the gods.

This was the kind of power that could drive a person mad.

CHAPTER 56

ALI

"Do you have the crystal?" asked Marroc.

"Why?" I asked, my mind no longer working logically. All I could think was: *We have to get out of here before we suffocate.*

"I'll use a spell to send it back to Boston."

A sort of euphoria blazed in my mind, so overwhelming I was on the verge of hysteria. "Oh, right! The wand. The wand can get us out of here."

A maniacal sort of laughter escaped my throat, which I regretted instantly. I wasn't sure I could ever be in an enclosed space again after this. Which meant I definitely had to find a way out of the Shadow Caverns.

With shaking hands, I dug in my pocket for the crystal. I tried to hand it to him, but he stopped me.

"Not yet. I'll tell you when I'm ready."

As I stood by Marroc's side, he waved the wand in a complex series of runic shapes. The air around us glowed, brighter and brighter. Once again, I could breathe. *We're getting out of here.* At last, this horror would be over. And if he was telling the truth, I'd finally get to Galin.

Slowly, a circle of blue light formed in the air, growing wider and wider. The ring expanded, revealing a portal. Through it, I could see a much cleaner place: a rug over a wooden floor and a blazing hearth. Marroc's living room. Oh, gods, it looked nice.

Marroc turned to me. "All right, put the crystal into the portal."

I lifted my vergr crystal and began to shove it toward the glowing portal.

"Watch your fingers. This magic is powerful."

Carefully, I reached through the hole into Marroc's living room and placed the crystal on the floor of his hall.

"Are you clear?"

I nodded, drawing back my hand. Then, with a blinding flash of light, the portal vanished.

"All right," he said. "Now all you have to do is teleport us to your crystal."

I turned to him, wrapping my arms around him, then quietly spoke the word that would save us: "Fara."

CHAPTER 57

ALI

I lay on a soft rug before the hearth and breathed in the clean air of Marroc's home. I couldn't help but grin as I opened my eyes. Wood crackled in the fireplace, and its warmth wavered over my skin. The soft chairs looked inviting for my exhausted muscles. Through the windows, I could see stars shining against a pitch-black sky.

I sat up straight and looked at Marroc, smiling broadly. But he was still gripping his stomach, looking like he was in pain.

"Are you okay?" I asked.

He nodded. "I'll be fine."

He was supposed to be able to heal fast. I looked down at myself. Marroc's magical light had cleaned some of the muck away, but I was still desperate to clean myself after the whole *Corpse Shore* situation.

Never again. I wanted to scrub myself for days.

"Marroc, I'm going to take a quick bath, okay? And probably burn these clothes."

"I suppose I could tell you where to find new ones." His deep, velvety voice wrapped around me.

With the adrenaline leaving my body, it was like all the exhaustion had returned to me at once. "Yes, thanks. I'd rather not walk around naked."

"Shame. Anyway, you'll find some in the wardrobe of the room you first stayed in." He pointed toward the kitchen. "But as they are my old clothes, they're unlikely to fit you properly."

"I'll make it work."

He nodded, still looking like he was going to be sick from his wound. That was worrying. He usually recovered so quickly.

I rose and headed for the kitchen. It seemed like ages since I'd first been here, investigating the human contraptions. My gaze snagged on the blender. What I really wanted, before I slaughtered my ancient enemy, was a smoothie...

I crossed to the stairwell, taking deep breaths of the clean air in Marroc's home. Never again would I take fresh air for granted. Or not being in the bowel of a monster. These were all things to be grateful for.

In the bedroom, I opened the wardrobe and picked out one of Marroc's sweaters—a thin sort of wool that would function as a dress on me. Good enough.

I carried it with me into the bathroom, the white marble floors inviting. I could *really* get used to a place like this.

I started filling the tub with hot water. I'd want it as hot as possible. Steam rose from the tub, and I peeled off my clothes, tossing them on the floor. Well, not quite. Marroc didn't have any replacement bras or underwear, so I filled the sink with soap and hot water and washed them until they were clean.

Then I stepped into the marble tub, nearly moaning with pleasure at the deliciously hot water. With a bar of soap in my hands, I started scrubbing hard. My hands, my legs and feet. I dunked my head under the water and washed my hair.

CURSED PRINCE

I scrubbed every inch of myself, then rinsed it in the hot water.

My skin had gone pink in the bath, and exhaustion burned through my muscles. I sighed with relief.

We'd actually succeeded, hadn't we? At least, as long as Marroc was telling the truth. As long as he could raise Galin for me to torture until I got the answers I needed.

My muscles burned with fatigue, but I forced myself out of the tub, rivulets of water dripping down my body. I toweled off, drying my hair. My bra and underwear were slightly damp, but it couldn't be helped. Lastly, I slid into the soft sweater. It skimmed over my hips, down my thighs and to my knees.

I shoved the vergr stone into my bra and slid the golden ring onto my remaining ring finger.

Clearly, I didn't need it anymore, but I'd never had anything that pretty before.

Freshly cleaned, I hurried back down to the living room, to the warmth of the hearth. Marroc sat in one of his chairs, wearing a new outfit—his damp hair hung over a crisp white shirt, his sleeves rolled up to the elbow. He clutched Loki's gleaming silver wand.

But something wasn't right with him. He was usually so stoic, but I could see the pain etched on his features.

"You're not okay," I said.

"It's Nidhogg's venom. Apparently the one thing I can't heal from."

I sat across from him in a soft armchair. "And Loki's wand? That can't heal it?"

"No, I'm afraid not. And if I return my soul to myself in this condition, I'd die quickly."

A little bit of panic rose in me. He couldn't die—then I'd never get to Galin. "What heals a lich? Blood?"

He gave me a wary look. "Technically the soul, or magic drunk through blood. But I'm not drinking your blood."

"Would it work?"

"Yes, it would work." He spoke in a deep, soft voice. "But I could lose control and drain you completely."

I stood. "Look, Marroc. I have waited my whole life to avenge the Night Elves. I have no other purpose than to free them. And I need you to bring Galin back to life, and you can't do that if you're dead. So, you need to drink a little bit of my blood and master control of yourself. And then we need to finish this. Okay?"

Unsure what to do, I thrust my wrist out before him and pulled up the long sleeve of my sweater dress. I wasn't about to offer up my neck, because that seemed, frankly, terrifying.

I saw his eyes blaze with hunger as he looked at the veins in my wrist. Then he grabbed it in his hands and brought it to his mouth.

I winced as his teeth pierced my skin. At first, his bite was gentle, his lips warm, his tongue gently caressing my skin.

A chill spread over my hand, and his mouth became hungry, drinking faster. A strangely pleasurable sensation raced up my arm—a tingling warmth that spread into my chest—which disturbed me. His scent of wood smoke and sage wrapped around me.

When I closed my eyes, I thought of the words *North Star*, a gleaming light in the night sky. Heat raced through my body, and I became acutely aware of my bare legs, as I was only in a long sweater. Strangely, I didn't want Marroc to stop.

But when he did, I felt a slight jolt of horror at what I'd just experienced. He pulled his teeth from my wrist, looking up at me.

Did I actually enjoy that?

Bizarre.

"Did it work?" I asked, tugging down the sleeve of my sweater.

He nodded, a smile slowly spreading on his lips. "Beautifully. I can return your magic to you soon."

It had felt incredible when he was drinking my blood, but now I could hardly move. My body was nearly drained of strength, and I slid down into the armchair, sighing.

Marroc looked at me with a satisfied smile on his face. "When this is all over, I'm going to set you up in a beautiful home like this one. You can even bring Barthol."

I was no longer sure what he was talking about, and I had the sense we were both a little delirious. "You're going to get my brother and me a house?"

His smile deepened. "Ah. He's your brother?"

I blinked. "What are we talking about?"

But from the corner of my eye, I saw a dark shape move in one of his windows. Was I hallucinating?

I turned and spotted the flicker of moth wings. "Marroc?"

Before he could answer, light flashed, and a spell shattered the glass. Not a hallucination. No, this was definitely real.

Marroc spun as more windows shattered. He leapt in front of me as High Elf soldiers poured into his atrium.

"Skalei." Mentally, I calculated my chances of taking out every one of these High Elves before they killed me.

My chances were not good.

The soldiers stalked toward us, wands trained on Marroc's chest. Curses hummed ominously at the ends of their wands.

Gorm, King of the High Elves, stepped to the front. His pale hair cascaded over golden robes, a spindly crown perched on his head.

"Don't move," he said in his stupid tinkling voice.

"What do you want?" Marroc boomed. He was standing before me, trying to shield me.

"I see you've found your voice again," said Gorm. "You will come with us."

"No," Marroc said. "I will not."

He raised Loki's wand. But before he could launch into a spell, his living room wall exploded.

I was thrown out of the chair onto the floor, and I scrambled to stand again. When I did, I saw the towering gray body of a troll.

"Ghhhrooooarrgh!" It snatched Marroc in its crushing grip and clamped a hand over his mouth, stopping him from uttering the spell.

Marroc had dropped Levateinn on the floor, the wand gleaming silver.

"Thank you, Porgor. Now, what have we here?" King Gorm bent down to pick up Levateinn, and his eyes widened. "Now this is quite the prize."

Oh *no.*

CHAPTER 58

MARROC

I knew where I was before I even opened my eyes. The stone beneath my back was as hard as I remembered, the scent of filth just as vile, and the warm body of a tiny rodent curled up at my feet confirmed it. I was in my cell in the Citadel, with my pet rat Gormie.

I sat up, my eyes adjusting to the darkness. I blinked slowly. There *was* something new. The bars I'd previously broken had been replaced with a thicker, heavier set. And, as if that wasn't enough, my hands were clamped in giant iron manacles. Escaping this time would not be so easy.

I peered into the cell across from me, hoping to see Ali's sleeping form, but it was empty.

"Fuck," I said under my breath.

I stood and paced the length of my cell, my arms bound behind my back. An intense rage, and a desperate need to get to Ali, was overtaking me. I no longer cared about my soul at this point; I only wanted to make sure she was safe.

At least my wound was healed now, thanks to Ali's blood. Gods, she had tasted sublime.

It had taken every ounce of my self-control not to drain her completely.

I returned to the familiar stone bench. Thick smoke gathered at my feet as the curse smoldered deep within my core.

Where would Ali be now? The question seared my brain, and fate be damned, I wished I'd never gotten her mixed up in this. I should have set her free, gotten the wand myself, and found her later.

Whatever was happening now, King Gorm certainly wouldn't be treating her to a manicure and clay face mask. He'd want to torture her, extract all the information he could. Worse, Ali was a Night Elf. She was supposed to be banished to the Shadow Caverns. Her very presence in Midgard was enough for a death sentence. And if they learned she was an assassin...

Cold rage slid through me, and I imagined ripping open the king's throat before I savaged his entire family.

And then there was Levateinn. The king now possessed Loki's wand, and he had the power of the gods in his grasp. He'd be nearly impossible to defeat.

I should have never set this sequence of events in motion. I shouldn't have used my magic to call Ali to me.

I stood and rested my head against the iron bars. Trapped in the cell, there was nothing I could do.

I frowned as an idea came to me. Actually, there *was* one thing I could do. I could access the astral plane.

I sat on my stone bench. Closing my eyes, I focused my inner eye on the ethereal realm. Without my soul, I couldn't traverse it, but I could still gaze upon its vast expanse. I could look for my mate again.

Where is Ali?

As I searched, the curse kindled, a low, throbbing pain in my stomach. I ignored the pain and scanned the astral plane, searching for Ali. I could see the souls of the castle guards stationed at the gates, the High Elves in their chambers, even a few humans as they walked Boston's icy streets.

In the distance, a pair of souls glowed, so close together they might have been one—it was Ali's and my souls together, shimmering faintly. Thank gods she was alive.

Heat began to fill my veins, but I gritted my teeth and pushed forward.

Horror slid through my bones. I knew exactly where she was. By the edge of the Well of Wyrd.

"Marroc?"

I opened my eyes to find a High Elf standing before the cell bars, her pale hair tumbling over a golden gown.

"Welcome home," she said with a smug smile. "We missed you."

Pure panic was claiming my mind now. "Revna. I want you to know that if you harm a hair on Ali's head, I will find a way out of here and personally destroy everyone in your family. I will make it hurt. And after I kill you all, I will take over the kingdom myself."

Her face paled, and her jaw dropped open. "You can speak?"

"Apparently. What are you doing with Ali?"

"I want the ring back."

A plan started to form in my mind. "The Night Elf has it," I said. "Why don't you ask her for it?"

Revna crossed her arms, pouting. "The king won't let me anywhere near her."

I was about to tell her she could find Ali by the Well of Wyrd. This, at least, would stop her from being thrown into it, and it would buy me a little time to get to her. I'd have said anything to forestall what was surely Ali's imminent demise.

But before Revna could reply, a group of guards burst in.

"Step aside, princess," shouted a burly guard. "The king

wishes to see the prisoner." Already, he was at the front of my cell, unlocking it.

Normally, I would have put up a fight, wet the floor with the guard's blood, but that wouldn't get me to Ali any faster. My best guess was that they wanted to throw us into the Well of Wyrd together.

I turned back to Revna as he led me away. "Princess," I called, "if you want your golden ring, you'd better make sure nothing happens to Ali."

As we started to climb the stairs to the amphitheater, frustration ripped through me. We were moving far too slowly, and panic was still searing my brain. What if we didn't get there in time? I had to expedite this.

I whirled to the guard closest to me and sank my teeth into his neck. With the power of his soul flowing into me, I ripped free from the manacles. I tore into the throat of another guard, reveling in the power that flowed into me from his blood.

Within moments, the stairwell was drenched in carnage, and I could hear Revna's screams fading as she ran away.

Now, imbued with the strength of two more souls, power flooded me. I surged up the stairs at the speed of lightning.

After racing up the stairs, covered in blood, I launched myself onto the roof of the Citadel. Snowflakes drifted down from a steel-gray sky in the amphitheater that encircled the Well of Wyrd.

Today, the seats were empty. On the dais overlooking the well, King Gorm stood, dressed in his usual golden robes. In his right hand, Levateinn shimmered. And that was where my power met its limits—because even with these souls in my body, I was no match for the wand.

Ali stood next to him swaying slightly. Her arms were bound tightly behind her. She looked completely drained of energy. Fear stole my breath. I'd do anything to get her out of this, even if it meant giving up my life.

"Where are your subjects?" I shouted to the king with all the confidence I could muster. I was still moving quickly, rushing down the steps toward them, desperate to be near Ali. "I thought your subjects were into spectacles," I went on, hoping to stall him. "That's what you have planned, isn't it? More tossing of bodies into your sacrificial pit. But you'll need an audience."

"I see you are soaked in the blood of my guards," Gorm said. "How charming. Unfortunately, it's just a small group of us today. Come down and speak with me."

I shrugged, feigning nonchalance. More slowly, I began to make my way toward the king. As I walked down the steps, my mind worked frantically. *What's his game plan? Is this an execution? A negotiation? Or something else entirely?*

Maybe a direct approach would work best. I had reached the stone platform that overlooked the well, and I stalked closer until I was only a few feet from Ali and the king. "What do you want?"

"Stop where you are!" Gorm commanded.

Ali stood perilously close to the edge, only inches from the king. I fought the urge to run to her, knowing that any sudden moments would result in him shoving her into the well.

King Gorm held up my ring. "It's time you were made whole again."

That was unexpected. What *was* his game plan?

He raised Levateinn to point at my chest. The wand shimmered with magic.

Like Revna, King Gorm didn't appear to realize that my soul was no longer contained within the gold circlet. This attempt to join the ring to me would be pointless, and I had no idea why he wanted to do it in the first place.

But it was buying us time, and time was what we needed.

The king began to chant. Magic unspooled from the end of the wand in silver sheets. They enveloped me, and a metallic taste filled my mouth. King Gorm chanted louder, holding up my ring.

"Fara ond!" he shouted as he finished the incantation. The metallic magic tightened.

Nothing happened.

Visibly frustrated, King Gorm waved the wand a few more times. "It's not bloody working!" he shouted, his face red. "Where is it?"

"What?"

"Tell me where it is!" The king stepped closer and pressed Levateinn against my chest as though he might run me through. "Where have you hidden your soul?"

"I don't know," I lied. "It's been a thousand years. I believe it's lost. But I can help you find it, if you let us both live."

"No!" shouted King Gorm. "You lie! You know where it is now. You will tell me."

I looked to the edges of the amphitheater, where guards now raised their wands. Killing hexes hummed at their tips, ready to end Ali's life. I'd have to bluff.

"You and I both know hexes are useless against me. As a lich, I am indestructible. Throw us back in the prison cells, let us live, and I will help you find my soul."

The king spun and pointed Levateinn at Ali's chest. "But this little tunnel-elf can die. If you take one more step, I will transform her into a bug and squash her."

Time seemed to stop.

"I thought so," Gorm said as I turned to face him once again. "Yes, the tunnel-elf is important to you." He pressed the wand against her temple as if it were a gun. "Now tell me where your soul is. I want it returned to you, and then you must pledge fealty to me once more. You will wear the crown, the Helm of Awe."

The Helm of Awe was a crown that could control your mind, and I had only a hazy understanding of why he wanted all this to happen. With my soul back, I would be a powerful sorcerer. And if I wore the Helm of Awe, I would be a powerful weapon in the king's arsenal. My magic would be completely under his control. Once, I'd worked for him, but I'd made my own decisions. If I wore the Helm, he'd be making them for me.

King Gorm was rotten to his core, and this would be a disaster. And yet—what choice did I have? I had an immediate problem, and that was saving Ali's life. The long-term problem would have to wait.

Hazy memories flickered of my past life with him, and a dreadful understanding began to dawn. I hadn't just worked for him, had I? No... I knew these people much more intimately than that.

King Gorm stepped closer to Ali. "You have three seconds to make your choice."

Cold fear chilled my blood. I saw the end game now. What I had to do, even if it would kill me inside. I was starting to remember him, to remember me.

"Fine," I said. "But you must guarantee to me that you will send her back to the Shadow Caverns."

"What?" said Ali.

I locked my gaze on hers. "You need to trust me. I will look out for you."

"How touching," said the king.

"I need your oath," I said to him. "That you will send Ali safely home if I give you what you want. I'll wear your crown."

"Fine." The king stood tall. "What do I care if a tunnel-elf is in a cave or dead? I give you my oath. I will send her back home safely."

Grief poisoned my blood at what I was about to say. I felt the weight of it like rocks crushing me.

"Your Majesty," I said, "if you let her live, I will wear the Helm of Awe. I will join the kingdom once again."

CHAPTER 59

ALI

Back to the Shadow Caverns? I didn't want to go back home. I wanted to free the Night Elves, or all of this would have been pointless. "But what about Galin?" I asked.

The king chuckled softly. "Come to me, my son."

His *what*? Marroc was a prince? The history books hadn't mentioned his name. I only knew of Revna and Sune.

What the Helheim was going on?

I gaped as Marroc—*Prince* Marroc—began to walk closer to us. "My soul is within Ali. Ali, I won't hurt you. You have my oath."

I tried to make sense of this. His soul was in me? It was hard to think straight with the king pressing the wand harder into my skull.

If I hadn't been bound, I'd have slashed the king's throat open and demanded answers from the prince. Answers to questions like "where is Galin?" and "how the fuck did I end up with your soul?"

Except the soldiers and their killing hexes would take me down before I got the answers.

Gorm pointed the wand at Marroc. "Kneel and take the pledge, prince. Your true name has been struck from our history for a thousand years, but now it will be restored."

Shock flickered through me as Marroc knelt. I couldn't quite believe this was happening, that I'd been with the *prince of Elfheim* the entire time. His true name...

Dread was sliding over my thoughts.

"Bring forth the crown!" shouted the king. "Place it on his head."

From the shadows, a guard stepped closer, carrying a silver crown, and he rested it on Marroc's head.

Slowly, Marroc began to speak. "I pledge my life, my ambitions, my desires, and my soul to Gorm, King of the High Elves." His deep voice boomed over the amphitheater. "Let the bond last until he releases me. Until then, I am his servant to command however he may desire."

The silver crown gleamed brighter.

"It is an honor to have you back in my service," Gorm said. "But you are useless to me in this form. Your magic is smothered by the curse. It is time you were made whole."

Casually, King Gorm handed him Levateinn. The silver wand hummed in his hand.

Marroc stood tall, peering down at me. Pain flickered in his eyes. He hated his father, didn't he? But he was doing this for me.

He held Levateinn straight out and slowly began to chant. Its tip shone in the winter light, and silvery magic collected on it. Then Marroc turned the wand so that it pointed at my head.

The magic slid over me, cold as quicksilver, freezing me in place. A liquid metal filled my mouth. It streamed down my throat in a silver torrent, rushing into my stomach. In seconds, it began mixing with my blood.

Pain like nothing I'd ever experienced coursed through

me. I spasmed as the magic arched my back, wrenched my lips open in a silent scream, and ripped my consciousness away. I seemed to float up until I was looking down at my shivering form. On the dais, everything moved in slow motion.

Marroc stood over me with regret in his eyes. He held the wand straight over his head. It had changed, transformed. The wand was now a sharp silver blade, flashing and shining as though lit by a thousand suns.

The king's guards stood around us, wands leveled at us. Marroc's hair blew in the winter wind. All around us, twined Levateinn's magic. Silver coils traced over the stones, twisted about my body, and continued to unspool down my throat in shining loops.

Marroc's voice rose, chanting louder than before, and the magic began to rush from the wand.

I saw it pool at Marroc's feet, saw him stumble, then fall to his knees. I watched as Levateinn's magic rushed up his massive thighs, over the smoldering runes on his chest. For a moment, it paused at his throat, then his head snapped back as Loki's magic began to pour into his mouth.

In seconds, he'd transformed, his pale skin glowing until he looked like he'd been dipped in liquid gold. The magic carried our bodies together. My body twisted, shuddering, and something burst from my chest.

Agony shot through me as my soul separated from my body. It hung there, suspended, an orb of pulsing light. Then the silver magic formed over it, and it dimmed until it faded away entirely. All that was left was a tiny silver ball hovering in the winter air.

For a second I thought I was dead, but my consciousness didn't dissipate. Instead, I continued to watch from above as the ball split in two. A pair of orbs now hung suspended above the dais.

Everything happened in an instant. With a crack like a thunderclap, one orb shot into my body, the other into Marroc's. My consciousness raced downward, plunged into my chest.

I opened my eyes, shocked by what had just happened. My entire body trembled.

And when I looked up at Marroc, I saw him completely transformed. His eyes were no longer blue but gold, the color of the rising sun. His black hair had transformed to blond, and it whirled around his head in the winter breeze. Now, he looked like the High Elf that he was—a golden warrior gleaming like the sun.

He rose to his feet like a conquering god, his gaze still fixed on me. The crown gleamed on his head.

Then, with one hand, he pulled me up from the floor. I hung limply as he drew me to his blazing chest. Heat from his body washed over me, and I felt like I was melting into him.

"Ali." His voice was deep and strong like the tolling of a church bell. "Ali," he repeated, holding me tighter. His expression was ecstatic, rapturous. His hair continued to swirl around his head.

Pressed against his chest, I could feel his heart beating thunderously. The smoky smell of his curse was gone, replaced by the scent of fresh sage. He lifted me up so that my face was level with his. For the first time, I got a clear view of his features. Golden eyes, tawny skin, sensual lips. Tingly warmth rushed over my skin.

"I need to return the magic I drank," he whispered, his voice smooth as whiskey.

Marroc leaned down and pressed his lips to mine, and my body warmed as magic flowed into me. My magic. Slowly, I could feel the strength filling me once more.

He pulled away, looking into my eyes. Marroc's golden

eyes held mine with a sort of magnetic connection neither of us could break. Whether I liked it or not, we were bonded in some way.

And that bond was so strong, so deliciously warm on my skin—I almost didn't notice who he really was.

All the warmth drained from my body.

"Galin?" I clenched my jaw. "What the fuck?"

"Oh, you've caught on?" King Gorm echoed in his flute-like voice. His eyes fixed on mine, flashing with unsurpassed glee. "Marroc is dead, but Galin now lives again. We'd banished the name Galin from our realms. But now, the curse is lifted. His soul is restored. He's Galin again. The greatest elven sorcerer who ever walked this earth."

I stared at him, and an icy tendril of horror coiled through me, winding around my insides.

This was the man I'd spent all my life wanting to kill, and he'd lied to me this entire time. But Galin had miscalculated. With that kiss, he'd just given me my strength back. I wasn't going to go down without a fight.

As quietly as I could, I whispered, "Skalei."

CHAPTER 60

MARROC

My memories of the people around me were flooding back into me in streams. King Gorm —my father—had ruled over Elfheim when it had still existed. My sister Revna and I had hated each other since we were young. Sune had always been an idiot. In Elfheim, I'd retreated to the mountains and mastered the power of sorcery greater than any elf who'd ever lived.

But I had to push out this overwhelming flood of memories to focus on the tragedy unfolding before me.

"You—" Ali's voice cracked.

I'd been beaten, branded, stabbed, tortured, lived a thousand years with a curse that boiled my blood, but none of it compared to the pain that clutched at my heart as I saw the look of horror in Ali's eyes.

I opened my mouth to explain this to her, why I'd done what I'd done. But the crown on my head shot a charge of agonizing magic into my skull. My father, King Gorm, was in control of me now.

Ali's rage was palpable.

"You," she repeated, more slowly, in a surprisingly even

voice. "You never mentioned that you were Galin, the great sorcerer. You were the one who locked the Dokkalfar in the Shadow Caverns. You're the reason we've been living in the dark, dying of cave sickness. You never had any intention of helping me to free the Night Elves, did you?"

That wasn't true.

Now, with the memories of my old life returned to me, I remembered it all. I remembered the terrible day when I'd cast the spell to imprison the Night Elves in the Shadow Caverns forever. And I remembered exactly why I'd done it. The way the crown worked, it would burn me if I disobeyed the King's will. But at this point, I was plenty used to the pain.

"It was the only way," I said. A flash of pain seared my skull. I *would* find a way out of this. The King was a monster, but he wasn't a genius.

The King was shouting at me to stop, but I kept going, my head shot with agony. "I did it to protect the Night Elves, to hide them from my kind. The decision cost me my life and turned me into the monster I was for the past thousand years. The alternative for the Night Elves was death, and the Shadow Caverns were the only way to save—" The searing pain now grew too intense, choking off my words.

"Silence!" shouted the king.

"You must trust me!" I said to Ali.

She was still staring at me, but I could see her mind working. She was planning something, wasn't she? I needed to get her out of here before she did anything rash.

The king paced around her. "Well, this is an interesting conversation, but I do believe I have an oath to make good on, sending this creature back to her pits. Make your portal, Galin."

Magic sparked down my arm, and my hand moved at his command. Power flooded my veins. With Levateinn clasped in my hand, I wove the runes through the air. This spell was perhaps the most crucial one of my life.

I began to chant.

Magic flowed from me, and for the first time in a thousand years, my skin didn't smoke and my body didn't burn. With Levateinn, I traced the rune *isa*. In front of me, the air brightened until it formed a pale circle, larger and larger, until it was big enough for a person to pass through.

"All right," I said, gasping with exertion. "It's ready."

CHAPTER 61

ALI

With subtle movements, I sawed at the rope binding my wrists. Skalei was razor-sharp, but with my hands tied behind my back, I couldn't see what I was doing. I didn't want to cut myself or drop the blade.

"Go through the portal, girl," King Gorm commanded from the far side of the dais.

Dammit, I need more time to get answers from Galin. "It's just been so magical watching this family reunion."

I was almost there. I could feel the rope parting. I just needed five more seconds.

One of the guards lunged for me, but I just managed to make it through the last of the rope's fibers, and it fell away. Skalei flashed as I slashed for him, and the guard stumbled, clutching his stomach. Blood pumped from between his fingers. I was free.

"Stop her," shouted Gorm.

I leapt for Galin. He tried to catch me, but I was too fast. I slipped behind him and pressed Skalei to his throat.

"Attack, and he dies," I shouted, fairly certain I was bluffing. Somehow, I'd trusted what he said—that the Shadow

Caverns spell could have been a way of keeping us safe. I just wanted more answers—now. "How do we free the Night Elves? If you die, would it break the spell?"

"No," said Galin. "You have my sacred oath."

"Then how do I do it? How do I break the spell?"

His words were so quiet that I could barely hear them. It was a whisper meant only for me. "I promise to help break the spell. I will come for you." I pulled the blade away from his neck just a little, and he turned, meeting my gaze. "I will find a way to fix this," he mouthed. His golden eyes were imploring me to believe him, to go through the portal while I still could. His hand touched mine and pressed something into it.

Then Galin grimaced, and I saw smoke rise for his hair. It seemed the Helm of Awe was hurting him. That meant he was disobeying the king—telling the truth.

Behind me, I heard a hex buzzing on the end of a wand. The king had given his oath to send me home, but that didn't mean his guards couldn't kill me on the way. Seemed I was out of time.

Before a guard could take a shot at me, I dove through the portal.

Electricity sizzled as I jumped through it. For an instant everything was pitch black, then I slammed hard onto rough stone. I opened my eyes, but it was completely dark. I lay still for a moment, feeling only wet grit on my cheek.

I scrambled to my feet, holding Skalei defensively as my eyes adjusted.

Now, I stood in a towering cavern. Jutting down from the gloom above me were the tips of giant stalactites. But I hardly noticed them, as my gaze was drawn to the center of the cavern, to a massive column of gray stone that extended all the way from the floor to the ceiling.

Covered in rippling flowstone, it stood as large as some

of Boston's skyscrapers. Small lights dotted along its sides. A thousand windows that'd been carved into the rock. I knew where I was. This was Sindri, the great hall where the Shadow Lords dwelled.

I slowly breathed out. *I'm back in the Shadow Caverns.* Sent here by Galin himself—the sorcerer I'd been sent to kill. This was not how I'd planned to return, but it was becoming clear that there was more to the story than I thought. King Gorm had struck his son's name from the history books for a reason—which lent credence to Galin's claim. Still, the Shadow Lords would never believe this version of events.

Maybe, at one time, the caverns were a way of keeping us safe from the rest of the High Elves. But now? It was time to live in the light again. And I still believed I would do it—I would lead us there.

I just didn't think that the Shadow Lords needed to know everything.

As I started to put Skalei away. I remembered how Galin had touched my hip, slipped something into my pocket. Gingerly I reached inside. I grinned when my fingers wrapped around the metallic object. The ring. He'd known exactly what I needed to keep the Shadow Lords happy.

I began to run as fast I could toward Sindri. I had to tell the Shadow Lords that I'd returned. I had to give them the ring, to buy myself a bit of time while I figured out the real way out of this.

I ran past fields of mushrooms, down the dark streets of the city of Myrk, until I reached the hall. I'd been to Sindri a hundred times, but I'd forgotten the enormity of its entrance, a massive tunnel carved directly into the living rock.

A guard stood before the opening. Silver hair hung to the shoulders of his black chain mail. In one hand, he held a long halberd.

"Who goes there?"

My lungs burned, but I managed to get it all out on the first try. "Astrid, daughter of Volundar, Chief Assassin of the Shadow Lords."

"What is your business?"

"I must speak to the Lords."

The guard's eyes narrowed, and his fingers tightened on the halberd's shaft. "You'll need to be more specific."

"No," I said, still trying to catch my breath. "This is for the Lords' ears only. Tell them Astrid has returned from her assignment in Midgard. Tell them I must speak to them now. It's extremely important."

The guard gave me a final suspicious look before he left his post. By the time he'd returned, I'd caught my breath.

"All right, Astrid," he said. "Come with me."

The guard led me into the entrance tunnel. It was just as I remembered. Even so, my breath caught when we stepped from the tunnel into the audience chamber, the ceilings as tall and grand as a cathedral.

Lit only by candlelight, the chamber was solemn and stark. Three stone thrones stood on one end of the hall, each carved directly from the bedrock. They might have been beautiful once, but a thousand years of dripping water had left them covered in strangely rippling deposits of calcite.

Seated in each throne was a figure dressed in thick gray fabric, only slightly darker than the stone itself. The ancient elves had long silver hair and skin lined with wrinkles. Their eyes shone brightly in the darkness. Ilvis, Thyra, and Lynheid. The eldest of our kind.

"Where is the safe deposit box?" said Ilvis, who sat in the center throne. "The one we sent you to fetch. You took longer than expected to return."

It took me a second to realize that he was asking about my original assignment. That seemed like years ago. "I'll get to that in a second." I was taking an enormous risk with this, but I needed to know this now more than I needed anything: "Did my brother Barthol return here?"

"Insolence!" shouted Thyra.

Ilvis sighed. "Yes, he did. The box?"

Relief flooded me. Barthol was alive. Somehow, he'd escaped, made his way back to the Shadow Caverns. "Okay, well, I was attacked while trying to break into the bank. I'm sure Barthol told you that."

"Yes, but what about the safe deposit box?" asked Thyra, sounding impatient. "Barthol had nothing to report. He thought you might have it. He's been frantically asking for permission to find you, but we refused to give him another vergr stone."

"I managed to get a hold of the contents. The golden ring."

Ilvis gave me a look that said I shouldn't know about the ring. "Where is the ring now?" he asked slowly.

"Right here," I said, reaching into my pocket. I held up the ring so the Shadow Lords could see it. It glinted faintly in the candlelight.

"Give it to me," said Ilvis, thrusting out a hand.

I walked to the base of his throne and handed up the ring. He slipped it into his pocket.

"That was good work," said Thyra. "But what took you so long to return?"

"I'm sure you heard about the troll. He managed to steal the box, but I located it again." I forced myself to smile. I hated having to lie to them, but if they suspected I'd failed to deliver what they really wanted, I could find myself in prison.

So I'd leave out a few details—my descent into the Well of Wyrd, my journey to the Helheim. The fight with Nidhogg. The bit about where Galin's soul had been returned, and how he was controlled by Gorm.

If they knew that, they'd strip me of my commission and send me to the Kolar mines to work myself to death shoveling coal. So let them wonder at why the ring didn't work the way they hoped. It would keep them distracted while I worked on a real solution.

Ilvis smiled at me indulgently. "Well done, Astrid. You will, of course, be heavily rewarded for your efforts."

I'd done what they'd asked, hadn't I? And in my own way, I was certain I'd achieve my destiny—that I was the North Star, and I would lead us out of here.

CHAPTER 62

ALI

I slipped through the shadowy streets of Myrk. I knew this town like the back of my hand. I'd literally been forced to memorize its every alley and passageway as part of my assassin training. Not that I was making use of any of those shadowy routes tonight.

I hung a right down Stone Cave Lane then a left at Batfoot Road. Before I knew it, I was just outside my family home. A light glimmered inside.

I peered in through the front window. Barthol sat in his chair, his legs up, his eyes closed. The remains of a fire glowed in the hearth. Old pictures of Jeremy the Alcoholic Goat gleamed on the walls, but he hadn't drawn any new ones. He must've been worried out of his mind about me.

I grinned wickedly. Then I slipped round back, to the rear of the house. My key was right where I'd left it, hidden under a rock.

And next to the key, I found a long, flat rock. I had an idea for that, too. As quietly as I could, I unlocked the back door and slipped inside.

Gripping the rock like a knife, I tiptoed into the living

room. Some strange music was playing on his antique boombox.

Barthol hadn't moved from his chair. He was fast asleep. Snoring softly. Gods, he was a terrible assassin, but I loved him anyway.

I slipped behind him and pressed the stone to his neck.

"What the fuck do you think you're doing?" I said in my best impression of a High Elf singsong voice.

Barthol's eyes flashed open. "What?"

He tried to stand, but I kept the stone at his neck. "Is it true that you pissed your pants when you saw the troll?"

"I absolutely did not!" Barthol stammered. Then he twisted his head around and looked at me. His jaw dropped. "You asshole."

I held up the stone. "I may be an asshole, Barthol, but I'm the asshole who's going to teach you to stay on your toes. I'm the asshole who will keep you alive."

A grin split his face. "You're back!" he shouted.

"Shh. You'll wake up the neighborhood."

But Barthol had wrapped me in a suffocating bear hug. "You're okay. I knew you'd be okay. I mean, I wasn't sure. I wanted to get a vergr stone to find you, but they wouldn't give me one. Where *were* you?" He was practically shouting, shaking me up and down with excitement. "When the troll appeared, I tried to call you, but you didn't answer. Oh my god, Ali. The only reason I knew you were alive was because I was sure I'd feel it if you died."

"Also, because I am a chief assassin for a reason. I don't die that easily."

Barthol put his hands on my shoulders and pushed me back. He frowned slightly.

"What are you wearing?"

"What do you mean?" I followed his eyes down. I'd forgotten that I was still wearing Galin's shirt. "I had to steal some clothes in Midgard," I lied, before changing the subject. The less Barthol knew, the better. Ignorance would keep him safe. "What's this music you're playing? I like it."

He grinned. "You like it too? This album is *so* good. Super rare. I had to sell my coat to get it, but it was totally worth it. It's called *Best of Nickelback Vol 1.*"

CHAPTER 63

GALIN

I sat in my chambers in the Citadel, staring out the window onto a city covered in snow. White-blanketed Boston. Happiness warmed me at the thought that I'd managed to slip the golden ring to Ali. With her mission achieved, she'd be celebrated as a hero in the Shadow Caverns.

I ran a fingertip over the crown on my head, where the words *Helm of Awe* were carved into it. My situation wasn't quite as rosy.

My mind whirled darkly with the power my father now had over me. The crown stopped me from hurting the king or from escaping the Citadel. When he was near me, he could control me completely. But on my own, I could conduct spells as I wanted, and speak freely.

I just needed to pick the right time to get to Ali. If I appeared when others were around her, I could land her in serious trouble. Right now, she had the ring, and that should keep the Shadow Lords happy for the time being. I needed to find a way to send spies into the caverns.

With my soul returned to me, memories of my past life

had come flooding back. At last, I remembered who I'd once been. As prince of Elfheim, we'd ruled the world of elves before it had been destroyed in Ragnarok. A palace called Gimli had towered over the kingdom, and we had worshipped the gods when they were still alive.

I'd revered Odin. With his power igniting my veins, I'd learned magic in the mountains and forests. I'd kept wolves and ravens as my pets, honoring him.

Revna, Sune, and my father had been a cruel little unit, but I spent the years practicing sorcery until even they feared me.

And then Ragnarok had descended on us—the end of the Worlds. First the floods, then disease had spread through all the realms. The High Elves had never known disease before, but we found ourselves sickening. The gods battled giants; the gods died. Elfheim had been destroyed completely, nothing left but rubble and the dead.

This was what fate had foretold, and it had come to pass.

But after losing so much, the High Elves wanted blood. So they blamed the Night Elves, and my father proposed a game—we were supposed to hunt the Night Elves to extinction. One by one, the High Elves began to run down the Dokkalfar. They'd be tortured in public, in excruciating ways. I remembered how it had delighted my sister when they screamed.

Because when something terrible happens, there's only one way to make it right, isn't there? Make something worse happen to someone else.

But the truth was that Ragnarok wasn't their fault. Because it had always been foretold, and it was written by fate. That was why I had intervened to save them. I'd done what I could to keep them safe. I'd cast a spell, hiding them in the Shadow Caverns. I knew it had to be terrible in there—no light, no fresh food. But they were alive, at least.

If I hadn't acted, they'd all be dead by now. Ali wouldn't exist.

I still remembered my father's fury at what I'd done. An anger powerful enough to level a city.

As I stared out onto the darkened city, I felt the power of Wyrd speaking to me like a voice: *You will rule this Citadel as king.*

When I closed my eyes, I saw myself as the king of the Citadel. But that wasn't the vision I wanted. The one I wanted was one where I found Ali again, and we freed the Night Elves together.

It didn't seem to be what fate was most interested in, but it was what I most desired, because that was what she needed.

So right now, maybe I didn't give a fuck about what fate wanted. I would make my own vision come to pass, one way or another. And then I wanted Ali alone with me. My blood heated at the thought of having her close to me.

And yet clearly, Ali had her own vision for the future. I would do what I could to help make it come to pass.

I had told her I would come for her, and I would. With my soul returned to me, I could pull the spell from the Shadow Caverns, bring down the magical wall. It was just a little matter of finding a way to do it without the High Elves immediately instituting another gruesome hunt. And yet I was sure, if we were careful, Ali and I could find a way to fight them together.

* * *

Thank you for reading **Cursed Prince**.

While you wait for Book 2, we suggest you checkout **Dark King**.

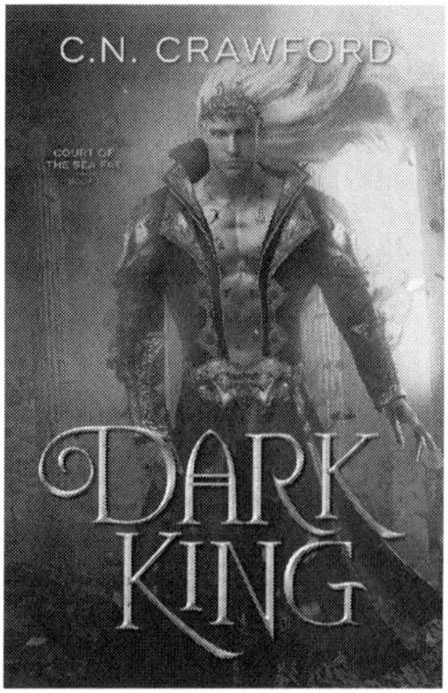
C.N. CRAWFORD
COURT OF
THE SEA FAE
DARK
KING

ALSO BY C.N. CRAWFORD

For a full list of our books, check out our website.
https://www.cncrawford.com/books/

And a possible reading order.
https://www.cncrawford.com/faq/

ACKNOWLEDGMENTS

This book was a bit of a struggle, so many many many thanks go to Christine for helping me become a better romance and first person POV writer (I love you Chunky)!

Robin, Bella, and Arran all contributed to the extensive editing and polishing that got this book ready for publication. Carlos made us another beautiful cover. And last but not least, thanks so much to our advanced reader team for their help, and to C.N. Crawford's Coven on Facebook!

Printed in Great Britain
by Amazon